# Steppenwolf

## Hermann Hesse

Translated By

Basil creighton

AF516846

Infinity Spectrum Books

Published by:
**INFINITY SPECTRUM BOOKS**
Email: infinityspectrumbooks@gmail.com

First published by Infinity Spectrum Books 2024


Title : **Steppenwolf**
Paperback ISBN : 9789361909177
Hardback ISBN: 9789361909566

# PREFACE

THIS BOOK CONTAINS THE RECORDS LEFT US by a man whom, according to the expression he often used himself, we called the Steppenwolf. Whether this manuscript needs any introductory remarks may be open to question. I, however, feel the need of adding a few pages to those of the Steppenwolf in which I try to record my recollections of him. What I know of him is little enough. Indeed, of his past life and origins I know nothing at all. Yet the impression left by his personality has remained, in spite of all, a deep and sympathetic one.

Some years ago the Steppenwolf, who was then approaching fifty, called on my aunt to inquire for a furnished room. He took the attic room on the top floor and the bedroom next it, returned a day or two later with two trunks and a big case of books and stayed nine or ten months with us. He lived by himself very quietly, and but for the fact that our bedrooms were next door to each other--which occasioned a good many chance encounters on the stairs and in the passage--we should have remained practically unacquainted. For he was not a sociable man. Indeed, he was unsociable to a degree I had never before experienced in anybody. He was, in fact, as he called himself, a real wolf of the Steppes, a strange, wild, shy--very shy--being from another world than mine. How deep the loneliness into which his life had drifted on account of his disposition and destiny and how consciously he accepted this loneliness as his destiny, I certainly did not know until I read the records he left behind him. Yet, before that, from our occasional talks and encounters, I became gradually acquainted with him, and I found that the portrait in his records was in substantial agreement with the paler and less complete one that our personal acquaintance had given me.

By chance I was there at the very moment when the Steppenwolf entered our house for the first time and became my aunt's lodger. He came at noon. The table had not been cleared and I still had half an hour before going back to the office. I have never forgotten the odd and very conflicting impressions he made on me at this first encounter. He came through the glazed door, having just rung the bell, and my aunt asked him in the dim light of the hall what he wanted. The Steppenwolf, however, first threw up his sharp, closely cropped head and sniffed around nervously before he either made any answer or announced his name.

"Oh, it smells good here," he said, and at that he smiled and my aunt smiled too. For my part, I found this matter of introducing himself ridiculous and was not favorably impressed.

"However," said he, "I've come about the room you have to let."

I did not get a good look at him until we were all three on our way up to the top floor. Though not very big, he had the bearing of a big man. He wore a fashionable and comfortable winter overcoat and he was well, though carelessly, dressed, clean-shaven, and his cropped head showed here and there a streak of grey. He carried himself in a way I did not at all like at first. There was something weary and undecided about it that did not go with his keen and striking profile nor with the tone of his voice. Later, I found out that his health was poor and that walking tired him. With a peculiar smile--at that time equally unpleasant to me--he contemplated the stairs, the walls, and windows, and the tall old cupboards on the staircase. All this seemed to please and at the same time to amuse him. Altogether he gave the impression of having come out of an alien world, from another continent perhaps. He found it all very charming and a little odd. I cannot deny that he was polite, even friendly. He agreed at once and without objection to the terms for lodging and breakfast and so forth, and yet about the whole man there was a foreign and, as I chose to think, disagreeable or hostile atmosphere. He took the room and the bedroom too, listened attentively and amiably to all he was told about the heating, the water, the service and the rules of the household, agreed to everything, offered at once to pay a sum in advance--and yet he seemed at the same time to be outside it all, to find it comic to be doing as he did and not to take it seriously. It was as though it were a very odd and new experience for him, occupied as he was with quite other concerns, to be renting a room and talking to people in German. Such more or less was my impression, and it would certainly not have been a good one if it had not been revised and corrected by many small instances. Above all, his face pleased me from the first, in spite of the foreign air it had. It was a rather original face and perhaps a sad one, but alert, thoughtful, strongly marked and highly intellectual. And then, to reconcile me further, there was his polite and friendly manner, which though it seemed to cost him some pains, was all the same quite without pretension; on the contrary, there was something almost touching, imploring in it. The explanation of it I found later, but it disposed me at once in his favor.

Before we had done inspecting the rooms and going into the arrangements, my luncheon hour was up and I had to go back to business. I took my leave and left him to my aunt. When I got back at night, she told me that he had taken the rooms and was coming in in a day or two. The only request he had made was that his arrival should not be notified to the police, as in his poor state of health he found these formalities and the standing about in official waiting rooms more than he could tolerate. I remember very well how this surprised me and how I warned my aunt against giving in to his stipulation. This fear of the police seemed to me to agree only too well with the mysterious and alien air the man had and struck me as suspicious. I explained to my aunt that she ought not on any account to put herself in this equivocal and in any case rather peculiar position for a complete stranger; it might well turn out to have very unpleasant consequences for her. But it then came out that my aunt had already granted his request, and, indeed, had let herself be altogether captivated and charmed by the strange gentleman. For she never took a lodger with whom she did not contrive to stand in some human, friendly, and as it were auntlike or, rather, motherly relation; and many a one has made full use of this weakness of hers. And thus for the first weeks things went on; I had many a fault to find with the new lodger, while my aunt every time warmly took his part.

As I was not at all pleased about this business of neglecting to notify the police, I wanted at least to know what my aunt had learnt about him; what sort of family he came of and what his intentions were. And, of course, she had learnt one thing and another, although he had only stayed a short while after I left at noon. He had told her that he thought of spending some months in our town to avail himself of the libraries and to see its antiquities. I may say it did not please my aunt that he was only taking the rooms for so short a time, but he had clearly quite won her heart in spite of his rather peculiar way of presenting himself. In short, the rooms were let and my objections came too late.

"Why on earth did he say that it smelt so good here?" I asked.

"I know well enough," she replied, with her usual insight. "There's a smell of cleanliness and good order here, of comfort and respectability. It was that that pleased him. He looks as if he weren't used to that of late and missed it."

Just so, thought I to myself.

"But," I said aloud, "if he isn't used to an orderly and respectable life, what is going to happen? What will you say if he has filthy habits and makes dirt everywhere, or comes home drunk at all hours of the night?"

"We shall see, we shall see," she said, and laughed; and I left it at that.

And in the upshot my fears proved groundless. The lodger, though he certainly did not live a very orderly or rational life, was no worry or trouble to us. Yet my aunt and I bothered our heads a lot about him, and I confess I have not by a long way done with him even now. I often dream of him at night, and the mere existence of such a man, much as I got to like him, has had a thoroughly disturbing and disquieting effect on me.

Two days after this the stranger's luggage--his name was Harry Haller--was brought in by a porter. He had a very fine leather trunk, which made a good impression on me, and a big flat cabin trunk that showed signs of having traveled far--at least it was plastered with labels of hotels and travel agencies of various countries, some overseas.

Then he himself appeared, and the time began during which I gradually got acquainted with this strange man. At first I did nothing on my side to encourage it. Although Haller interested me from the moment I saw him, I took no steps for the first two or three weeks to run across him or to get into conversation with him. On the other hand I confess that I did, all the same and from the very first, keep him under observation a little, and also went into his room now and again when he was out and my curiosity drove me to do a little spy work.

I have already given some account of the Steppenwolf's outward appearance. He gave at the very first glance the impression of a significant, an uncommon, and unusually gifted man. His face was intellectual, and the abnormally delicate and mobile play of his features reflected a soul of extremely emotional and unusually delicate sensibility. When one spoke to him and he, as was not always the case, dropped conventionalities and said personal and individual things that came out of his own alien world, then a man like myself came under his spell on the spot. He had thought more than other men, and in matters of the intellect he had that calm objectivity, that certainty of thought and knowledge, such as only really intellectual men have, who have no axe to grind, who never wish to shine, or to talk others down, or to appear always in the right.

I remember an instance of this in the last days he was here, if I can call a mere fleeting glance he gave me an example of what I mean. It was when a celebrated historian, philosopher, and critic, a man of European fame, had announced a lecture in the school auditorium. I had succeeded in persuading the Steppenwolf to attend it, though at first he had little desire to do so. We went together and sat next to each other in the lecture hall. When the lecturer ascended the platform and began his address, many of his hearers, who had expected a sort of prophet, were disappointed by his rather dapper appearance and conceited air. And when he proceeded, by way of introduction, to say a few flattering things to the audience, thanking them for their attendance in such numbers, the Steppenwolf threw me a quick look, a look which criticized both the words and the speaker of them--an unforgettable and frightful look which spoke volumes! It was a look that did not simply criticize the lecturer, annihilating the famous man with its delicate but crushing irony. That was the least of it. It was more sad than ironical; it was indeed utterly and hopelessly sad; it conveyed a quiet despair, born partly of conviction, partly of a mode of thought which had become habitual with him. This despair of his not only unmasked the conceited lecturer and dismissed with its irony the matter at hand, the expectant attitude of the public, the somewhat presumptuous title under which the lecture was announced--no, the Steppenwolf's look pierced our whole epoch, its whole overwrought activity, the whole surge and strife, the whole vanity, the whole superficial play of a shallow, opinionated intellectuality. And alas! the look went still deeper, went far below the faults, defects and hopelessness of our time, our intellect, our culture alone. It went right to the heart of all humanity, it bespoke eloquently in a single second the whole despair of a thinker, of one who knew the full worth and meaning of man's life. It said: "See what monkeys we are! Look, such is man!" and at once all renown, all intelligence, all the attainments of the spirit, all progress towards the sublime, the great and the enduring in man fell away and became a monkey's trick!

With this I have gone far ahead and, contrary to my actual plan and intention, already conveyed what Haller essentially meant to me; whereas my original aim was to uncover his picture by degrees while telling the course of my gradual acquaintance with him.

Now that I have gone so far ahead it will save time to say a little more about Haller's puzzling "strangeness" and to tell in detail how I gradually guessed and became aware of the causes and meaning of this strangeness, this extraordinary and frightful loneliness. It will be better so, for I wish to leave my own personality as far as possible in the background. I do not want to put down my own confessions, to tell a story or to write an essay on psychology, but simply as an eyewitness to contribute something to the picture of the peculiar individual who left this Steppenwolf manuscript behind him.

At the very first sight of him, when he came into my aunt's home, craning his head like a bird and praising the smell of the house, I was at once astonished by something curious about him; and my first natural reaction was repugnance. I suspected (and my aunt, who unlike me is the very reverse of an intellectual person, suspected very much the same thing)--I suspected that the man was ailing, ailing in the spirit in some way, or in his temperament or character, and I shrank from him with the instinct of the healthy. This shrinking was in course of time replaced by a sympathy inspired by pity for one who had suffered so long and deeply, and whose loneliness and inward death I witnessed. In course of time I was more and more conscious, too, that this affliction was not due to any defects of nature, but rather to a profusion of gifts and powers which had not attained to harmony. I saw that Haller was a genius of suffering and that in the meaning of many sayings of Nietzsche he had created within himself with positive genius a boundless and frightful capacity for pain. I saw at the same time that the root of his pessimism was not world-contempt but self-contempt; for however mercilessly he might annihilate institutions and persons in his talk he never spared himself. It was always at himself first and foremost that he aimed the shaft, himself first and foremost whom he hated and despised.

And here I cannot refrain from a psychological observation. Although I know very little of the Steppenwolf's life, I have all the same good reason to suppose that he was brought up by devoted but severe and very pious parents and teachers in accordance with that doctrine that makes the breaking of the will the corner-stone of education and upbringing. But in this case the attempt to destroy the personality and to break the will did not succeed. He was much too strong and hardy, too proud and spirited. Instead of destroying his personality they succeeded only in teaching him to hate himself. It was against himself that, innocent and noble as he was, he directed during his whole life the whole wealth of his fancy, the whole of his thought; and in so far as he let loose upon himself every barbed criticism, every anger and hate he could command, he was, in spite of all, a real Christian and a real martyr. As for others and the world around him he never ceased in his heroic and earnest endeavor to love them, to be just to them, to do them no harm, for the love of his neighbor was as deeply in him as the hatred of himself, and so his whole life was an example that love of one's neighbor is not possible without love of oneself, and that self-hate is really the same thing as sheer egoism, and in the long run breeds the same cruel isolation and despair.

It is now time, however, to put my own thoughts aside and to get to facts. What I first discovered about Haller, partly through my espionage, partly from my aunt's remarks, concerned his way of living. It was soon obvious that his days were spent with his thoughts and his books, and that he pursued no practical calling. He lay always very late in bed. Often he was not up much before noon and went across from his bedroom, to his sitting room in his dressing gown. This sitting room, a large and comfortable attic room with two windows, after a few days was not at all the same as when occupied by other tenants. It filled up more and more as time went on. Pictures were hung on the walls, drawings tacked up--sometimes illustrations cut out from magazines and often changed. A southern landscape, photographs of a little German country town, apparently Haller's home, hung there, and between them were some brightly painted water colors, which, as we discovered later, he had painted himself. Then there were photographs of a pretty young woman, or--rather--girl. For a long while a Siamese Buddha hung on the wall, to be replaced first by Michelangelo's "Night," then by a portrait of Mahatma Gandhi. Books filled the large bookcase and lay everywhere else as well, on the table, on the pretty old bureau, on the sofa, on the chairs and all about on the floor, books with notes slipped into them which were continually changing. The books constantly increased, for besides bringing whole armfuls back with him from the libraries he was always getting parcels of them by post. The occupant of this room might well be a learned man; and to this the all-pervading smell of cigar smoke might testify as well as the stumps and ash of cigars all about the room. Many of the books, however, were not of a scholarly nature. The majority were works of the poets of all times and peoples. For a long while there lay about on the sofa where he often spent whole days all six volumes of a work with the title *Sophia's Journey from Memet to Saxony*--a work of the latter part of the eighteenth century. A complete edition of Goethe and one of Jean Paul showed signs of wear, also Novalis, while Lessing, Jacobi and Lichtenberg were in the same condition. A few volumes of Dostoievski bristled with penciled slips. On the big table among the books and papers there was often a vase of flowers. There, too, a paint box, generally full of dust, reposed among flakes of cigar ash and (to leave nothing out) sundry bottles of wine. There was a straw-covered bottle usually containing Italian red wine, which he procured from a little shop in the neighborhood; often, too, a bottle of Burgundy as well as Malaga; and a squat bottle of Cherry brandy was, as I saw, nearly emptied in a very brief space--after which it disappeared in a corner of the room, there to collect the dust without further diminution of its contents. I will not pretend to justify this espionage I carried on, and I will say openly that all these signs of a life full of intellectual curiosity, but thoroughly slovenly and disorderly all the same, inspired me at first with aversion and mistrust. I am not only a middle-class man, living a regular life, fond of work and punctuality; I am also an abstainer and nonsmoker, and these bottles in Haller's room pleased me even less than the rest of his artistic disorder.

He was just as irregular and irresponsible about his meal times as he was about his hours of sleep and work. There were days when he did not go out at all and had nothing but his coffee in the morning. Sometimes my aunt found nothing but a banana peel to show that he had dined. Other days, however, he took his meals in restaurants, sometimes in the best and most fashionable, sometimes in little out-lying taverns. His health did not seem good. Besides his limping gait that often made the stairs fatiguing to him, he seemed to be plagued with other troubles, and he once said to me that it was years since he had had either good digestion or sound sleep. I put it down first and last to his drinking. When, later on, I accompanied him sometimes to his haunts I often saw with my own eyes how he drank when the mood was on him, though neither I nor anyone else ever saw him really drunk.

I have never forgotten our first encounter. We knew each other then only as fellow lodgers whose rooms were adjoining ones. Then one evening I came home from business and to my astonishment found Haller seated on the landing between the first and second floors. He was sitting on the top step and he moved to one side to let me pass. I asked him if he was all right and offered to take him up to the top.

Haller looked at me and I could see that I had awoken him from a kind of trance. Slowly he began to smile his delightful sad smile that has so often filled my heart with pity. Then he invited me to sit beside him. I thanked him, but said it was not my custom to sit on the stairs at other people's doors.

"Ah, yes," he said, and smiled the more. "You're quite right. But wait a moment, for I really must tell you what it was made me sit here for a bit."

He pointed as he spoke to the entrance of the first floor flat, where a widow lived. In the little space with parquet flooring between the stairs, the window and the glazed front door there stood a tall cupboard of mahogany, with some old pewter on it, and in front of the cupboard on the floor there were two plants, an azalea and an araucaria, in large pots which stood on low stands. The plants looked very pretty and were always kept spotlessly neat and clean, as I had often noticed with pleasure.

"Look at this little vestibule," Haller went on, "with the araucaria and its wonderful smell. Many a time I can't go by without pausing a moment. At your aunt's too, there reigns a wonderful smell of order and extreme cleanliness, but this little place of the araucaria, why, it's so shiningly clean, so dusted and polished and scoured, so inviolably clean that it positively glitters. I always have to take a deep breath of it as I go by. Don't you smell it too, a fragrance given off by the odor of floor polish and a faint whiff of turpentine together with the mahogany and the washed leaves of the plants--the very essence of bourgeois cleanliness, of neatness and meticulousness, of duty and devotion shown in little things. I don't know who lives here, but behind that glazed door there must be a paradise of cleanliness and spotless mediocrity, of ordered ways, a touching and anxious devotion to life's little habits and tasks.

"Do not, please, think for a moment," he went on when I said nothing in reply, "that I speak with irony. My dear sir, I would not for the world laugh at the bourgeois life. It is true that I live myself in another world, and perhaps I could not endure to live a single day in a house with araucarias. But though I am a shabby old Steppenwolf, still I'm the son of a mother, and my mother too was a middle-class man's wife and raised plants and took care to have her house and home as clean and neat and tidy as ever she could make it. All that is brought back to me by this breath of turpentine and by the araucaria, and so I sit down here every now and again; and I look into this quiet little garden of order and rejoice that such things still are."

He wanted to get up, but found it difficult; and he did not repulse me when I offered him a little help. I was silent, but I submitted just as my aunt had done before me to a certain charm the strange man could sometimes exercise. We went slowly up the stairs together, and at his door, the key in his hand, he looked me once more in the eyes in a friendly way and said; "You've come from business? Well, of course, I know little of all that. I live a bit to one side, on the edge of things, you see. But you too, I believe, interest yourself in books and such matters. Your aunt told me one day that you had been through the high school and were a good Greek scholar. Now, this morning I came on a passage in Novalis. May I show it you? It would delight you, I know."

He took me into his room, which smelt strongly of tobacco, and took out a book from one of the heaps, turned the leaves and looked for the passage.

"This is good too, very good," he said, "listen to this: 'A man should be proud of suffering. All suffering is a reminder of our high estate.' Fine! Eighty years before

Nietzsche. But that is not the sentence I meant. Wait a moment, here I have it. This: 'Most men will not swim before they are able to.' Is not that witty? Naturally, they won't swim! They are born for the solid earth, not for the water. And naturally they won't think. They are made for life, not for thought. Yes, and he who thinks, what's more, he who makes thought his business, he may go far in it, but he has bartered the solid earth for the water all the same, and one day he will drown."

He had got hold of me now. I was interested; and I stayed on a short while with him; and after that we often talked when we met on the stairs or in the street. On such occasions I always had at first the feeling that he was being ironical with me. But it was not so. He had a real respect for me, just as he had for the araucaria. He was so convinced and conscious of his isolation, his swimming in the water, his uprootedness, that a glimpse now and then of the orderly daily round--the punctuality, for example, that kept me to my office hours, or an expression let fall by a servant or tramway conductor--acted on him literally as a stimulus without in the least arousing his scorn. At first all this seemed to me a ridiculous exaggeration, the affectation of a gentleman of leisure, a playful sentimentality. But I came to see more and more that from the empty spaces of his lone wolfishness he actually really admired and loved our little bourgeois world as something solid and secure, as the home and peace which must ever remain far and unattainable, with no road leading from him to them. He took off his hat to our charwoman, a worthy person, every time he met her, with genuine respect; and when my aunt had any little occasion to talk to him, to draw his attention, it might be, to some mending of his linen or to warn him of a button hanging loose on his coat, he listened to her with an air of great attention and consequence, as though it were only with an extreme and desperate effort that he could force his way through any crack into our little peaceful world and be at home there, if only for an hour.

During that very first conversation, about the araucaria, he called himself the Steppenwolf, and this too estranged and disturbed me a little. What an expression! However, custom did not only reconcile me to it, but soon I never thought of him by any other name; nor could I today hit on a better description of him. A wolf of the Steppes that had lost its way and strayed into the towns and the life of the herd, a more striking image could not be found for his shy loneliness, his savagery, his restlessness, his homesickness, his homelessness.

I was able once to observe him for a whole evening. It was at a Symphony concert, where to my surprise I found him seated near me. He did not see me. First some Handel was played, noble and lovely music. But the Steppenwolf sat absorbed in his own thoughts, paying attention neither to the music nor to his surroundings. He sat there detached, a lonely stranger, with downcast eyes and a cold but troubled expression on his face. After the Handel came a little symphony by Friedemann Bach, and I saw with surprise how after a few bars my stranger began to smile and abandon himself to the music. He was completely absorbed in himself, and for about ten minutes so happily lost and rapt in pleasant dreams that I paid more attention to him than to the music. When the piece ended he woke up, and made a movement to go; but after all he kept his seat and heard the last piece too. It was *Variations* by Reger, a composition that many found rather long and tiresome. The Steppenwolf, too, who at first made up his mind to listen, wandered again, put his hands into his pockets and sank once more into his own thoughts, not happily and dreamily as before, but sadly and finally irritated. His face was once more vacant and grey. The light in it was quenched and he looked old, ill, and discontented.

I saw him again after the concert in the street and walked along behind him. Wrapped in his cloak he went his way joylessly and wearily in the direction of our quarter, but stopped in front of a small old-fashioned inn, and after looking irresolutely at the time, went in. I obeyed a momentary impulse and followed him; and there he sat at a table in the backroom of the bar, greeted by hostess and waitress as a well-known guest. Greeting him, too, I took my seat beside him. We sat there for an hour, and while I drank two glasses of mineral water, he accounted for a pint of red wine and then called for another half. I remarked that I had been to the concert, but he did not follow up this topic. He read the label on my bottle and asked whether I would not drink some wine. When I declined his offer and said that I never drank it, the old helpless expression came over his face.

"You're quite right there," he said. "I have practised abstinence myself for years, and had my time of fasting, too, but now I find myself once more beneath the sign of Aquarius, a dark and humid constellation."

And then, when I playfully took up his allusion and remarked how unlikely it seemed to me that he really believed in astrology, he promptly resumed the too polite tone which often hurt me and said: "You are right. Unfortunately, I cannot believe in that science either."

I took my leave and went. It was very late before he came in, but his step was as usual, and as always, instead of going straight to bed, he stayed up an hour longer in his sitting room, as I from my neighboring room could hear plainly enough.

There was another evening which I have not forgotten. My aunt was out and I was alone in the house, when the doorbell rang. I opened the door and there stood a young and very pretty woman, whom, as soon as she asked for Mr. Haller, I recognized from the photograph in his room. I showed her his door and withdrew. She stayed a short while above, but soon I heard them both come down stairs and go out, talking and laughing together very happily. I was much astonished that the hermit had his love, and one so young and pretty and elegant;

and all my conjectures about him and his life were upset once more. But before an hour had gone he came back alone and dragged himself wearily upstairs with his sad and heavy tread. For hours on end he paced softly to and fro in his sitting room, exactly like a wolf in its cage. The whole night, nearly until dawn, there was light in his room. I know nothing at all about this occasion, and have only this to add. On one other occasion I saw him in this lady's company. It was in one of the streets of the town. They were arm in arm and he looked very happy; and again I wondered to see how much charm--what an even childlike expression--his care-ridden face had sometimes. It explained the young lady to me, also the predilection my aunt had for him. That day, too, however, he came back in the evening, sad, and wretched as usual. I met him at the door and under his cloak, as many a time before, he had the bottle of Italian wine, and he sat with it half the night in his hell upstairs. It grieved me. What a comfortless, what a forlorn and shiftless life he led!

And now I have gossiped enough. No more is needed to show that the Steppenwolf lived a suicidal existence. But all the same I do not believe that he took his own life when, after paying all he owed but without a word of warning or farewell, he left our town one day and vanished. We have not heard from him since and we are still keeping some letters that came for him after he had left. He left nothing behind but his manuscript. It was written during the time he was here, and he left it with a few lines to say that I might do what I liked with it.

It was not in my power to verify the truth of the experiences related in Haller's manuscript. I have no doubt that they are for the most part fictitious, not, however, in the sense of arbitrary invention. They are rather the deeply lived spiritual events which he has attempted to express by giving them the form of tangible experiences. The partly fantastic occurrences in Haller's fiction come presumably from the later period of his stay here, and I have no doubt that even they have some basis in real occurrence. At that time our guest did in fact alter very much in behavior and in appearance. He was out a great deal, for whole nights sometimes; and his books lay untouched. On the rare occasions when I saw him at that time I was very much struck, by his air of vivacity and youth. Sometimes, indeed, he seemed positively happy. This does not mean that a new and heavy depression did not follow immediately. All day long he lay in bed. He had no desire for food. At that time the young lady appeared once more on the scene, and an extremely violent, I may even say brutal, quarrel occurred which upset the whole house and for which Haller begged my aunt's pardon for days after.

No, I am sure he has not taken his life. He is still alive, and somewhere wearily goes up and down the stairs of strange houses, stares somewhere at clean-scoured parquet floors and carefully tended araucarias, sits for days in libraries and nights in taverns, or lying on a hired sofa, listens to the world beneath his window and the hum of human life from which he knows that he is excluded. But he has not killed himself, for a glimmer of belief still tells him that he is to drink this frightful suffering in his heart to the dregs, and that it is of this suffering he must die. I think of him often. He has not made life lighter for me. He had not the gift of fostering strength and joy in me. Oh, on the contrary! But I am not he, and I live my own life, a narrow, middle-class life, but a solid one, filled with duties. And so we can think of him peacefully and affectionately, my aunt and I. She would have more to say of him than I have, but that lies buried in her good heart.

And now that we come to these records of Haller's, these partly diseased, partly beautiful, and thoughtful fantasies, I must confess that if they had fallen into my hands by chance and if I had not known their author, I should most certainly have thrown them away in disgust. But owing to my acquaintance with Haller I have been able, to some extent, to understand them, and even to appreciate them. I should hesitate to share them with others if I saw in them nothing but the pathological fancies of a single and isolated case of a diseased temperament. But I see something more in them. I see them as a document of the times, for Haller's sickness of the soul, as I now know, is not the eccentricity of a single individual, but the sickness of the times themselves, the neurosis of that generation to which Haller belongs, a sickness, it seems, that by no means attacks the weak and worthless only but, rather, precisely those who are strongest in spirit and richest in gifts.

These records, however much or however little of real life may lie at the back of them, are not an attempt to disguise or to palliate this widespread sickness of our times. They are an attempt to present the sickness itself in its actual manifestation. They mean, literally, a journey through hell, a sometimes fearful, sometimes courageous journey through the chaos of a world whose souls dwell in darkness, a journey undertaken with the determination to go through hell from one end to the other, to give battle to chaos, and to suffer torture to the full.

A remark of Haller's gave me the key to this interpretation. He said to me once when we were talking of the so-called horrors of the Middle Ages: "These horrors were really nonexistent. A man of the Middle Ages would detest the whole mode of our present-day life as something far more than horrible, far more than barbarous. Every age, every culture, every custom and tradition has its own character, its own weakness and its own strength, its beauties and ugliness; accepts certain sufferings as matters of course, puts up patiently with certain evils. Human life is reduced to real suffering, to hell, only when two ages, two cultures and religions overlap. A man of the Classical Age who had to live in medieval times would suffocate miserably just as a savage does in the midst of our civilisation. Now there are times when a whole generation is caught in this way between two ages, two modes of life, with the consequence that it loses all power to understand itself and has no standard, no security, no simple acquiescence.

Naturally, every one does not feel this equally strongly. A nature such as Nietzsche's had to suffer our present ills more than a generation in advance. What he had to go through alone and misunderstood, thousands suffer today."

I often had to think of these words while reading the records. Haller belongs to those who have been caught between two ages, who are outside of all security and simple acquiescence. He belongs to those whose fate it is to live the whole riddle of human destiny heightened to the pitch of a personal torture, a personal hell.

Therein, it seems to me, lies the meaning these records can have for us, and because of this I decided to publish them. For the rest, I neither approve nor condemn them. Let every reader do as his conscience bids him.

# HARRY HALLER'S RECORDS
## "FOR MADMEN ONLY"

THE DAY HAD GONE BY JUST AS DAYS GO BY. I had killed it in accordance with my primitive and retiring way of life. I had worked for an hour or two and perused the pages of old books. I had had pains for two hours, as elderly people do. I had taken a powder and been very glad when the pains consented to disappear. I had lain in a hot bath and absorbed its kindly warmth. Three times the mail had come with undesired letters and circulars to look through. I had done my breathing exercises, but found it convenient today to omit the thought exercises. I had been for an hour's walk and seen the loveliest feathery cloud patterns penciled against the sky. That was very delightful. So was the reading of the old books. So was the lying in the warm bath. But, taken all in all, it had not been exactly a day of rapture. No, it had not even been a day brightened with happiness and joy. Rather, it had been just one of those days which for a long while now had fallen to my lot; the moderately pleasant, the wholly bearable and tolerable, lukewarm days of a discontented middle-aged man; days without special pains, without special cares, without particular worry, without despair; days when I calmly wonder, objective and fearless, whether it isn't time to follow the example of Adalbert Stifter and have an accident while shaving.

He who has known the other days, the angry ones of gout attacks, or those with that wicked headache rooted behind the eyeballs that casts a spell on every nerve of eye and ear with a fiendish delight in torture, or soul-destroying, evil days of inward vacancy and despair, when, on this distracted earth, sucked dry by the vampires of finance, the world of men and of so-called culture grins back at us with the lying, vulgar, brazen glamor of a Fair and dogs us with the persistence of an emetic, and when all is concentrated and focused to the last pitch of the intolerable upon your own sick self--he who has known these days of hell may be content indeed with normal half-and-half days like today. Thankfully you sit by the warm stove, thankfully you assure yourself as you read your morning paper that another day has come and no war broken out, no new dictatorship has been set up, no particularly disgusting scandal been unveiled in the worlds of politics or finance. Thankfully you tune the strings of your moldering lyre to a moderated, to a passably joyful, nay, to an even delighted psalm of thanksgiving and with it bore your quiet, flabby and slightly stupefied half-and-half god of contentment; and in the thick warm air of a contented boredom and very welcome painlessness the nodding mandarin of a half-and-half god and the nodding middle-aged gentleman who sings his muffled psalm look as like each other as two peas.

There is much to be said for contentment and painlessness, for these bearable and submissive days, on which neither pain nor pleasure is audible, but pass by whispering and on tip-toe. But the worst of it is that it is just this contentment that I cannot endure. After a short time it fills me with irrepressible hatred and nausea. In desperation I have to escape and throw myself on the road to pleasure, or, if that cannot be, on the road to pain. When I have neither pleasure nor pain and have been breathing for a while the lukewarm insipid air of these so-called good and tolerable days, I feel so bad in my childish soul that I smash my moldering lyre of thanksgiving in the face of the slumbering god of contentment and would rather feel the very devil burn in me than this warmth of a well-heated room. A wild longing for strong emotions and sensations seethes in me, a rage against this toneless, flat, normal and sterile life. I have a mad impulse to smash something, a warehouse, perhaps, or a cathedral, or myself, to commit outrages, to pull off the wigs of a few revered idols, to provide a few rebellious schoolboys with the longed-for ticket to Hamburg, or to stand one or two representatives of the established order on their heads. For what I always hated and detested and cursed above all things was this contentment, this healthiness and comfort, this carefully preserved optimism of the middle classes, this fat and prosperous brood of mediocrity.

It was in such a mood then that I finished this not intolerable and very ordinary day as dusk set in. I did not end it in a manner becoming a rather ailing man and go to bed tempted by a hot water bottle. Instead I put on my shoes ill-humoredly, discontented and disgusted with the little work I had done, and went out into the dark and foggy streets to drink what men according to an old convention call "a glass of wine," at the sign of the Steel Helmet.

So I went down the stairs from my room in the attic, those difficult stairs of this alien world, those thoroughly bourgeois, well-swept and scoured stairs of a very respectable three-family apartment house under whose roof I have my refuge. I don't know how it comes about, but I, the homeless Steppenwolf, the solitary, the hater of life's petty conventions, always take up my quarters in just such houses as this. It is an old weakness of mine. I live neither in palatial houses nor in those of the humble poor, but instead and deliberately in these respectable and wearisome and spotless middle-class homes, which smell of turpentine and soap and where there is a panic if you bang the door or come in with dirty shoes. The love of this atmosphere comes, no doubt, from the days of my childhood, and a secret yearning I have for something homelike drives me, though with little hope, to follow the same old stupid road. Then again, I like the contrast between my lonely, loveless, hunted, and thoroughly disorderly existence and this middle-class family life. I like to breathe in on the stairs this odor of quiet and order, of cleanliness and respectable domesticity. There is something in it that touches me in spite of my hatred for all it stands for. I like to step across the threshold of my room where all this suddenly stops; where, instead, cigar ash and wine bottles lie among the heaped-up books and there is nothing but disorder and neglect; and where everything--books, manuscript, thoughts--is marked and saturated with the plight of lonely men, with the problem of existence and with the yearning after a new orientation for an age that has lost its bearings.

And now I came to the araucaria. I must tell you that on the first floor of this house the stairs pass by a little vestibule at the entrance to a flat which, I am convinced, is even more spotlessly swept and garnished than the others; for this little vestibule shines with a superhuman housewifery. It is a little temple of order. On the parquet floor, where it seems desecration to tread, are two elegant stands and on each a large pot. In the one grows an azalea. In the other a stately araucaria, a thriving, straight-grown baby tree, a perfect specimen, which to the last needle of the topmost twig reflects the pride of frequent ablutions. Sometimes, when I know that I am unobserved, I use this place as a temple. I take my seat on a step of the stairs above the araucaria and, resting awhile with folded hands, I contemplate this little garden of order and let the touching air it has and its somewhat ridiculous loneliness move me to the depths of my soul. I imagine behind this vestibule, in the sacred shadow, one may say, of the araucaria, a home full of shining mahogany, and a life full of sound respectability--early rising, attention to duty, restrained but cheerful family gatherings, Sunday church going, early to bed.

Affecting lightheartedness, I trod the moist pavements of the narrow streets. As though in tears and veiled, the lamps glimmered through the chill gloom and sucked their reflections slowly from the wet ground. The forgotten years of my youth came back to me. How I used to love the dark, sad evenings of late autumn and winter, how eagerly I imbibed their moods of loneliness and melancholy when wrapped in my cloak I strode for half the night through rain and storm, through the leafless winter landscape, lonely enough then too, but full of deep joy, and full of poetry which later I wrote down by candlelight sitting on the edge of my bed! All that was past now. The cup was emptied and would never be filled again. Was that a matter for regret? No, I did not regret the past. My regret was for the present day, for all the countless hours and days that I lost in mere passivity and that brought me nothing, not even the shocks of awakening. But, thank God, there were exceptions. There were now and then, though rarely, the hours that brought the welcome shock, pulled down the walls and brought me back again from my wanderings to the living heart of the world. Sadly and yet deeply moved, I set myself to recall the last of these experiences. It was at a concert of lovely old music. After two or three notes of the piano the door was opened of a sudden to the other world. I sped through heaven and saw God at work. I suffered holy pains. I dropped all my defences and was afraid of nothing in the world. I accepted all things and to all things I gave up my heart. It did not last very long, a quarter of an hour perhaps; but it returned to me in a dream at night, and since, through all the barren days, I caught a glimpse of it now and then. Sometimes for a minute or two I saw it clearly, threading my life like a divine and golden track. But nearly always it was blurred in dirt and dust. Then again it gleamed out in golden sparks as though never to be lost again and yet was soon quite lost once more. Once it happened, as I lay awake at night, that I suddenly spoke in verses, in verses so beautiful and strange that I did not venture to think of writing them down, and then in the morning they vanished; and yet they lay hidden within me like the hard kernel within an old brittle husk. Once it came to me while reading a poet, while pondering a thought of Descartes, of Pascal; again it shone out and drove its gold track far into the sky while I was in the presence of my beloved. Ah, but it is hard to find this track of the divine in the midst of this life we lead, in this besotted humdrum age of spiritual blindness, with its architecture, its business, its politics, its men! How could I fail to be a lone wolf, and an uncouth hermit, as I did not share one of its aims nor understand one of its pleasures? I cannot remain for long in either theater or picture-house. I can scarcely read a paper, seldom a modern book. I cannot understand what pleasures and joys they are that drive people to the overcrowded railways and hotels, into the packed cafés with the suffocating and oppressive music, to the Bars and variety entertainments, to World Exhibitions, to the Corsos. I cannot understand nor share these joys, though they are within my reach, for which thousands of others strive. On the other hand, what happens to me in my rare hours of joy, what for me is bliss and life and ecstasy and exaltation, the world in general seeks at most in imagination; in life it finds it absurd. And in fact, if the world is right, if this music of the cafés, these mass enjoyments and these Americanised men who are pleased with so little are right, then I am wrong, I am crazy. I am in truth the Steppenwolf that I often call myself; that beast astray who finds neither home nor joy nor nourishment in a world that is strange and incomprehensible to him.

With these familiar thoughts I went along the wet street through one of the quietest and oldest quarters of the town. On the opposite side there stood in the darkness an old stone wall which I always noticed with pleasure. Old and serene, it stood between a little church and an old hospital and often during the day I let my eyes rest on its rough surface. There were few such quiet and peaceful spaces in the center of the town where from every square foot some lawyer, or quack, or doctor, or barber, or chiropodist shouted his name at you. This time, too, the wall was peaceful and serene and yet something was altered in it. I was amazed to see a small and pretty doorway with a Gothic arch in the middle of the wall, for I could not make up my mind whether this doorway had always been there or whether it had just been made. It looked old without a doubt, very old;

apparently this closed portal with its door of blackened wood had opened hundreds of years ago onto a sleepy convent yard, and did so still, even though the convent was no longer there. Probably I had seen it a hundred times and simply not noticed it. Perhaps it had been painted afresh and caught my eye for that reason. I paused to examine it from where I stood without crossing over, as the street between was so deep in mud and water. From the sidewalk where I stood and looked across, it seemed to me in the dim light that a garland, or something gaily colored, was festooned round the doorway, and now that I looked more closely I saw over the portal a bright shield, on which, it seemed to me, there was something written. I strained my eyes and at last, in spite of the mud and puddles, went across, and there over the door I saw a stain showing up faintly on the grey-green of the wall, and over the stain bright letters dancing and then disappearing, returning and vanishing once more. So that's it, thought I. They've disfigured this good old wall with an electric sign. Meanwhile I deciphered one or two of the letters as they appeared again for an instant; but they were hard to read even by guess work, for they came with very irregular spaces between them and very faintly, and then abruptly vanished. Whoever hoped for any result from a display like that was not very smart. He was a Steppenwolf, poor fellow. Why have his letters playing on this old wall in the darkest alley of the Old Town on a wet night with not a soul passing by, and why were they so fleeting, so fitful and illegible? But wait, at last I succeeded in catching several words on end. They were:

MAGIC THEATER
ENTRANCE NOT FOR EVERYBODY

I tried to open the door, but the heavy old latch would not stir. The display too was over. It had suddenly ceased, sadly convinced of its uselessness. I took a few steps back, landing deep into the mud, but no more letters came. The display was over. For a long time I stood waiting in the mud, but in vain.

Then, when I had given up and gone back to the alley, a few colored letters were dropped here and there, reflected on the asphalt in front of me. I read:

FOR MADMEN ONLY!

My feet were wet and I was chilled to the bone. Nevertheless, I stood waiting. Nothing more. But while I waited, thinking how prettily the letters had danced in their ghostly fashion over the damp wall and the black sheen of the asphalt, a fragment of my former thoughts came suddenly to my mind; the similarity to the track of shining gold which suddenly vanishes and cannot be found.

I was freezing and walked on following that track in my dreams, longing too for that doorway to an enchanted theater, which was for madmen only. Meanwhile I had reached the market place, where there is never a lack of evening entertainments. At every other step were placards and posters with their various attractions, Ladies' Orchestra, Variété, Cinema, Ball. But none of these was for me. They were for "everybody," for those normal persons whom I saw crowding every entrance. In spite of that my sadness was a little lightened. I had had a greeting from another world, and a few dancing, colored letters had played upon my soul and sounded its secret strings. A glimmer of the golden track had been visible once again.

I sought out the little ancient tavern where nothing had altered since my first visit to this town a good twenty-five years before. Even the landlady was the same as then and many of the patrons who sat there in those days sat there still at the same places before the same glasses. There I took refuge. True, it was only a refuge, something like the one on the stairs opposite the araucaria. Here, too, I found neither home nor company, nothing but a seat from which to view a stage where strange people played strange parts. Nonetheless, the quiet of the place was worth something; no crowds, no music; only a few peaceful townsfolk at bare wooden tables (no marble, no enamel, no plush, no brass) and before each his evening glass of good old wine. Perhaps this company of habitués, all of whom I knew by sight, were all regular Philistines and had in their Philistine dwellings their altars of the home dedicated to sheepish idols of contentment; perhaps, too, they were solitary fellows who had been sidetracked, quiet, thoughtful topers of bankrupt ideals, lone wolves and poor devils like me. I could not say. Either homesickness or disappointment, or need of change drew them there, the married to recover the atmosphere of his bachelor days, the old official to recall his student years. All of them were silent, and all were drinkers who would rather, like me, sit before a pint of Elsasser than listen to a Ladies' Orchestra. Here I cast anchor, for an hour, or it might be two. With the first sip of Elsasser I realised that I had eaten nothing that day since my morning roll.

It is remarkable, all that men can swallow. For a good ten minutes I read a newspaper. I allowed the spirit of an irresponsible man who chews and munches another's words in his mouth, and gives them out again undigested, to enter into me through my eyes. I absorbed a whole column of it. And then I devoured a large piece cut from the liver of a slaughtered calf. Odd indeed! The best was the Elsasser. I am not fond, for everyday at least, of racy, heady wines that diffuse a potent charm and have their own particular flavor. What I like the best is a clean, light, modest country vintage of no special name. One can carry plenty of it and it has the good and homely flavor of the land, and of earth and sky and woods. A pint of Elsasser and a piece of good bread is the best of all meals. By this time, however, I had already eaten my portion of liver, an unusual indulgence for me, as I seldom eat meat, and the second pint had been set before me. And this too was odd: that somewhere in a green valley vines were tended by good, strong fellows and the wine pressed so that here and there in the world, far away, a few disappointed, quietly drinking townsfolk and dispirited Steppenwolves could sip a little heart and courage from their glasses.

I didn't really care whether all this was odd or not. It was good, it helped, it raised my spirits. As I thought again of that newspaper article and its jumble of words, a refreshing laughter rose in me, and suddenly the forgotten melody of those notes of the piano came back to me again. It soared aloft like a soap bubble, reflecting the whole world in miniature on its rainbow surface, and then softly burst. Could I be altogether lost when that heavenly little melody had been secretly rooted within me and now put forth its lovely bloom with all its tender hues? I might be a beast astray, with no sense of its environment, yet there was some meaning in my foolish life, something in me gave an answer and was the receiver of those distant calls from worlds far above. In my brain were stored a thousand pictures:

Giotto's flock of angels from the blue vaulting of a little church in Padua, and near them walked Hamlet and the garlanded Ophelia, fair similitudes of all sadness and misunderstanding in the world, and there stood Gianozzo, the aeronaut, in his burning balloon and blew a blast on his horn, Attila carrying his new headgear in his hand, and the Borobudur reared its soaring sculpture in the air. And though all these figures lived in a thousand other hearts as well, there were ten thousand more unknown pictures and tunes there which had no dwelling place but in me, no eyes to see, no ears to hear them but mine. The old hospital wall with its grey-green weathering, its cracks and stains in which a thousand frescoes could be fancied, who responded to it, who looked into its soul, who loved it, who found the charm of its colors ever delicately dying away? The old books of the monks, softly illumined with their miniatures, and the books of the German poets of two hundred and a hundred years ago whom their own folk have forgotten, all the thumbed and damp-stained volumes, and the works in print and manuscripts of the old composers, the stout and yellowing music sheets dreaming their music through a winter sleep--who heard their spirited, their roguish and yearning tones, who carried through a world estranged from them a heart full of their spirit and their charm? Who still remembered that slender cypress on a hill over Gubbio, that though split and riven by a fall of stone yet held fast to life and put forth with its last resources a new sparse tuft at top? Who read by night above the Rhine the cloudscript of the drifting mists? It was the Steppenwolf. And who over the ruins of his life pursued its fleeting, fluttering significance, while he suffered its seeming meaninglessness and lived its seeming madness, and who hoped in secret at the last turn of the labyrinth of Chaos for revelation and God's presence?

I held my hand over my glass when the landlady wanted to fill it once more, and got up. I needed no more wine. The golden trail was blazed and I was reminded of the eternal, and of Mozart, and the stars. For an hour I could breathe once more and live and face existence, without the need to suffer torment, fear, or shame.

A cold wind was sifting the fine rain as I went out into the deserted street. It drove the drops with a patter against the streetlamps where they glimmered with a glassy sparkle. And now, whither? If I had had a magic wand at this moment I should have conjured up a small and charming Louis Seize music room where a few musicians would have played me two or three pieces of Handel and Mozart. I was in the very mood for it, and would have sipped the cool and noble music as gods sip nectar. Oh, if I had had a friend at this moment, a friend in an attic room, dreaming by candlelight and with a violin lying ready at his hand! How I should have slipped up to him in his quiet hour, noiselessly climbing the winding stair to take him by surprise, and then with talk and music we should have held heavenly festival throughout the night! Once, in years gone by, I had often known such happiness, but this too time had taken away. Withered years lay between those days and now.

I loitered as I wended my way homeward; turned up my collar and struck my stick on the wet pavement. However long I lingered outside I should find myself all too soon in my top-floor room, my makeshift home, which I could neither love nor do without; for the time had gone by when I could spend a wet winter's night in the open. And now my prayer was not to let the good mood the evening had given me be spoiled, neither by the rain, nor by gout, nor by the araucaria; and though there was no chamber music to be had nor a lonely friend with his violin, still that lovely melody was in my head and I could play it through to myself after a fashion, humming the rhythm of it as I drew my breath. Reflecting thus, I walked on and on. Yes, even without the chamber music and the friend. How foolish to wear oneself out in vain longing for warmth! Solitude is independence. It had been my wish and with the years I had attained it. It was cold. Oh, cold enough! But it was also still, wonderfully still and vast like the cold stillness of space in which the stars revolve.

From a dance hall there met me as I passed by the strains of lively jazz music, hot and raw as the steam of raw flesh. I stopped a moment. This kind of music, much as I detested it, had always had a secret charm for me. It was repugnant to me, and yet ten times preferable to all the academic music of the day. For me too, its raw and savage gaiety reached an underworld of instinct and breathed a simple honest sensuality.

I stood for a moment on the scent, smelling this shrill and blood-raw music, sniffing the atmosphere of the hall angrily, and hankering after it a little too. One half of this music, the melody, was all pomade and sugar and sentimentality. The other half was savage, temperamental and vigorous. Yet the two went artlessly well together and made a whole. It was the music of decline. There must have been such music in Rome under the later emperors. Compared with Bach and Mozart and real music it was, naturally, a miserable affair; but so was all our art, all our thought, all our makeshift culture in comparison with real culture. This music was at least sincere, unashamedly primitive and childishly happy. There was something of the Negro in it, and something of the American, who with all his strength seems so boyishly fresh and childlike to us Europeans. Was Europe to become the same? Was it on the way already? Were we, the old connoisseurs, the reverers of Europe as it used to be, of genuine music and poetry as once they were, nothing but a pig-headed minority suffering from a complex neurosis, whom tomorrow would forget or deride? Was all that we called culture, spirit, soul, all that we called beautiful and sacred, nothing but a ghost long dead, which only a few fools like us took for true and living? Had it perhaps indeed never been true and living? Had all that we poor fools bothered our heads about never been anything but a phantom?

I was now in the old quarter of the town. The little church stood up dim and grey and unreal. At once the experience of the evening came back to me, the mysterious Gothic doorway, the mysterious tablet above it and the illuminated letters dancing in mockery. How did the writing run? "Entrance not for Everybody." And: "For madmen only." I scrutinised the old wall opposite in the secret hope that the magic night might begin again; the writing invite me, the madman; the little doorway give me admittance. There perhaps lay my desire, and there perhaps would my music be played.

The dark stone wall looked back at me with composure, shut off in a deep twilight, sunk in a dream of its own. And there was no gateway anywhere and no pointed arch; only the dark unbroken masonry. With a smile I went on, giving it a friendly nod. "Sleep well. I will not awake you. The time will come when you will be pulled down or plastered with covetous advertisements. But for the present, there you stand, beautiful and quiet as ever, and I love you for it."

From the black mouth of an alley a man appeared with startling suddenness at my elbow, a lone man going his homeward way with weary step. He wore a cap and a blue blouse, and above his shoulders he carried a signboard fixed on a pole, and in front of him an open tray suspended by straps such as pedlars carry at fairs. He walked on wearily in front of me without looking round. Otherwise I should have bidden him a good evening and given him a cigar. I tried to read the device on his standard--a red signboard on a pole--in the light of the next lamp; but it swayed to and fro and I could decipher nothing. Then I called out and asked him to let me read his placard. He stopped and held his pole a little steadier. Then I could read the dancing reeling letters:

ANARCHIST EVENING ENTERTAINMENT
MAGIC THEATER
ENTRANCE NOT FOR EVERYBODY

"I've been looking for you," I shouted with delight. "What is this Evening Entertainment? Where is it? When?"

He was already walking on.

"Not for everybody," he said dully with a sleepy voice. He had had enough. He was for home, and on he went.

"Stop," I cried, and ran after him. "What have you got there in your box? I want to buy something from you."

Without stopping, the man felt mechanically in his box, pulled out a little book and held it out to me. I took it quickly and put it in my pocket. While I felt for the buttons of my coat to get out some money, he turned in at a doorway, shut the door behind him and disappeared. His heavy steps rang on a flagged yard, then on wooden stairs; and then I heard no more. And suddenly I too felt very tired. It came over me that it must be very late--and high time to go home. I walked on faster and, following the road to the suburb, I was soon in my own neighborhood among the well-kept gardens, where in, clean little apartment houses behind lawn and ivy are the dwellings of officialdom and people of modest means. Passing the ivy and the grass and the little fir tree I reached the door of the house, found the keyhole and the switch, slipped past the glazed doors, and the polished cupboards and the potted plants and unlocked the door of my room, my little pretence of a home, where the armchair and the stove, the ink-pot and the paint-box, Novalis and Dostoievski, awaited me just as do the mother, or the wife, the children, maids, dogs and cats in the case of more sensible people.

As I threw off my wet coat I came upon the little book, and took it out. It was one of those little books wretchedly printed on wretched paper that are sold at fairs, "Were you born in January?" or "How to be twenty years younger in a week."

However, when I settled myself in my armchair and put on my glasses, it was with great astonishment and a sudden sense of impending fate that I read the title on the cover of this companion volume to fortune-telling booklets. *"Treatise on the*

*Steppenwolf. Not for Everybody."*

I read the contents at a sitting with an engrossing interest that deepened page by page.

## TREATISE ON THE STEPPENWOLF

There was once a man, Harry, called the Steppenwolf. He went on two legs, wore clothes and was a human being, but nevertheless he was in reality a wolf of the Steppes. He had learned a good deal of all that people of a good intelligence can, and was a fairly clever fellow. What he had not learned, however, was this: to find contentment in himself and his own life. The cause of this apparently was that at the bottom of his heart he knew all the time (or thought he knew) that he was in reality not a man, but a wolf of the Steppes. Clever men might argue the point whether he truly was a wolf, whether, that is, he had been changed, before birth perhaps, from a wolf into a human being, or had been given the soul of a wolf, though born as a human being; or whether, on the other hand, this belief that he was a wolf was no more than a fancy or a disease of his. It might, for example, be possible that in his childhood he was a little wild and disobedient and disorderly, and that those who brought him up had declared a war of extinction against the beast in him; and precisely this had given him the idea and the belief that he was in fact actually a beast with only a thin covering of the human. On this point one could speak at length and entertainingly, and indeed write a book about it. The Steppenwolf, however, would be none the better for it, since for him it was all one whether the wolf had been bewitched or beaten into him, or whether it was merely an idea of his own. What others chose to think about it or what he chose to think himself was no good to him at all. It left the wolf inside him just the same.

And so the Steppenwolf had two natures, a human and a wolfish one. This was his fate, and it may well be that it was not a very exceptional one. There must have been many men who have had a good deal of the dog or the fox, of the fish or the serpent in them without experiencing any extraordinary difficulties on that account. In such cases, the man and the fish lived on together and neither did the other any harm. The one even helped the other. Many a man indeed has carried this condition to such enviable lengths that he has owed his happiness more to the fox or the ape in him than to the man. So much for common knowledge. In the case of Harry, however, it was just the opposite. In him the man and the wolf did not go the same way together, but were in continual and deadly enmity. One existed simply and solely to harm the other, and when there are two in one blood and in one soul who are at deadly enmity, then life fares ill. Well, to each his lot, and none is light.

Now with our Steppenwolf it was so that in his conscious life he lived now as a wolf, now as a man, as indeed the case is with all mixed beings. But, when he was a wolf, the man in him lay in ambush, ever on the watch to interfere and condemn, while at those times that he was a man the wolf did just the same. For example, if Harry, as man, had a beautiful thought, felt a fine and noble emotion, or performed a so-called good act, then the wolf bared his teeth at him and laughed and showed him with bitter scorn how laughable this whole pantomime was in the eyes of a beast, of a wolf who knew well enough in his heart what suited him, namely, to trot alone over the Steppes and now and then to gorge himself with blood or to pursue a female wolf. Then, wolfishly seen, all human activities became horribly absurd and misplaced, stupid and vain. But it was exactly the same when Harry felt and behaved as a wolf and showed others his teeth and felt hatred and enmity against all human beings and their lying and degenerate manners and customs. For then the human part of him lay in ambush and watched the wolf, called him brute and beast, and spoiled and embittered for him all pleasure in his simple and healthy and wild wolf's being.

Thus it was then with the Steppenwolf, and one may well imagine that Harry did not have an exactly pleasant and happy life of it. This does not mean, however, that he was unhappy in any extraordinary degree (although it may have seemed so to himself all the same, inasmuch as every man takes the sufferings that fall to his share as the greatest). That cannot be said of any man. Even he who has no wolf in him, may be none the happier for that. And even the unhappiest life has its sunny moments and its little flowers of happiness between sand and stone. So it was, then, with the Steppenwolf too. It cannot be denied that he was generally very unhappy; and he could make others unhappy also, that is, when he loved them or they him. For all who got to love him, saw always only the one side in him. Many loved him as a refined and clever and interesting man, and were horrified and disappointed when they had come upon the wolf in him. And they had to because Harry wished, as every sentient being does, to be loved as a whole and therefore it was just with those whose love he most valued that he could least of all conceal and belie the wolf. There were those, however, who loved precisely the wolf in him, the free, the savage, the untamable, the dangerous and strong, and these found it peculiarly disappointing and deplorable when suddenly the wild and wicked wolf was also a man, and had hankerings after goodness and refinement, and wanted to hear Mozart, to read poetry and to cherish human ideals. Usually these were the most disappointed and angry of all; and so it was that the Steppenwolf brought his own dual and divided nature into the destinies of others besides himself whenever he came into contact with them.

Now, whoever thinks that he knows the Steppenwolf and that he can imagine to himself his lamentably divided life is nevertheless in error. He does not know all by a long way. He does not know that, as there is no rule without an exception and as one sinner may under certain circumstances be dearer to God than ninety and nine righteous persons, with Harry too there were now and then exceptions and strokes of good luck, and that he could breathe and think and feel sometimes as the wolf, sometimes as the man, clearly and without confusion of the two; and even on very rare occasions, they made peace and lived for one another in such fashion that not merely did one keep watch whilst the other slept but each strengthened and confirmed the other. In the life of this man, too, as well as in all things else in the world, daily use and the accepted and common knowledge seemed sometimes to have no other aim than to be arrested now and again for an instant, and broken through, in order to yield the place of honor to the exceptional and miraculous. Now whether these short and occasional hours of happiness balanced and alleviated the lot of the Steppenwolf in such a fashion that in the upshot happiness and suffering held the scales even, or whether perhaps the short but intense happiness of those few hours outweighed all suffering and left a balance over is again a question over which idle persons may meditate to their hearts' content. Even the wolf brooded often over this, and those were his idle and unprofitable days.

In this connection one thing more must be said. There are a good many people of the same kind as Harry. Many artists are of his kind. These persons all have two souls, two beings within them. There is God and the devil in them; the mother's blood and the father's; the capacity for happiness and the capacity for suffering; and in just such a state of enmity and entanglement towards and within each other as were the wolf and man in Harry. And these men, for whom life has no repose, live at times in their rare moments of happiness with such strength and indescribable beauty, the spray of their moment's happiness is flung so high and dazzlingly over the wide sea of suffering, that the light of it, spreading its radiance, touches others too with its enchantment. Thus, like a precious, fleeting foam over the sea of suffering arise all those works of art, in which a single individual lifts himself for an hour so high above his personal destiny that his happiness shines like a star and appears to all who see it as something eternal and as a happiness of their own. All these men, whatever their deeds and works may be, have really no life; that is to say, their lives are not their own and have no form. They are not heroes, artists or thinkers in the same way that other men are judges, doctors, shoemakers, or schoolmasters. Their life consists of a perpetual tide, unhappy and torn with pain, terrible and meaningless, unless one is ready to see its meaning in just those rare experiences, acts, thoughts and works that shine out above the chaos of such a life. To such men the desperate and horrible thought has come that perhaps the whole of human life is but a bad joke, a violent and ill-fated abortion of the primal mother, a savage and dismal catastrophe of nature. To them, too, however, the other thought has come that man is perhaps not merely a half-rational animal but a child of the gods and destined to immortality.

Men of every kind have their characteristics, their features, their virtues and vices and their deadly sins. Prowling about at night was one of the Steppenwolf's favorite tendencies. The morning was a wretched time of day for him. He feared it and it never brought him any good. On no morning of his life had he ever been in good spirits nor done any good before midday, nor ever had a happy idea, nor devised any pleasure for himself or others. By degrees during the afternoon he warmed and became alive, and only towards evening, on his good days, was he productive, active and, sometimes, aglow with joy. With this was bound up his need for loneliness and independence. There was never a man with a deeper and more passionate craving for independence than he. In his youth when he was poor and had difficulty in earning his bread, he preferred to go hungry and in torn clothes rather than endanger his narrow limit of independence. He never sold himself for money or an easy life or to women or to those in power; and had thrown away a hundred times what in the world's eyes was his advantage and happiness in order to safeguard his liberty. No prospect was more hateful and distasteful to him than that he should have to go to an office and conform to daily and yearly routine and obey others. He hated all kinds of offices, governmental or commercial, as he hated death, and his worst nightmare was confinement in barracks. He contrived, often at great sacrifice, to avoid all such predicaments. It was here that his strength and his virtue rested. On this point he could neither be bent nor bribed. Here his character was firm and indeflectable. Only, through this virtue, he was bound the closer to his destiny of suffering. It happened to him as it does to all; what he strove for with the deepest and most stubborn instinct of his being fell to his lot, but more than is good for men. In the beginning his dream and his happiness, in the end it was his bitter fate. The man of power is ruined by power, the man of money by money, the submissive man by subservience, the pleasure seeker by pleasure. He achieved his aim. He was ever more independent. He took orders from no man and ordered his ways to suit no man. Independently and alone, he decided what to do and to leave undone. For every strong man attains to that which a genuine impulse bids him seek. But in the midst of the freedom he had attained Harry suddenly became aware that his freedom was a death and that he stood alone. The world in an uncanny fashion left him in peace. Other men concerned him no longer. He was not even concerned about himself. He began to suffocate slowly in the more and more rarefied atmosphere of remoteness and solitude. For now it was his wish no longer, nor his aim, to be alone and independent, but rather his lot and his sentence. The magic wish had been fulfilled and could not be cancelled, and it was no good now to open his arms with longing and goodwill to welcome the bonds of society. People left him alone now. It was not, however, that he was an object of hatred and repugnance. On the contrary, he had many friends. A great many people liked him. But it was no more than sympathy and friendliness. He received invitations, presents, pleasant letters; but no more. No one came near to him. There was no link left, and no one could have had any part in his life even had anyone wished it. For the air of lonely men surrounded him now, a still atmosphere in which the world around him slipped away, leaving him incapable of relationship, an atmosphere against which neither will nor longing availed. This was one of the significant earmarks of his life.

Another was that he was numbered among the suicides. And here it must be said that to call suicides only those who actually destroy themselves is false. Among these, indeed, there are many who in a sense are suicides only by accident and in whose being suicide has no necessary place. Among the common run of men there are many of little personality and stamped with no deep impress of fate, who find their end in suicide without belonging on that account to the type of the suicide by inclination; while on the other hand, of those who are to be counted as suicides by the very nature of their beings are many, perhaps a majority, who never in fact lay hands on themselves. The "suicide," and Harry was one, need not necessarily live in a peculiarly close relationship to death. One may do this without being a suicide. What is peculiar to the suicide is that his ego, rightly or wrongly, is felt to be an extremely dangerous, dubious, and doomed germ of nature; that he is always in his own eyes exposed to an extraordinary risk, as though he stood with the slightest foothold on the peak of a crag whence a slight push from without or an instant's weakness from within suffices to precipitate him into the void. The line of fate in the case of these men is marked by the belief they have that suicide is their most probable manner of death. It might be presumed that such temperaments, which usually manifest themselves in early youth and persist through life, show a singular defect of vital force. On the contrary, among the "suicides" are to be found unusually tenacious and eager and also hardy natures. But just as there are those who at the least indisposition develop a fever, so do those whom we call suicides, and who are always very emotional and sensitive, develop at the least shock the notion of suicide. Had we a science with the courage and authority to concern itself with mankind, instead of with the mechanism merely of vital phenomena, had we something of the nature of an anthropology, or a psychology, these matters of fact would be familiar to every one.

What was said above on the subject of suicides touches obviously nothing but the surface. It is psychology, and, therefore, partly physics. Metaphysically considered, the matter has a different and a much clearer aspect. In this aspect suicides present themselves as those who are overtaken by the sense of guilt inherent in individuals, these souls that find the aim of life not in the perfecting and molding of the self, but in liberating themselves by going back to the mother, back to God, back to the all. Many of these natures are wholly incapable of ever having recourse to real suicide, because they have a profound consciousness of the sin of doing so. For us they are suicides nonetheless; for they see death and not life as the releaser. They are ready to cast themselves away in surrender, to be extinguished and to go back to the beginning.

As every strength may become a weakness (and under some circumstances must) so, on the contrary, may the typical suicide find a strength and a support in his apparent weakness. Indeed, he does so more often than not. The case of Harry, the Steppenwolf, is one of these. As thousands of his like do, he found consolation and support, and not merely the melancholy play of youthful fancy, in the idea that the way to death was open to him at any moment. It is true that with him, as with all men of his kind, every shock, every pain, every untoward predicament at once called forth the wish to find an escape in death. By degrees, however, he fashioned for himself out of this tendency a philosophy that was actually serviceable to life. He gained strength through familiarity with the thought that the emergency exit stood always open, and became curious, too, to taste his suffering to the dregs. If it went too badly with him he could feel sometimes with a grim malicious pleasure: "I am curious to see all the same just how much a man can endure. If the limit of what is bearable is reached, I have only to open the door to escape." There are a great many suicides to whom this thought imparts an uncommon strength.

On the other hand, all suicides have the responsibility of fighting against the temptation of suicide. Every one of them knows very well in some corner of his soul that suicide, though a way out, is rather a mean and shabby one, and that it is nobler and finer to be conquered by life than to fall by one's own hand. Knowing this, with a morbid conscience whose source is much the same as that of the militant conscience of so-called self-contented persons, the majority of suicides are left to a protracted struggle against their temptation. They struggle as the kleptomaniac against his own vice. The Steppenwolf was not unfamiliar with this struggle. He had engaged in it with many a change of weapons. Finally, at the age of forty-seven or thereabouts, a happy and not unhumorous idea came to him from which he often derived some amusement. He appointed his fiftieth birthday as the day on which he might allow himself to take his own life. On this day, according to his mood, so he agreed with himself, it should be open to him to employ the emergency exit or not. Let happen to him what might, illness, poverty, suffering and bitterness, there was a time-limit. It could not extend beyond these few years, months, days whose number daily diminished. And in fact he bore much adversity, which previously would have cost him severer and longer tortures and shaken him perhaps to the roots of his being, very much more easily. When for any reason it went particularly badly with him, when peculiar pains and penalties were added to the desolateness and loneliness and savagery of his life, he could say to his tormentors: "Only wait, two years and I am your master." And with this he cherished the thought of the morning of his fiftieth birthday. Letters of congratulation would arrive, while he, relying on his razor, took leave of all his pains and closed the door behind him. Then gout in the joints, depression of spirits, and all pains of head and body could look for another victim.

. . . . . . .

It still remains to elucidate the Steppenwolf as an isolated phenomenon, in his relation, for example, to the bourgeois world, so that his symptoms may be traced to their source. Let us take as a starting point, since it offers itself, his relation to the bourgeoisie.

To take his own view of the matter, the Steppenwolf stood entirely outside the world of convention, since he had neither family life nor social ambitions. He felt himself to be single and alone, whether as a queer fellow and a hermit in poor health, or as a person removed from the common run of men by the prerogative of talents that had something of genius in them. Deliberately, he looked down upon the ordinary man and was proud that he was not one. Nevertheless his life in many aspects was thoroughly ordinary. He had money in the bank and supported poor relations. He was dressed respectably and inconspicuously, even though without particular care. He was glad to live on good terms with the police and the tax collectors and other such powers. Besides this, he was secretly and persistently attracted to the little bourgeois world, to those quiet and respectable homes with tidy gardens, irreproachable stair-cases and their whole modest air of order and comfort. It pleased him to set himself outside it, with his little vices and extravagances, as a queer fellow or a genius, but he never had his domicile in those provinces of life where the bourgeoisie had ceased to exist. He was not at ease with violent and exceptional persons or with criminals and outlaws, and he took up his abode always among the middle classes, with whose habits and standards and atmosphere he stood in a constant relation, even though it might be one of contrast and revolt. Moreover, he had been brought up in a provincial and conventional home and many of the notions and much of the examples of those days had never left him. In theory he had nothing whatever against the servant class, yet in practice it would have been beyond him to take a servant quite seriously as his equal. He was capable of loving the political criminal, the revolutionary or intellectual seducer, the outlaw of state and society, as his brother, but as for theft and robbery, murder and rape, be would not have known how to deplore them otherwise than in a thoroughly bourgeois manner.

In this way he was always recognising and affirming with one half of himself, in thought and act, what with the other half he fought against and denied. Brought up, as he was, in a cultivated home in the approved manner, he never tore part of his soul loose from its conventionalities even after he had long since individualised himself to a degree beyond its scope and freed himself from the substance of its ideals and beliefs.

Now what we call "bourgeois," when regarded as an element always to be found in human life, is nothing else than the search for a balance. It is the striving after a mean between the countless extremes and opposites that arise in human conduct. If we take any one of these coupled opposites, such as piety and profligacy, the analogy is immediately comprehensible. It is open to a man to give himself up wholly to spiritual views, to seeking after God, to the ideal of saintliness. On the other hand, he can equally give himself up entirely to the life of instinct, to the lusts of the flesh, and so direct all his efforts to the attainment of momentary pleasures. The one path leads to the saint, to the martyrdom of the spirit and surrender to God. The other path leads to the profligate, to the martyrdom of the flesh, the surrender to corruption. Now it is between the two, in the middle of the road, that the bourgeois seeks to walk. He will never surrender himself either to lust or to asceticism. He will never be a martyr or agree to his own destruction. On the contrary, his ideal is not to give up but to maintain his own identity. He strives neither for the saintly nor its opposite. The absolute is his abhorrence. He may be ready to serve God, but not by giving up the fleshpots. He is ready to be virtuous, but likes to be easy and comfortable in this world as well. In short, his aim is to make a home for himself between two extremes in a temperate zone without violent storms and tempests; and in this he succeeds though it be at the cost of that intensity of life and feeling which an extreme life affords. A man cannot live intensely except at the cost of the self. Now the bourgeois treasures nothing more highly than the self (rudimentary as his may be). And so at the cost of intensity he achieves his own preservation and security. His harvest is a quiet mind which he prefers to being possessed by God, as he does comfort to pleasure, convenience to liberty, and a pleasant temperature to that deathly inner consuming fire. The bourgeois is consequently by nature a creature of weak impulses, anxious, fearful of giving himself away and easy to rule. Therefore, he has substituted majority for power, law for force, and the polling booth for responsibility.

It is clear that this weak and anxious being, in whatever numbers he exists, cannot maintain himself, and that qualities such as his can play no other role in the world than that of a herd of sheep among free roving wolves. Yet we see that, though in times when commanding natures are uppermost, the bourgeois goes at once to the wall, he never goes under; indeed at times he even appears to rule the world. How is this possible? Neither the great numbers of the herd, nor virtue, nor common sense, nor organization could avail to save it from destruction. No medicine in the world can keep a pulse beating that from the outset was so weak. Nevertheless the bourgeoisie prospers. Why?

The answer runs: Because of the Steppenwolves. In fact, the vital force of the bourgeoisie resides by no means in the qualities of its normal members, but in those of its extremely numerous "outsiders" who by virtue of the extensiveness and elasticity of its ideals it can embrace. There is always a large number of strong and wild natures who share the life of the fold. Our Steppenwolf, Harry, is a characteristic example. He who is developed far beyond the level possible to the bourgeois, he who knows the bliss of meditation no less than the gloomy joys of hatred and self-hatred, he who despises law, virtue and common sense, is nevertheless captive to the bourgeoisie and cannot escape it. And so all through the mass of the real bourgeoisie are interposed numerous layers of humanity, many thousands of lives and minds, every one of whom, it is true, would have outgrown it and have obeyed the call to unconditioned life, were they not fastened to it by sentiments of their childhood and infected for the most part with its less intense life; and so they are kept lingering, obedient and bound by obligation and service. For with the bourgeoisie the opposite of the formula for the great is true: He who is not against me is with me.

If we now pause to test the soul of the Steppenwolf, we find him distinct from the bourgeois in the higher development of his individuality--for all extreme individuation turns against itself, intent upon its own destruction. We see that he had in him strong impulses both to be a saint and a profligate; and yet he could not, owing to some weakness or inertia, make the plunge into the untrammelled realms of space. The parent constellation of the bourgeoisie binds him with its spell. This is his place in the universe and this his bondage. Most intellectuals and most artists belong to the same type. Only the strongest of them force their way through the atmosphere of the bourgeois earth and attain to the cosmic. The others all resign themselves or make compromises. Despising the bourgeoisie, and yet belonging to it, they add to its strength and glory; for in the last resort they have to share their beliefs in order to live. The lives of these infinitely numerous persons make no claim to the tragic; but they live under an evil star in a quite considerable affliction; and in this hell their talents ripen and bear fruit. The few who break free seek their reward in the unconditioned and go down in splendor. They wear the thorn crown and their number is small. The others, however, who remain in the fold and from whose talents the bourgeoisie reaps much gain, have a third kingdom left open to them, an imaginary and yet a sovereign world, humor. The lone wolves who know no peace, these victims of unceasing pain to whom the urge for tragedy has been denied and who can never break through the starry space, who feel themselves summoned thither and yet cannot survive in its atmosphere--for them is reserved, provided suffering has made their spirits tough and elastic enough, a way of reconcilement and an escape into humor. Humor has always something bourgeois in it, although the true bourgeois is incapable of understanding it. In its imaginary realm the intricate and many-faceted ideal of all Steppenwolves finds its realisation. Here it is possible not only to extol the saint and the profligate in one breath and to make the poles meet, but to include the bourgeois, too, in the same affirmation. Now it is possible to be possessed by God and to affirm the sinner, and vice versa, but it is not possible for either saint or sinner (or for any other of the unconditioned) to affirm as well that lukewarm mean, the bourgeois. Humor alone, that magnificent discovery of those who are cut short in their calling to highest endeavor, those who falling short of tragedy are yet as rich in gifts as in affliction, humor alone (perhaps the most inborn and brilliant achievement of the spirit) attains to the impossible and brings every aspect of human existence within the rays of its prism. To live in the world as though it were not the world, to respect the law and yet to stand above it, to have possessions as though "one possessed nothing," to renounce as though it were no renunciation, all these favorite and often formulated propositions of an exalted worldly wisdom, it is in the power of humor alone to make efficacious.

And supposing the Steppenwolf were to succeed, and he has gifts and resources in plenty, in decocting this magic draught in the sultry mazes of his hell, his rescue would be assured. Yet there is much lacking. The possibility, the hope only are there. Whoever loves him and takes his part may wish him this rescue. It would, it is true, keep him forever tied to the bourgeois world, but his suffering would be bearable and productive. His relation to the bourgeois world would lose its sentimentality both in its love and in its hatred, and his bondage to it would cease to cause him the continual torture of shame.

To attain to this, or, perhaps it may be, to be able at least to dare the leap into the unknown, a Steppenwolf must once have a good look at himself. He must look deeply into the chaos of his own soul and plumb its depths. The riddle of his existence would then be revealed to him at once in all its changelessness, and it would be impossible for him ever after to escape first from the hell of the flesh to the comforts of a sentimental philosophy and then back to the blind orgy of his wolfishness. Man and wolf would then be compelled to recognise one another without the masks of false feeling and to look one another straight in the eye. Then they would either explode and separate forever, and there would be no more Steppenwolf, or else they would come to terms in the dawning light of humor.

It is possible that Harry will one day be led to this latter alternative. It is possible that he will learn one day to know himself. He may get hold of one of our little mirrors. He may encounter the Immortals. He may find in one of our magic theaters the very thing that is needed to free his neglected soul. A thousand such possibilities await him. His fate brings them on, leaving him no choice; for those outside of the bourgeoisie live in the atmosphere of these magic possibilities. A mere nothing suffices--and the lightning strikes.

And all this is very well known to the Steppenwolf, even though his eye may never fall on this fragment of his inner biography. He has a suspicion of his allotted place in the world, a suspicion of the Immortals, a suspicion that he may meet himself face to face; and he is aware of the existence of that mirror in which he has such bitter need to look and from which he shrinks in such deathly fear.

. . . . . . .

For the close of our study there is left one last fiction, a fundamental delusion to make clear. All interpretation, all psychology, all attempts to make things comprehensible, require the medium of theories, mythologies and lies; and a self-respecting author should not omit, at the close of an exposition, to dissipate these lies so far as may be in his power. If I say "above" or "below," that is already a statement that requires explanation, since an above and a below exist only in thought, only as abstractions. The world itself knows nothing of above or below.

So too, to come to the point, is the Steppenwolf a fiction. When Harry feels himself to be a were-wolf, and chooses to consist of two hostile and opposed beings, he is merely availing himself of a mythological simplification. He is no were-wolf at all, and if we appeared to accept without scrutiny this lie which he invented for himself and believes in, and tried to regard him literally as a two-fold being and a Steppenwolf, and so designated him, it was merely in the hope of being more easily understood with the assistance of a delusion, which we must now endeavor to put in its true light.

The division into wolf and man, flesh and spirit, by means of which Harry tries to make his destiny more comprehensible to himself is a very great simplification. It is a forcing of the truth to suit a plausible, but erroneous, explanation of that contradiction which this man discovers in himself and which appears to himself to be the source of his by no means negligible sufferings. Harry finds in himself a human being, that is to say, a world of thoughts and feelings, of culture and tamed or sublimated nature, and besides this he finds within himself also a wolf, that is to say, a dark world of instinct, of savagery and cruelty, of unsublimated or raw nature. In spite of this apparently clear division of his being between two spheres, hostile to one another, he has known happy moments now and then when the man and the wolf for a short while were reconciled with one another. Suppose that Harry tried to ascertain in any single moment of his life, any single act, what part the man had in it and what part the wolf, he would find himself at once in a dilemma, and his whole beautiful wolf-theory would go to pieces. For there is not a single human being, not even the primitive Negro, not even the idiot, who is so conveniently simple that his being can be explained as the sum of two or three principal elements; and to explain so complex a man as Harry by the artless division into wolf and man is a hopelessly childish attempt. Harry consists of a hundred or a thousand selves, not of two. His life oscillates, as everyone's does, not merely between two poles, such as the body and the spirit, the saint and the sinner, but between thousand and thousands.

We need not be surprised that even so intelligent and educated a man as Harry should take himself for a Steppenwolf and reduce the rich and complex organism of his life to a formula so simple, so rudimentary and primitive. Man is not capable of thought in any high degree, and even the most spiritual and highly cultivated of men habitually sees the world and himself through the lenses of delusive formulas and artless simplifications--and most of all himself. For it appears to be an inborn and imperative need of all men to regard the self as a unit. However often and however grievously this illusion is shattered, it always mends again. The judge who sits over the murderer and looks into his face, and at one moment recognizes all the emotions and potentialities and possibilities of the murderer in his own soul and hears the murderer's voice as his own, is at the next moment one and indivisible as the judge, and scuttles back into the shell of his cultivated self and does his duty and condemns the murderer to death. And if ever the suspicion of their manifold being dawns upon men of unusual powers and of unusually delicate perceptions, so that, as all genius must, they break through the illusion of the unity of the personality and perceive that the self is made up of a bundle of selves, they have only to say so and at once the majority puts them under lock and key, calls science to aid, establishes schizomania and protects humanity from the necessity of hearing the cry of truth from the lips of these unfortunate persons. Why then waste words, why utter a thing that every thinking man accepts as self-evident, when the mere utterance of it is a breach of taste? A man, therefore, who gets so far as making the supposed unity of the self two-fold is already almost a genius, in any case a most exceptional and interesting person. In reality, however, every ego, so far from being a unity is in the highest degree a manifold world, a constellated heaven, a chaos of forms, of states and stages, of inheritances and potentialities. It appears to be a necessity as imperative as eating and breathing for everyone to be forced to regard this chaos as a unity and to speak of his ego as though it were a one-fold and clearly detached and fixed phenomenon. Even the best of us shares the delusion.

The delusion rests simply upon a false analogy. As a body everyone is single, as a soul never. In literature, too, even in its ultimate achievement, we find this customary concern with apparently whole and single personalities. Of all literature up to our days the drama has been the most highly prized by writers and critics, and rightly, since it offers (or might offer) the greatest possibilities of representing the ego as a manifold entity, but for the optical illusion which makes us believe that the characters of the play are one-fold entities by lodging each one in an undeniable body, singly, separately and once and for all. An artless esthetic criticism, then, keeps its highest praise for this so-called character-drama in which each character makes his appearance unmistakably as a separate and single entity. Only from afar and by degrees the suspicion dawns here and there that all this is perhaps a cheap and superficial esthetic philosophy, and that we make a mistake in attributing to our great dramatists those magnificent conceptions of beauty that come to us from antiquity. These conceptions are not native to us, but are merely picked up at second hand, and it is in them, with their common source in the visible body, that the origin of the fiction of an ego, an individual, is really to be found. There is no trace of such a notion in the poems of ancient India. The heroes of the epics of India are not individuals, but whole reels of individualities in a series of incarnations. And in modern times there are poems, in which, behind the veil of a concern with individuality and character that is scarcely, indeed, in the author's mind, the motive is to present a manifold activity of soul. Whoever wishes to recognize this must resolve once and for all not to regard the characters of such a poem as separate beings, but as the various facets and aspects of a higher unity, in my opinion, of the poet's soul. If "Faust" is treated in this way, Faust, Mephistopheles, Wagner and the rest form a unity and a supreme individuality; and it is in this higher unity alone, not in the several characters, that something of the true nature of the soul is revealed. When Faust, in a line immortalized among schoolmasters and greeted with a shudder of astonishment by the Philistine, says: "Two souls, alas, do dwell within my breast!" he has forgotten Mephisto and a whole crowd of other souls that he has in his breast likewise. The Steppenwolf, too, believes that he bears two souls (wolf and man) in his breast and even so finds his breast disagreeably cramped because of them. The breast and the body are indeed one, but the souls that dwell in it are not two, nor five, but countless in number. Man is an onion made up of a hundred integuments, a texture made up of many threads. The ancient Asiatics knew this well enough, and in the Buddhist Yoga an exact technique was devised for unmasking the illusion of the personality. The human merry-go-round sees many changes: the illusion that cost India the efforts of thousands of years to unmask is the same illusion that the West has labored just as hard to maintain and strengthen.

If we consider the Steppenwolf from this standpoint it will be clear to us why he suffered so much under his ludicrous dual personality. He believes, like Faust, that two souls are far too many for a single breast and must tear the breast asunder. They are on the contrary far too few, and Harry does shocking violence to his poor soul when he endeavors to apprehend it by means of so primitive an image. Although he is a most cultivated person, he proceeds like a savage that cannot count further than two. He calls himself part wolf, part man, and with that he thinks .he has come to an end and exhausted the matter. With the "man" he packs in everything spiritual and sublimated or even cultivated to be found in himself, and with the wolf all that is instinctive, savage and chaotic. But things are not so simple in life as in our thoughts, nor so rough and ready as in our poor idiotic language; and Harry lies about himself twice over when he employs this niggardly wolf-theory. He assigns, we fear, whole provinces of his soul to the "man" which are a long way from being human, and parts of his being to the wolf that long ago have left the wolf behind.

Like all men Harry believes that he knows very well what man is and yet does not know at all, although in dreams and other states not subject to control he often has his suspicions. If only he might not forget them, but keep them, as far as possible at least, for his own. Man is not by any means of fixed and enduring form (this, in spite of suspicions to the contrary on the part of their wise men, was the ideal of the ancients). He is much more an experiment and a transition. He is nothing else than the narrow and perilous bridge between nature and spirit. His innermost destiny drives him on to the spirit and to God. His innermost longing draws him back to nature, the mother. Between the two forces his life hangs tremulous and irresolute. "Man," whatever people think of him, is never anything more than a temporary bourgeois compromise. Convention rejects and bans certain of the more naked instincts, a little consciousness, morality and debestialization is called for, and a modicum of spirit is not only permitted but even thought necessary. The "man" of this concordat, like every other bourgeois ideal, is a compromise, a timid and artlessly sly experiment, with the aim of cheating both the angry primal mother Nature and the troublesome primal father Spirit of their pressing claims, and of living in a temperate zone between the two of them. For this reason the bourgeois today burns as heretics and hangs as criminals those to whom he erects monuments tomorrow.

That man is not yet a finished creation but rather a challenge of the spirit; a distant possibility dreaded as much as it is desired; that the way towards it has only been covered for a very short distance and with terrible agonies and ecstasies even by those few for whom it is the scaffold today and the monument tomorrow--all this the Steppenwolf, too, suspected. What, however, he calls the "man" in himself, as opposed to the wolf, is to a great extent nothing else than this very same average man of the bourgeois convention.

As for the way to true manhood, the way to the immortals, he has, it is true, an inkling of it and starts upon it now and then for a few hesitating steps and pays for them with much suffering and many pangs of loneliness. But as for striving with assurance, in response to that supreme demand, towards the genuine manhood of the spirit, and going the one narrow way to immortality, he is deeply afraid of it. He knows too well that it leads to still greater sufferings, to proscription, to the last renunciation, perhaps to the scaffold, and even though the enticement of immortality lies at the journey's end, he is still unwilling to suffer all these sufferings and to die all these deaths. Though the goal of manhood is better known to him than to the bourgeois, still he shuts his eyes. He is resolved to forget that the desperate clinging to the self and the desperate clinging to life are the surest way to eternal death, while the power to die, to strip one's self naked, and the eternal surrender of the self bring immortality with them. When he worships his favorites among the immortals, Mozart, perchance, he always looks at him in the long run through bourgeois eyes. His tendency is to explain Mozart's perfected being, just as a schoolmaster would, as a supreme and special gift rather than as the outcome of his immense powers of surrender and suffering, of his indifference to the ideals of the bourgeois, and of his patience under that last extremity of loneliness which rarefies the atmosphere of the bourgeois world to an ice-cold ether, around those who suffer to become men, that loneliness of the Garden of Gethsemane.

This Steppenwolf of ours has always been aware of at least the Faustian two-fold nature within him. He has discovered that the one-fold of the body is not inhabited by a one-fold of the soul, and that at best he is only at the beginning of a long pilgrimage towards this ideal harmony. He would like either to overcome the wolf and become wholly man or to renounce mankind and at last to live wholly a wolf's life. It may be presumed that he has never carefully watched a real wolf. Had he done so he would have seen, perhaps, that even animals are not undivided in spirit. With them, too, the well-knit beauty of the body hides a being of manifold states and strivings. The wolf, too, has his abysses. The wolf, too, suffers. No, back to nature is a false track that leads nowhere but to suffering and despair. Harry can never turn back again and become wholly wolf, and could he do so he would find that even the wolf is not of primeval simplicity, but already a creature of manifold complexity. Even the wolf has two, and more than two, souls in his wolf's breast, and he who desires to be a wolf falls into the same forgetfulness as the man who sings: "If I could be a child once more!" He who sentimentally sings of blessed childhood is thinking of the return to nature and innocence and the origin of things, and has quite forgotten that these blessed children are beset with conflict and complexities and capable of all suffering.

There is, in fact, no way back either to the wolf or to the child. From the very start there is no innocence and no singleness. Every created thing, even the simplest, is already guilty, already multiple. It has been thrown into the muddy stream of being and may never more swim back again to its source. The way to innocence, to the uncreated and to God leads on, not back, not back to the wolf or to the child, but ever further into sin, ever deeper into human life. Nor will suicide really solve your problem, unhappy Steppenwolf. You will, instead, embark on the longer and wearier and harder road of life. You will have to multiply many times your two-fold being and complicate your complexities still further. Instead of narrowing your world and simplifying your soul, you will have to absorb more and more of the world and at last take all of it up in your painfully expanded soul, if you are ever to find peace. This is the road that Buddha and every great man has gone, whether consciously or not, insofar as fortune favored his quest. All births mean separation from the All, the confinement within limitation, the separation from God, the pangs of being born ever anew. The return into the All, the dissolution of painful individuation, the reunion with God means the expansion of the soul until it is able once more to embrace the All.

We are not dealing here with man as he is known to economics and statistics, as he is seen thronging the streets by the million, and of whom no more account can be made than of the sand of the sea or the spray of its waves. We are not concerned with the few millions less or more. They are a stock-in-trade, nothing else. No, we are speaking of man in the highest sense, of the end of the long road to true manhood, of kingly men, of the immortals. Genius is not so rare as we sometimes think; nor, certainly, so frequent as may appear from history books or, indeed, from the newspapers. Harry has, we should say, genius enough to attempt the quest of true manhood instead of discoursing pitifully about his stupid Steppenwolf at every difficulty encountered.

It is as much a matter for surprise and sorrow that men of such possibilities should fall back on Steppenwolves and "Two souls, alas!" as that they reveal so often that pitiful love for the bourgeoisie. A man who can understand Buddha and has an intuition of the heaven and hell of humanity ought not to live in a world ruled by "common sense" and democracy and bourgeois standards. It is only from cowardice that he lives in it; and when its dimensions are too cramping for him and the bourgeois parlor too confining, he lays it at the wolf's door, and refuses to see that the wolf is as often as not the best part of him. All that is wild in himself he calls wolf and considers it wicked and dangerous and the bugbear of all decent life. He cannot see, even though he thinks himself an artist and possessed of delicate perceptions, that a great deal else exists in him besides and behind the wolf. He cannot see that not all that bites is wolf and that fox, dragon, tiger, ape and bird of paradise are there also. And he cannot see that this whole world, this Eden and its manifestations of beauty and terror, of greatness and meanness, of strength and tenderness is crushed and imprisoned by the wolf legend just as the real man in him is crushed and imprisoned by that sham existence, the bourgeois.

Man designs for himself a garden with a hundred kinds of trees, a thousand kinds of flowers, a hundred kinds of fruit and vegetables. Suppose, then, that the gardener of this garden knew no other distinction than between edible and inedible, nine-tenths of this garden would be useless to him. He would pull up the most enchanting flowers and hew down the noblest trees and even regard them with a loathing and envious eye. This is what the Steppenwolf does with the thousand flowers of his soul. What does not stand classified as either man or wolf he does not see at all. And consider all that he imputes to "man"! All that is cowardly and apish, stupid and mean--while to the wolf, only because he has not succeeded in making himself its master, is set down all that is strong and noble.

Now we bid Harry good-bye and leave him to go on his way alone. Were he already among the immortals--were he already there at the goal to which his difficult path seems to be taking him, with what amazement he would look back to all this coming and going, all this indecision and wild zig-zag trail. With what a mixture of encouragement and blame, pity and joy, he would smile at this Steppenwolf.

When I had read to the end it came to my mind that some weeks before I had written one night a rather peculiar poem, likewise about the Steppenwolf. I looked for it in the pile of papers on my cluttered writing table, found it, and read:

The Wolf trots to and fro,
The world lies deep in snow,
The raven from the birch tree flies,
But nowhere a hare, nowhere a roe,
The roe--she is so dear, so sweet--
If such a thing I might surprise
In my embrace, my teeth would meet,
What else is there beneath the skies?
The lovely creature I would so treasure,
And feast myself deep on her tender thigh,
I would drink of her red blood full measure,
Then howl till the night went by.
Even a hare I would not despise;
Sweet enough its warm flesh in the night.
Is everything to be denied
That could make life a little bright?
The hair on my brush is getting grey.
The sight is failing from my eyes.
Years ago my dear mate died.
And now I trot and dream of a roe.
I trot and dream of a hare.
I hear the wind of midnight howl.
I cool with the snow my burning jowl,
And on to the devil my wretched soul I bear.

So now I had two portraits of myself before me, one a self-portrait in doggerel verse, as sad and sorry as myself; the other painted with the air of a lofty impartiality by one who stood outside and who knew more and yet less of me than I did myself. And both these pictures of myself, my dispirited and halting poem and the clever study by an unknown hand, equally afflicted me. Both were right. Both gave the unvarnished truth about my shiftless existence. Both showed clearly how unbearable and untenable my situation was. Death was decreed for this Steppenwolf. He must with his own hand make an end of his detested existence--unless, molten in the fire of a renewed self-knowledge, he underwent a change and passed over to a self, new and undisguised. Alas! this transition was not unknown to me. I had already experienced it several times, and always in periods of utmost despair. On each occasion of this terribly uprooting experience, my self, as it then was, was shattered to fragments. Each time deep-seated powers had shaken and destroyed it; each time there had followed the loss of a cherished and particularly beloved part of my life that was true to me no more. Once, I had lost my profession and livelihood. I had had to forfeit the esteem of those who before had touched their caps to me. Next, my family life fell in ruins over night, when my wife, whose mind was disordered, drove me from house and home. Love and confidence had changed of a sudden to hate and deadly enmity and the neighbors saw me go with pitying scorn. It was then that my solitude had its beginning. Years of hardship and bitterness went by. I had built up the ideal of a new life, inspired by the asceticism of the intellect. I had attained a certain serenity and elevation of life once more, submitting myself to the practice of abstract thought and to a rule of austere meditation. But this mold, too, was broken and lost at one blow all its exalted and noble intent. A whirl of travel drove me afresh over the earth; fresh sufferings were heaped up, and fresh guilt. And every occasion when a mask was torn off, an ideal broken, was preceded by this hateful vacancy and stillness, this deathly constriction and loneliness and unrelatedness, this waste and empty hell of lovelessness and despair, such as I had now to pass through once more.

It is true that every time my life was shattered in this way I had in the end gained something, some increase in liberty and in spiritual growth and depth, but with it went an increased loneliness, an increasing chill of severance and estrangement. Looked at with the bourgeois eye, my life had been a continuous descent from one shattering to the next that left me more remote at every step from all that was normal, permissible and healthful. The passing years had stripped me of my calling, my family, my home. I stood outside all social circles, alone, beloved by none, mistrusted by many, in unceasing and bitter conflict with public opinion and morality; and though I lived in a bourgeois setting, I was all the same an utter stranger to this world in all I thought and felt. Religion, country, family, state, all lost their value and meant nothing to me any more. The pomposity of the sciences, societies, and arts disgusted me. My views and tastes and all that I thought, once the shining adornments of a gifted and sought-after person, had run to seed in neglect and were looked at askance. Granting that I had in the course of all my painful transmutations made some invisible and unaccountable gain, I had had to pay dearly for it; and at every turn my life was harsher, more difficult, lonely and perilous. In truth, I had little cause to wish to continue in that way which led on into ever thinner air, like the smoke in Nietzsche's harvest song.

Oh, yes, I had experienced all these changes and transmutations that fate reserves for her difficult children, her ticklish customers. I knew them only too well. I knew them as well as a zealous but unsuccessful sportsman knows the stands at a shoot; as an old gambler on the Exchange knows each stage of speculation, the scoop, the weakening market, the break and bankruptcy. Was I really to live through all this again? All this torture, all this pressing need, all these glimpses into the paltriness and worthlessness of my own self, the frightful dread lest I succumb, and the fear of death. Wasn't it better and simpler to prevent a repetition of so many sufferings and to quit the stage? Certainly, it was simpler and better. Whatever the truth of all that was said in the little book on the Steppenwolf about "suicides," no one could forbid me the satisfaction of invoking the aid of coal gas or a razor or revolver, and so sparing myself this repetition of a process whose bitter agony I had had to drink often enough, surely, and to the dregs. No, in all conscience, there was no power in the world that could prevail with me to go through the mortal terror of another encounter with myself, to face another reorganisation, a new incarnation, when at the end of the road there was no peace or quiet--but forever destroying the self, in order to renew the self. Let suicide be as stupid, cowardly, shabby as you please, call it an infamous and ignominious escape; still, any escape, even the most ignominious, from this treadmill of suffering was the only thing to wish for. No stage was left for the noble and heroic heart. Nothing was left but the simple choice between a slight and swift pang and an unthinkable, a devouring and endless suffering. I had played Don Quixote often enough in my difficult, crazed life, had put honor before comfort, and heroism before reason. There was an end of it!

Daylight was dawning through the window panes, the leaden, infernal daylight of a rainy winter's day, when at last I got to bed. I took my resolution to bed with me. At the very last, however, on the last verge of consciousness in the moment of falling asleep, the remarkable passage in the Steppenwolf pamphlet which deals with the immortals flashed through me. With it came the enchanting recollection that several times, the last quite recently, I had felt near enough to the immortals to share in one measure of old music their cool, bright, austere and yet smiling wisdom. The memory of it soared, shone out, then died away; and heavy as a mountain, sleep descended on my brain.

I woke about midday, and at once the situation, as I had disentangled it, came back to me. There lay the little book on my night stand, and my poem. My resolution, too, was there. After the nights sleep it had taken shape and looked at me out of the confusion of my youth with a calm and friendly greeting. Haste makes no speed. My resolve to die was not the whim of an hour. It was the ripe, sound fruit that had grown slowly to full size, lightly rocked by the winds of fate whose next breath would bring it to the ground.

I had in my medicine chest an excellent means of stilling pain--an unusually strong tincture of laudanum. I indulged very rarely in it and often refrained from using it for months at a time. I had recourse to the drug only when physical pain plagued me beyond endurance. Unfortunately, it was of no use in putting an end to myself. I had proved this some years before. Once when despair had again got the better of me I had swallowed a big dose of it--enough to kill six men, and yet it had not killed me. I fell asleep, it is true, and lay for several hours completely stupefied; but then to my frightful disappointment I was half awakened by violent convulsions of the stomach and fell asleep once more. It was the middle of the next day when I woke up in earnest in a state of dismal sobriety. My empty brain was burning and I had almost lost my memory. Apart from a spell of insomnia and severe pains in the stomach no trace of the poison was left.

This expedient, then, was no good. But I put my resolution in this way: the next time I felt that I must have recourse to the opium, I might allow myself to use big means instead of small, that is, a death of absolute certainty with a bullet or a razor. Then I could be sure. As for waiting till my fiftieth birthday, as the little book wittily prescribed--this seemed to me much too long a delay. There were still two years till then. Whether it were a year hence or a month, were it even the following day, the door stood open.

I cannot say that the resolution altered my life very profoundly. It made me a little more indifferent to my afflictions, a little freer in the use of opium and wine, a little more inquisitive to know the limits of endurance, but that was all. The other experiences of that evening had a stronger after-effect. I read the Steppenwolf treatise through again many times, now submitting gratefully to an invisible magician because of his wise conduct of my destiny, now with scorn and contempt for its futility, and the little understanding it showed of my actual disposition and predicament. All that was written there of Steppenwolves and suicides was very good, no doubt, and very clever. It might do for the species, the type; but it was too wide a mesh to catch my own individual soul, my unique and unexampled destiny.

What, however, occupied my thoughts more than all else was the hallucination, or vision, of the church wall. The announcement made by the dancing illuminated letters promised much that was hinted at in the treatise, and the voices of that strange world had powerfully aroused my curiosity. For hours I pondered deeply over them. On these occasions I was more and more impressed by the warning of that inscription--"Not for everybody!" and "For madmen only!" Madman, then, I must certainly be and far from the mold of "everybody" if those voices reached me and that world spoke to me. In heaven's name, had I not long ago been remote from the life of everybody and from normal thinking and normal existence? Had I not long ago given ample margin to isolation and madness? All the same, I understood the summons well enough in my innermost heart. Yes, I understood the invitation to madness and the jettison of reason and the escape from the clogs of convention in surrender to the unbridled surge of spirit and fantasy.

One day after I had made one more vain search through streets and squares for the man with the signboard and prowled several times past the wall of the invisible door with watchful eye, I met a funeral procession in St. Martin's. While I was contemplating the faces of the mourners who followed the hearse with halting step, I thought to myself, "Where in this town or in the whole world is the man whose death would be a loss to me? And where is the man to whom my death would mean anything?" There was Erica, it is true, but for a long while we had lived apart. We rarely saw one another without quarreling and at the moment I did not even know her address. She came to see me now and then, or I made the journey to her, and since both of us were lonely, difficult people related somehow to one another in soul, and sickness of soul, there was a link between us that held in spite of all. But would she not perhaps breathe more freely if she heard of my death? I did not know. I did not know either how far my own feeling for her was to be relied upon. To know anything of such matters one needs to live in a world of practical possibilities.

Meanwhile, obeying my fancy, I had fallen in at the rear of the funeral procession and jogged along behind the mourners to the cemetery, an up-to-date set-up all of concrete, complete with crematorium and what not. The deceased in question was not however to be cremated. His coffin was set down before a simple hole in the ground, and I saw the clergyman and the other vultures and functionaries of a burial establishment going through their performances, to which they endeavored to give all the appearance of great ceremony and sorrow and with such effect that they outdid themselves and from pure acting they got caught in their own lies and ended by being comic. I saw how their black professional robes fell in folds, and what pains they took to work up the company of mourners and to force them to bend the knee before the majesty of death. It was labor in vain. Nobody wept. The deceased did not appear to have been indispensable. Nor could anyone be talked into a pious frame of mind; and when the clergyman addressed the company repeatedly as "dear fellow-Christians," all the silent faces of these shop people and master bakers and their wives were turned down in embarrassment and expressed nothing but the wish that this uncomfortable function might soon be over. When the end came, the two foremost of the fellow-Christians shook the clergyman's hand, scraped the moist clay in which the dead had been laid from their shoes at the next scraper and without hesitation their faces again showed their natural expression; and then it was that one of them seemed suddenly familiar. It was, so it seemed to me, the man who had carried the signboard and thrust the little book into my hands.

At the moment when I thought I recognized him he stopped and, stooping down, carefully turned up his black trousers, and then walked away at a smart pace with his umbrella clipped under his arm. I walked after him, but when I overtook him and gave him a nod, he did not appear to recognize me.

"Is there no show tonight?" I asked with an attempt at a wink such as two conspirators give each other. But it was long ago that such pantomime was familiar to me. Indeed, living as I did, I had almost lost the habit of speech, and I felt myself that I only made a silly grimace.

"Show tonight?" he growled, and looked at me as though he had never set eyes on me before. "Go to the Black Eagle, man, if that's what you want."

And, in fact, I was no longer certain it was he. I was disappointed and feeling the disappointment I walked on aimlessly. I had no motives, no incentives to exert myself, no duties. Life tasted horribly bitter. I felt that the long-standing disgust was coming to a crisis and that life pushed me out and cast me aside. I walked through the grey streets in a rage and everything smelt of moist earth and burial. I swore that none of these death-vultures should stand at my grave, with cassock and sentimental Christian murmurings. Ah, look where I might and think what I might, there was no cause for rejoicing and nothing beckoned me. There was nothing to charm me or tempt me. Everything was old, withered, grey, limp and spent, and stank of staleness and decay. Dear God, how was it possible? How had I, with the wings of youth and poetry, come to this? Art and travel and the glow of ideals--and now this! How had this paralysis crept over me so slowly and furtively, this hatred against myself and everybody, this deep-seated anger and obstruction of all feelings, this filthy hell of emptiness and despair.

Passing by the Library I met a young professor of whom in earlier years I used occasionally to see a good deal. When I last stayed in the town, some years before, I had even been several times to his house to talk Oriental mythology, a study in which I was then very much interested. He came in my direction walking stiffly and with a short-sighted air and only recognized me at the last moment as I was passing by. In my lamentable state I was half-thankful for the cordiality with which he threw himself on me. His pleasure in seeing me became quite lively as he recalled the talks we had had together and assured me that he owed a great deal to the stimulus they had given him and that he often thought of me. He had rarely had such stimulating and productive discussions with any colleague since. He asked how long I had been in the town (I lied and said "a few days") and why I had not looked him up. The learned man held me with his friendly eye and, though I really found it all ridiculous, I could not help enjoying these crumbs of warmth and kindliness, and was lapping them up like a starved dog. Harry, the Steppenwolf, was moved to a grin. Saliva collected in his parched throat and against his will he bowed down to sentiment. Yes, zealously piling lie upon lie, I said that I was only here in passing, for the purpose of research, and should of course have paid him a visit but that I had not been feeling very fit. And when he went on to invite me very heartily to spend the evening with him, I accepted with thanks and sent my greetings to his wife, until my cheeks fairly ached with the unaccustomed efforts of all these forced smiles and speeches. And while I, Harry Haller, stood there in the street, flattered and surprised and studiously polite and smiling into the good fellow's kindly, shortsighted face, there stood the other

Harry, too, at my elbow and grinned likewise. He stood there and grinned as he thought what a funny, crazy, dishonest fellow I was to show my teeth in rage and curse the whole world one moment and, the next, to be falling all over myself in the eagerness of my response to the first amiable greeting of the first good honest fellow who came my way, to be wallowing like a suckling-pig in the luxury of a little pleasant feeling and friendly esteem. Thus stood the two Harrys, neither playing a very pretty part, over against the worthy professor, mocking one another, watching one another, and spitting at one another, while as always in such predicaments, the eternal question presented itself whether all this was simple stupidity and human frailty, a common depravity, or whether this sentimental egoism and perversity, this slovenliness and two-facedness of feeling was merely a personal idiosyncrasy of the Steppenwolves. And if this nastiness was common to men in general, I could rebound from it with renewed energy into hatred of all the world, but if it was a personal frailty, it was good occasion for an orgy of hatred of myself.

While my two selves were thus locked in conflict, the professor was almost forgotten; and when the oppressiveness of his presence came suddenly back to me, I made haste to be relieved of it. I looked after him for a long while as he disappeared into the distance along the leafless avenue with the good-natured and slightly comic gait of an ingenuous idealist. Within me, the battle raged furiously. Mechanically I bent and unbent my stiffened fingers as though to fight the ravages of a secret poison, and at the same time had to realize that I had been nicely framed. Round my neck was the invitation for 8:30, with all its obligations of politeness, of talking shop and of contemplating another's domestic bliss. And so home--in wrath. Once there, I poured myself out some brandy and water, swallowed some of my gout pills with it, and, lying on the sofa, tried to read. No sooner had I succeeded in losing myself for a moment in *Sophia's Journey from Memel to Saxony,* a delightful old book of the eighteenth century, than the invitation came over me of a sudden and reminded me that I was neither shaved nor dressed. Why, in heaven's name, had I brought all this on myself? Well, get up, so I told myself, lather yourself, scrape your chin till it bleeds, dress and show an amiable disposition towards your fellow-men. And while I lathered my face, I thought of that sordid hole in the clay of the cemetery into which some unknown person had been lowered that day. I thought of the pinched faces of the bored fellow-Christians and I could not even laugh. There in that sordid hole in the clay, I thought, to the accompaniment of stupid and insincere ministrations and the no less stupid and insincere demeanor of the group of mourners, in the discomforting sight of all the metal crosses and marble slabs and artificial flowers of wire and glass, ended not only that unknown man, and, tomorrow or the day after, myself as well, buried in the soil with a hypocritical show of sorrow--no, there and so ended everything; all our striving, all our culture, all our beliefs, all our joy and pleasure in life--already sick and soon to be buried there too. Our whole civilization was a cemetery where Jesus Christ and Socrates, Mozart and Haydn, Dante and Goethe were but the indecipherable names on moldering stones; and the mourners who stood round affecting a pretence of sorrow would give much to believe in these inscriptions which once were holy, or at least to utter one heart-felt word of grief and despair about this world that is no more. And nothing was left them but the embarrassed grimaces of a company round a grave. As I raged on like this I cut my chin in the usual place and had to apply a caustic to the wound; and even so there was my clean collar, scarce put on, to change again, and all this for an invitation that did not give me the slightest pleasure. And yet a part of me began play-acting again, calling the professor a sympathetic fellow, yearning after a little talk and intercourse with my fellow men, reminding me of the professor's pretty wife, prompting me to believe that an evening spent with my pleasant host and hostess would be in reality positively cheering, helping me to clap some court plaster to my chin, to put on my clothes and tie my tie well, and gently putting me, in fact, far from my genuine desire of staying at home. Whereupon it occurred to me--so it is with every one. Just as I dress and go out to visit the professor and exchange a few more or less insincere compliments with him, without really wanting to at all, so it is with the majority of men day by day and hour by hour in their daily lives and affairs. Without really wanting to at all, they pay calls and carry on conversations, sit out their hours at desks and on office chairs; and it is all compulsory, mechanical and against the grain, and it could all be done or left undone just as well by machines; and indeed it is this never-ceasing machinery that prevents their being, like me, the critics of their own lives and recognizing the stupidity and shallowness, the hopeless tragedy and waste of the lives they lead, and the awful ambiguity grinning over it all. And they are right, right a thousand times to live as they do, playing their games and pursuing their business, instead of resisting the dreary machine and staring into the void as I do, who have left the track. Let no one think that I blame other men, though now and then in these pages I scorn and even deride them, or that I accuse them of the responsibility of my personal misery. But now that I have come so far, and standing as I do on the extreme verge of life where the ground falls away before me into bottomless darkness, I should do wrong and I should lie if I pretended to myself or to others that that machine still revolved for me and that I was still obedient to the eternal child's play of that charming world.

On all this the evening before me afforded a remarkable commentary. I paused a moment in front of the house and looked up at the windows. There he lives, I thought, and carries on his labors year by year, reads and annotates texts, seeks for analogies between western Asiatic and Indian mythologies, and it satisfies him, because he believes in the value of it all. He believes in the studies whose servant he is; he believes in the value of mere knowledge and its acquisition, because he believes in progress and evolution. He has not been through the war, nor is he acquainted with the shattering of the foundations of thought by Einstein (that, thinks he, only concerns the mathematicians). He sees nothing of the preparations for the next war that are going on all round him. He hates Jews and Communists. He is a good, unthinking, happy child, who takes himself seriously; and, in fact, he is much to be envied. And so, pulling myself together, I entered the house. A maid in cap and apron opened the door. Warned by some premonition, I noticed with care where she laid my hat and coat, and was then shown into a warm and well-lighted room and requested to wait. Instead of saying a prayer or taking a nap, I followed a wayward impulse and picked up the first thing I saw. It chanced to be a small picture in a frame that stood on the round table leaning back on its paste-board support. It was an engraving and it represented the poet Goethe as an old man full of character, with a finely chiseled face and a genius' mane. Neither the renowned fire of his eyes nor the lonely and tragic expression beneath the courtly whitewash was lacking. To this the artist had given special care, and he had succeeded in combining the elemental force of the old man with a somewhat professional make-up of self-discipline and righteousness, without prejudice to his profundity; and had made of him, all in all, a really charming old gentleman, fit to adorn any drawing room. No doubt this portrait was no worse than others of its description. It was much the same as all those representations by careful craftsmen of saviors, apostles, heroes, thinkers and statesmen. Perhaps I found it exasperating only because of a certain pretentious virtuosity. In any case, and whatever the cause, this empty and self-satisfied presentation of the aged Goethe shrieked at me at once as a fatal discord, exasperated and oppressed as I was already. It told me that I ought never to have come. Here fine Old Masters and the Nation's Great Ones were at home, not Steppenwolves.

If only the master of the house had come in now, I might have had the luck to find some favorable opportunity for finding my way out. As it was, his wife came in, and I surrendered to fate though I scented danger. We shook hands and to the first discord there succeeded nothing but new ones. The lady complimented me on my looks, though I knew only too well how sadly the years had aged me since our last meeting. The clasp of her hand on my gouty fingers had reminded me of it already. Then she went on to ask after my dear wife, and I had to say that my wife had left me and that we were divorced. We were glad enough when the professor came in. He too gave me a hearty welcome and the awkward comedy came to a beautiful climax. He was holding a newspaper to which he subscribed, an organ of the militarist and jingoist party, and after shaking hands he pointed to it and commented on a paragraph about a namesake of mine--a publicist called Haller, a bad fellow and a rotten patriot--who had been making fun of the Kaiser and expressing the view that his own country was no less responsible for the outbreak of war than the enemy nations. There was a man for you! The editor had given him his deserts and put him in the pillory. However, when the professor saw that I was not interested, we passed to other topics, and the possibility that this horrid fellow might be sitting in front of them did not even remotely occur to either of them. Yet so it was, I myself was that horrid fellow. Well, why make a fuss and upset people? I laughed to myself, but gave up all hope now of a pleasant evening.

I have a clear recollection of the moment when the professor spoke of Haller as a traitor to his country. It was then that the horrid feeling of depression and despair which had been mounting in me and growing stronger and stronger ever since the burial scene condensed to a dreary dejection. It rose to the pitch of a bodily anguish, arousing within me a dread and suffocating foreboding. I had the feeling that something lay in wait for me, that a danger stalked me from behind. Fortunately the announcement that dinner was on the table supervened. We went into the dining room, and while I racked my brains again and again for something harmless to say, I ate more than I was accustomed to do and felt myself growing more wretched with every moment. Good heavens, I thought all the while, why do we put ourselves to such exertions? I felt distinctly that my hosts were not at their ease either and that their liveliness was forced, whether it was that I had a paralyzing effect on them or because of some other and domestic embarrassment. There was not a question they put to me that I could answer frankly, and I was soon fairly entangled in my lies and wrestling with my nausea at every word. At last, for the sake of changing the subject, I began to tell them of the funeral which I had witnessed earlier in the day. But I could not hit the right note. My efforts at humor fell entirely flat and we were more than ever at odds. Within me the Steppenwolf bared his teeth in a grin. By the time we had reached dessert, silence had descended on all three of us.

We went back to the room we had come from to invoke the aid of coffee and cognac. There, however, my eye fell once more on the magnate of poetry, although he had been put on a chest of drawers at one side of the room. Unable to get away from him, I took him once more in my hands, though warning voices were plainly audible, and proceeded to attack him. I was as though obsessed by the feeling that the situation was intolerable and that the time had come either to warm my hosts up, to carry them off their feet and put them in tune with myself, or else to bring about a final explosion.

"Let us hope," said I, "that Goethe did not really look like this. This conceited air of nobility, the great man ogling the distinguished company, and beneath the manly exterior what a world of charming sentimentality! Certainly, there is much to be said against him. I have a good deal against his venerable pomposity myself. But to represent him like this--no, that is going too far."

The lady of the house finished pouring out the coffee with a deeply wounded expression and then hurriedly left the room; and her husband explained to me with mingled embarrassment and reproach that the picture of Goethe belonged to his wife and was one of her dearest possessions. "And even if, objectively speaking, you are right, though I don't agree with you, you need not have been so outspoken."

"There you are right," I admitted. "Unfortunately it is a habit, a vice of mine, always to speak my mind as much as possible, as indeed Goethe did, too, in his better moments. In this chaste drawing room Goethe would certainly never have allowed himself to use an outrageous, a genuine and unqualified expression. I sincerely beg your wife's pardon and your own. Tell her, please, that I am a schizomaniac. And now, if you will allow me, I will take my leave."

To this he made objections in spite of his perplexity. He even went back to the subject of our former discussions and said once more how interesting and stimulating they had been and how deep an impression my theories about Mithras and Krishna had made on him at the time. He had hoped that the present occasion would have been an opportunity to renew these discussions. I thanked him for speaking as he did. Unfortunately, my interest in Krishna had vanished and also my pleasure in learned discussions. Further, I had told him several lies that day. For example, I had been many months in the town, and not a few days, as I had said. I lived, however, quite by myself, and was no longer fit for decent society; for in the first place, I was nearly always in a bad temper and afflicted with the gout, and in the second place, usually drunk. Lastly, to make a clean slate, and not to go away, at least, as a liar, it was my duty to inform him that he had grievously insulted me that evening. He had endorsed the attitude taken up by a reactionary paper towards Haller's opinions; a stupid bull-necked paper, fit for an officer on half-pay, not for a man of learning. This bad fellow and rotten patriot, Haller, however, and myself were one and the same person, and it would be better for our country and the world in general, if at least the few people who were capable of thought stood for reason and the love of peace instead of heading wildly with a blind obsession for a new war. And so I would bid him good-bye.

With that I got up and took leave of Goethe and of the professor. I seized my hat and coat from the rack outside and left the house. The wolf in me howled in gleeful triumph, and a dramatic struggle between my two selves followed. For it was at once clear to me that this disagreeable evening had much more significance for me than for the indignant professor. For him, it was a disillusionment and a petty outrage. For me, it was a final failure and flight. It was my leave-taking from the respectable, moral and learned world, and a complete triumph for the Steppenwolf. I was sent flying and beaten from the field, bankrupt in my own eyes, dismissed without a shred of credit or a ray of humor to comfort me. I had taken leave of the world in which I had once found a home, the world of convention and culture, in the manner of the man with a weak stomach who has given up pork. In a rage I went on my way beneath the street lamps, in a rage and sick unto death. What a hideous day of shame and wretchedness it had been from morning to night, from the cemetery to the scene with the professor. For what? And why? Was there any sense in taking up the burden of more such days as this or of sitting out any more such suppers? There was not. This very night I would make an end of the comedy, go home and cut my throat. No more tarrying.

I paced the streets in all directions, driven on by wretchedness. Naturally it was stupid of me to bespatter the drawing-room ornaments of the worthy folk, stupid and ill-mannered, but I could not help it; and even now I could not help it. I could not bear this tame, lying, well-mannered life any longer. And since it appeared that I could not bear my loneliness any longer either, since my own company had become so unspeakably hateful and nauseous, since I struggled for breath in a vacuum and suffocated in hell, what way out was left me? There was none. I thought of my father and mother, of the sacred flame of my youth long extinct, of the thousand joys and labors and aims of my life. Nothing of them all was left me, not even repentance, nothing but agony and nausea. Never had the clinging to mere life seemed so grievous as now.

I rested a moment in a tavern in an outlying part of the town and drank some brandy and water; then to the streets once more, with the devil at my heels, up and down the steep and winding streets of the Old Town, along the avenues, across the station square. The thought of going somewhere took me into the station. I scanned the time tables on the walls; drank some wine and tried to come to my senses. Then the specter that I went in dread of came nearer, till I saw it plain. It was the dread of returning to my room and coming to a halt there, faced by my despair. There was no escape from this moment though I walked the streets for hours. Sooner or later I should be at my door, at the table with my books, on the sofa with the photograph of Erica above it. Sooner or later the moment would come to take out my razor and cut my throat. More and more plainly the picture rose before me. More and more plainly, with a wildly beating heart, I felt the dread of all dreads, the fear of death. Yes, I was horribly afraid of death. Although I saw no other way out, although nausea, agony and despair threatened to engulf me; although life had no allurement and nothing to give me either of joy or hope, I shuddered all the same with an unspeakable horror of a gaping wound in a condemned man's flesh.

I saw no other way of escape from this dreadful specter. Suppose that today cowardice won a victory over despair, tomorrow and each succeeding day I would again face despair heightened by self-contempt. It was merely taking up and throwing down the knife till at last it was done. Better today then. I reasoned with myself as though with a frightened child. But the child would not listen. It ran away. It wanted to live. I renewed my fitful wanderings through the town, making many detours not to return to the house which I had always in my mind and always deferred. Here and there I came to a stop and lingered, drinking a glass or two, and then, as if pursued, ran around in a circle whose center had the razor as a goal, and meant death. Sometimes from utter weariness I sat on a bench, on a fountain's rim, or a curbstone and wiped the sweat from my forehead and listened to the beating of my heart. Then on again in mortal dread and an intense yearning for life.

Thus it was I found myself late at night in a distant and unfamiliar part of the town; and there I went into a public house from which there came the lively sound of dance music. Over the entrance as I went in I read "The Black Eagle" on the old signboard. Within I found it was a free night--crowds, smoke, the smell of wine, and the clamor of voices, with dancing in a room at the back, whence issued the frenzy of music. I stayed in the nearer room where there were none but simple folk, some of them poorly dressed, whereas behind in the dance hall fashionable people were also to be seen. Carried forward by the crowd, I soon found myself near the bar, wedged against a table at which sat a pale and pretty girl against the wall. She wore a thin dance-frock cut very low and a withered flower in her hair. She gave me a friendly and observant look as I came up and with a smile moved to one side to make room for me.

"May I?" I asked and sat down beside her.

"Of course, you may," she said. "But who are you?"

"Thanks," I replied. "I cannot possibly go home, cannot, cannot. I'll stay here with you if you'll let me. No, I can't go back home."

She nodded as though to humor me, and as she nodded I observed the curl that fell from her temple to her ear, and I saw that the withered flower was a camellia. From within crashed the music and at the buffet the waitresses hurriedly shouted their orders.

"Well, stay here then," she said with a voice that comforted me. "Why can't you go home?"

"I can't. There's something waiting for me there. No, I can't--it's too frightful."

"Let it wait then and stay here. First wipe your glasses. You can see nothing like that. Give me your handkerchief. What shall we drink? Burgundy?"

While she wiped my glasses, I had the first clear impression of her pale, firm face, with its clear grey eyes and smooth forehead, and the short, tight curl in front of her ear. Good-naturedly and with a touch of mockery she began to take me in hand. She ordered the wine, and as she clinked her glass with mine, her eyes fell on my shoes.

"Good Lord, wherever have you come from? You look as though you had come from Paris on foot. That's no state to come to a dance in."

I answered "yes" and "no," laughed now and then, and let her talk. I found her charming, very much to my surprise, for I had always avoided girls of her kind and regarded them with suspicion. And she treated me exactly in the way that was best for me at that moment, and so she has since without an exception. She took me under her wing just as I needed, and mocked me, too, just as I needed. She ordered me a sandwich and told me to eat it. She filled my glass and bade me sip it and not drink too fast. Then she commended my docility.

"That's fine," she said to encourage me. "You're not difficult. I wouldn't mind betting it's a long while since you have had to obey anyone."

"You'd win the bet. How did you know it?"

"Nothing in that. Obeying is like eating and drinking. There's nothing like it if you've been without it too long. Isn't it so, you're glad to do as I tell you?"

"Very glad. You know everything."

"You make it easy to. Perhaps, my friend, I could tell you, too, what it is that's waiting for you at home and what you dread so much. But you know that for yourself. We needn't talk about it, eh? Silly business! Either a man goes and hangs himself, and then he hangs sure enough, and he'll have his reasons for it, or else he goes on living and then he has only living to bother himself with. Simple enough."

"Oh," I cried, "if only it were so simple. I've bothered myself enough with life, God knows, and little use it has been to me. To hang oneself is hard, perhaps. I don't know. But to live is far, far harder. God, how hard it is!"

"You'll see it's child's play. We've made a start already. You've polished your glasses, eaten something and had a drink. Now we'll go and give your shoes and trousers a brush and then you'll dance a shimmy with me."

"Now that shows," I cried in a fluster, "that I was right! Nothing could grieve me more than not to be able to carry out any command of yours, but I can dance no shimmy, nor waltz, nor polka, nor any of the rest of them. I've never danced in my life. Now you can see it isn't all as easy as you think."

Her bright red lips smiled and she firmly shook her waved and shingled head; and as I looked at her, I thought I could see a resemblance to Rosa Kreisler, with whom I had been in love as a boy. But she had a dark complexion and dark hair. I could not tell of whom it was she reminded me. I knew only that it was of someone in my early youth and boyhood.

"Wait a bit," she cried. "So you can't dance? Not at all? Not even a one step? And yet you talk of the trouble you've taken to live? You told a fib there, my boy, and you shouldn't do that at your age. How can you say that you've taken any trouble to live when you won't even dance?"

"But if I can't--I've never learned!"

She laughed.

"But you learned reading and writing and arithmetic, I suppose, and French and Latin and a lot of other things? I don't mind betting you were ten or twelve years at school and studied whatever else you could as well. Perhaps you've even got your doctor's degree and know Chinese or Spanish. Am I right? Very well then. But you couldn't find the time and money for a few dancing lessons! No, indeed!"

"It was my parents," I said to justify myself. "They let me learn Latin and Greek and all the rest of it. But they didn't let me learn to dance. It wasn't the thing with us. My parents had never danced themselves."

She looked at me quite coldly, with real contempt, and again something in her face reminded me of my youth.

"So your parents must take the blame then. Did you ask them whether you might spend the evening at the Black Eagle? Did you? They're dead a long while ago, you say? So much for that. And now supposing you were too obedient to learn to dance when you were young (though I don't believe you were such a model child), what have you been doing with yourself all these years?"

"Well," I confessed, "I scarcely know myself--studied, played music, read books, written books, traveled--"

"Fine views of life, you have. You have always done the difficult and complicated things and the simple ones you haven't even learned. No time, of course. More amusing things to do. Well, thank God, I'm not your mother. But to do as you do and then say you've tested life to the bottom and found nothing in it is going a bit too far."

"Don't scold me," I implored. "It isn't as if I didn't know I was mad."

"Oh, don't make a song of your sufferings. You are no madman, Professor. You're not half mad enough to please me. It seems to me you're much too clever in a silly way, just like a professor. Have another roll. You can tell me some more later."

She got another roll for me, put a little salt and mustard on it, cut a piece for herself and told me to eat it. I did all she told me except dance. It did me a prodigious lot of good to do as I was told and to have some one sitting by me who asked me things and ordered me about and scolded me. If the professor or his wife had done so an hour or two earlier, it would have spared me a lot. But no, it was well as it was. I should have missed much.

"What's your name?" she asked suddenly.

"Harry."

"Harry? A babyish sort of name. And a baby you are, Harry, in spite of your few grey hairs. You're a baby and you need some one to look after you. I'll say no more of dancing. But look at your hair! Have you no wife, no sweetheart?"

"I haven't a wife any longer. We are divorced. A sweetheart, yes, but she doesn't live here. I don't see her very often. We don't get on very well."

She whistled softly.

"You must be difficult if nobody sticks to you. But now tell me what was up in particular this evening? What sent you chasing round out of your wits? Down on your luck? Lost at cards?"

This was not easy to explain.

"Well," I began, "you see, it was really a small matter. I had an invitation to dinner with a professor--I'm not one myself, by the way--and really I ought not to have gone. I've lost the habit of being in company and making conversation. I've forgotten how it's done. As soon as I entered the house I had the feeling something would go wrong, and when I hung my hat on the peg I thought to myself that perhaps I should want it sooner than I expected. Well, at the professor's there was a picture that stood on the table, a stupid picture. It annoyed me--"

"What sort of picture? Annoyed you--why?" she broke in.

"Well, it was a picture representing Goethe, the poet Goethe, you know. But it was not in the least as he really looked. That, of course, nobody can know exactly. He has been dead a hundred years. However, some artist of today had painted his portrait as he imagined him to have been and prettified him, and this picture annoyed me. It made me perfectly sick. I don't know whether you can understand that."

"I understand all right. Don't you worry. Go on."

"Before this in any case I didn't see eye to eye with the professor. Like nearly all professors, he is a great patriot, and during the war did his bit in the way of deceiving the public, with the best intentions, of course. I, however, am opposed to war. But that's all one. To continue my story, there was not the least need for me to look at the picture--"

"Certainly not."

"But in the first place it made me sorry because of Goethe, whom I love very dearly, and then, besides, I thought--well, I had better say just how I thought, or felt. There I was, sitting with people as one of themselves and believing that they thought of Goethe as I did and had the same picture of him in their minds as I, and there stood that tasteless, false and sickly affair and they thought it lovely and had not the least idea that the spirit of that picture and the spirit of Goethe were exact opposites. They thought the picture splendid, and so they might for all I cared, but for me it ended, once and for all, any confidence, any friendship, any feeling of affinity I could have for these people. In any case, my friendship with them did not amount to very much. And so I got furious, and sad, too, when I saw that I was quite alone with no one to understand me. Do you see what I mean?"

"It is very easy to see. And next? Did you throw the picture at them?"

"No, but I was rather insulting and left the house. I wanted to go home, but--"

"But you'd have found no mummy there to comfort the silly baby or scold it. I must say, Harry, you make me almost sorry for you. I never knew such a baby."

So it seemed to me, I must own. She gave me a glass of wine to drink. In fact, she was like a mother to me. In a glimpse, though, now and then I saw how young and beautiful she was.

"And so," she began again, "Goethe has been dead a hundred years, and you're very fond of him, and you have a wonderful picture in your head of what he must have looked like, and you have the right to, I suppose. But the artist who adores Goethe too, and makes a picture of him, has no right to do it, nor the professor either, nor anybody else--because you don't like it. You find it intolerable. You have to be insulting and leave the house. If you had sense, you would laugh at the artist and the professor--laugh and be done with it. If you were out of your senses, you'd smash the picture in their faces. But as you're only a little baby, you run home and want to hang yourself. I've understood your story very well, Harry. It's a funny story. You make me laugh. But don't drink so fast. Burgundy should be sipped. Otherwise you'll get hot. But you have to be told everything--like a little child."

She admonished me with the look of a severe governess of sixty.

"Oh, I know," I said contentedly. "Only tell me everything."

"What shall I tell you?"

"Whatever you feel like telling me."

"Good. Then I'll tell you something. For an hour I've been saying 'thou' to you, and you have been saying 'you' to me. Always Latin and Greek, always as complicated as possible. When a girl addresses you intimately and she isn't disagreeable to you, then you should address her in the same way. So now you've learned something. And secondly--for half an hour I've known that you're called Harry. I know it because I asked you. But you don't care to know my name."

"Oh, but indeed--I'd like to know very much."

"You're too late! If we meet again, you can ask me again. Today I shan't tell you. And now I'm going to dance."

At the first sign she made of getting up, my heart sank like lead. I dreaded her going and leaving me alone, for then it would all come back as it was before. In a moment, the old dread and wretchedness took hold of me like a toothache that has passed off and then comes back of a sudden and burns like fire. Oh, God, had I forgotten, then, what was waiting for me? Had anything altered?

"Stop," I implored, "don't go. You can dance of course, as much as you please, but don't stay away too long. Come back again, come back again."

She laughed as she got up. I expected her to be taller. She was slender, but not tall. Again I was reminded of some one. Of whom? I could not make out.

"You're coming back?"

"I'm coming back, but it may be half an hour or an hour, perhaps. I want to tell you something. Shut your eyes and sleep for a little. That's what you need."

I made room for her to pass. Her skirt brushed my knees and she looked, as she went, in a little pocket mirror, lifted her eyebrows, and powdered her chin; then she disappeared into the dance hall. I looked round me; strange faces, smoking men, spilled beer on marble-tops, clatter and clamor everywhere, the dance music in my ear. I was to sleep, she had said. Ah, my good child, you know a lot about my sleep that is shyer than a weasel! Sleep in this hurly-burly, sitting at a table, amidst the clatter of beer steins! I sipped the wine and, taking out a cigar, looked round for matches, but as I had after all no inclination to smoke, I put down the cigar on the table in front of me. "Shut your eyes," she had said. God knows where the girl got her voice; it was so deep and good and maternal. It was good to obey such a voice, I had found that out already. Obediently I shut my eyes, leaned my head against the wall and heard the roar of a hundred mingled noises surge around me and smiled at the idea of sleep in such a place. I made up my mind to go to the door of the dance hall and from there catch a glimpse of my beautiful girl as she danced. I made a movement to go, then felt at last how unutterably tired out I was from my hours of wandering and remained seated; and, thereupon I fell asleep as I had been told. I slept greedily, thankfully, and dreamed more lightly and pleasantly than I had for a long while.

I dreamed that I was waiting in an old-fashioned anteroom. At first I knew no more than that my audience was with some Excellency or other. Then it came to me that it was Goethe who was to receive me. Unfortunately I was not there quite on a personal call. I was a reporter, and this worried me a great deal and I could not understand how the devil I had got into such a fix. .Besides this, I was upset by a scorpion that I had seen a moment before trying to climb up my leg. I had shaken myself free of the black crawling beast, but I did not know where it had got to next and did not dare make a grab after it.

Also I was not very sure whether I had been announced by a mistake to Matthisson instead of to Goethe, and him again I mixed up in my dream with Bürger, for I took him for the author of the poem to Molly. Moreover I would have liked extremely to meet Molly. I imagined her wonderful, tender, musical. If only I were not here at the orders of that cursed newspaper office. My ill-humor over this increased until by degrees it extended even to Goethe, whom I suddenly treated to all manner of reflections and reproaches. It was going to be a lively interview. The scorpion, however, dangerous though he was and hidden no doubt somewhere within an inch of me, was all the same not so bad perhaps. Possibly he might even betoken something friendly. It seemed to me extremely likely that he had something to do with Molly. He might be a kind of messenger from her--or an heraldic beast, dangerously and beautifully emblematic of woman and sin. Might not his name perhaps be Vulpius? But at that moment a flunkey threw open the door. I rose and went in.

There stood old Goethe, short and very erect, and on his classic breast, sure enough, was the corpulent star of some Order. Not for a moment did he relax his commanding attitude, his air of giving audience, and of controlling the world from that museum of his at Weimar. Indeed, he had scarcely looked at me before with a nod and a jerk like an old raven he began pompously: "Now, you young people have, I believe, very little appreciation of us and our efforts."

"You are quite right," said I, chilled by his ministerial glance. "We young people have, indeed, very little appreciation of you. You are too pompous for us, Excellency, too vain and pompous, and not outright enough. That is, no doubt, at the bottom of it--not outright enough."

The little old man bent his erect head forward, and as his hard mouth with its official folds relaxed in a little smile and became enchantingly alive, my heart gave a sudden bound; for all at once the poem came to my mind--"The dusk with folding wing"--and I remembered that it was from the lips of this man that the poem came. Indeed, at this moment I was entirely disarmed and overwhelmed and would have chosen of all things to kneel before him. But I held myself erect and heard him say with a smile: "Oh, so you accuse me of not being outright? What a thing to say! Will you explain yourself a little more fully?"

I was very glad indeed to do so.

"Like all great spirits, Herr von Goethe, you have clearly recognised and felt the riddle and the hopelessness of human life, with its moments of transcendence that sink again to wretchedness, and the impossibility of rising to one fair peak of feeling except at the cost of many days' enslavement to the daily round; and, then, the ardent longing for the realm of the spirit in eternal and deadly war with the equally ardent and holy love of the lost innocence of nature, the whole frightful suspense in vacancy and uncertainty, this condemnation to the transient that can never be valid, that is ever experimental and dilettantish; in short, the utter lack of purpose to which the human state is condemned--to its consuming despair. You have known all this, yes, and said as much over and over again; yet you gave up your whole life to preaching its opposite, giving utterance to faith and optimism and spreading before yourself and others the illusion that our spiritual strivings mean something and endure. You have lent a deaf ear to those that plumbed the depths and suppressed the voices that told the truth of despair, and not in yourself only, but also in Kleist and Beethoven. Year after year you lived on at Weimar accumulating knowledge and collecting objects, writing letters and gathering them in, as though in your old age you had found the real way to discover the eternal in the momentary, though you could only mummify it, and to spiritualise nature though you could only hide it with a pretty mask. This is why we reproach you with insincerity."

The old bigwig kept his eyes musingly on mine, smiling as before.

Then to my surprise, he asked, "You must have a strong objection, then, to the *Magic Flute* of Mozart?"

And before I could protest, he went on:

"The *Magic Flute* presents life to us as a wondrous song. It honors our feelings, transient, as they are, as something eternal and divine. It agrees neither with Herr von Kleist nor with Herr Beethoven. It preaches optimism and faith."

"I know, I know," I cried in a rage. "God knows why you hit of all things on the *Magic Flute* that is dearer to me than anything else in the world. But Mozart did not live to be eighty-two. He did not make pretensions in his own life to the enduring and the orderly and to exalted dignity as you did. He did not think himself so important! He sang his divine melodies and died. He died young--poor and misunderstood--"

I lost my breath. A thousand things ought to have been said in ten words. My forehead began to sweat.

Goethe, however, said very amiably: "It may be unforgivable that I lived to be eighty-two. My satisfaction on that account was, however, less than you may think. You are right that a great longing for survival possessed me continually. I was in continual fear of death and continually struggling with it. I believe that the struggle against death, the unconditional and self-willed determination to live, is the motive power behind the lives and activities of all outstanding men. My eighty-two years showed just as conclusively that we must all die in the end as if I had died as a schoolboy. If it helps to justify me I should like to say this too: my nature had much of the child in it, its curiosity and love for idleness and play. Well, and so it went on and on, till I saw that sooner or later there must be enough of play."

As he said this, his smile was quite cunning--a downright roguish leer. He had grown taller and his erect bearing and the constrained dignity of his face had disappeared. The air, too, around us was now ringing with melodies, all of them songs of Goethe's. I heard Mozart's "Violets" and Schubert's "Again thou fillest brake and vale" quite distinctly. And Goethe's face was rosy and youthful, and he laughed; and now he resembled Mozart like a brother, now Schubert, and the star on his breast was composed entirely of wild flowers. A yellow primrose blossomed luxuriantly in the middle of it.

It did not altogether suit me to have the old gentleman avoid my questions and accusations in this sportive manner, and I looked at him reproachfully. At that he bent forward and brought his mouth, which had now become quite like a child's, close to my ear and whispered softly into it: "You take the old Goethe much too seriously, my young friend. You should not take old people who are already dead seriously. It does them injustice. We immortals do not like things to be taken seriously. We like joking. Seriousness, young man, is an accident of time. It consists, I don't mind telling you in confidence, in putting too high a value on time. I, too, once put too high a value on time. For that reason I wished to be a hundred years old. In eternity, however, there is no time, you see. Eternity is a mere moment, just long enough for a joke."

And indeed there was no saying another serious word to the man. He capered joyfully and nimbly up and down and made the primrose shoot out from his star like a rocket and then he made it shrink and disappear. While he flickered to and fro with his dance steps and figures, it was borne in upon me that he at least had not neglected learning to dance. He could do it wonderfully. Then I remembered the scorpion, or Molly, rather, and I called out to Goethe: "Tell me, is Molly there?"

Goethe laughed aloud. He went to his table and opened a drawer; took out a handsome leather or velvet box, and held it open under my eyes. There, small, faultless, and gleaming, lay a diminutive effigy of a woman's leg on the dark velvet, an enchanting leg, with the knee a little bent and the foot pointing downwards to end in the daintiest of toes.

I stretched out my hand, for I had quite fallen in love with the little leg and I wanted to have it, but just as I was going to take hold of it with my finger and thumb, the little toy seemed to move with a tiny start and it occurred to me suddenly that this might be the scorpion. Goethe seemed to read my thought, and even to have wanted to cause this deep timidity, this hectic struggle between desire and dread. He held the provoking little scorpion close to my face and watched me start forward with desire, then start back with dread; and this seemed to divert him exceedingly. While he was teasing me with the charming, dangerous thing, he became quite old once more, very, very old, a thousand years old, with hair as white as snow, and his withered graybeard's face laughed a still and soundless laughter that shook him to the depths with abysmal old-man's humor.

When I woke I had forgotten the dream; it did not come back to me till later. I had slept for nearly an hour, as I never thought I could possibly have done at a café table with the music and the bustle all round me. The dear girl stood in front of me with one hand on my shoulder.

"Give me two or three marks," she said. "I've spent something in there."

I gave her my purse. She took it and was soon back again.

"Well, now I can sit with you for a little and then I have to go. I have an engagement."

I was alarmed.

"With whom?" I asked quickly.

"With a man, my dear Harry. He has invited me to the Odéon Bar."

"Oh! I didn't think you would leave me alone."

"Then you should have invited me yourself. Someone has got in before you. Well, there's good money saved. Do you know the Odéon? Nothing but champagne after midnight. Armchairs like at a club, Negro band, very smart."

I had never considered all this.

"But let me invite you," I entreated her. "I thought it was an understood thing, now that we've made friends. Invite yourself wherever you like. Do, please, I beg you."

"That is nice of you. But, you see, a promise is a promise, and I've given my word and I shall keep it and go. Don't worry any more over that. Have another drink of wine. There's still some in the bottle. Drink it up and then go comfortably home and sleep. Promise me."

"No, you know that's just what I can't do--go home."

"Oh--you--with your tales! Will you never be done--with your Goethe?" (The dream about Goethe came back to me at that moment.) "But if you really can't go home, stay here. There are bedrooms. Shall I see about one for you?"

I was satisfied with that and asked where I could find her again? Where did she live? She would not tell me. I should find her in one place or another if I looked.

"Mayn't I invite you somewhere?"

"Where?"

"Where and when you like."

"Good. Tuesday for dinner at the old Franciscan. First floor. Good-bye."

She gave me her hand. I noticed for the first time how well it matched her voice--a beautiful hand, firm and intelligent and good-natured. She laughed at me when I kissed it.

Then at the last moment she turned once more and said: "I'll tell you something else--about Goethe. What you felt about him and finding the picture of him more than you could put up with, I often feel about the saints."

"The saints? Are you so religious?"

"No, I'm not religious, I'm sorry to say. But I was once and shall be again. There is no time now to be religious."

"No time. Does it need time to be religious?"

"Oh, yes. To be religious you must have time and, even more, independence of time. You can't be religious in earnest and at the same time live in actual things and still take them seriously, time and money and the Odéon Bar and all that."

"Yes, I understand. But what was that you said about the saints?"

"Well, there are many saints I'm particularly fond of--Stephen, St. Francis and others. I often see pictures of them and of the Savior and the Virgin--such utterly lying and false and silly pictures--and I can put up with them just as little as you could with that picture of Goethe. When I see one of those sweet and silly Saviors or St. Francises and see how other people find them beautiful and edifying, I feel it is an insult to the real Savior and it makes me think: Why did He live and suffer so terribly if people find a picture as silly as that satisfactory to them! But in spite of this I know that my own picture of the Savior or St. Francis is only a human picture and falls short of the original, and that the Savior Himself would find the picture I have of Him within me just as stupid as I do those sickly reproductions. I don't say this to justify you in your ill temper and rage with the picture of Goethe. There's no justification. I say it simply to show you that I can understand you. You learned people and artists have, no doubt, all sorts of superior things in your heads; but you're human beings like the rest of us, and we, too, have our dreams and fancies. I noticed, for example, learned sir, that you felt a slight embarrassment when it came to telling me your Goethe story. You had to make a great effort to make your ideas comprehensible to a simple girl like me. Well, and so I wanted to show you that you needn't have made such an effort. I understand you all right. And now I've finished, and your place is in bed."

She went away and an old house porter took me up two flights of stairs. But first he asked me where my luggage was, and when he heard that I hadn't any, I had to pay down what he called "sleep money." Then he took me up an old dark staircase to a room upstairs and left me alone. There was a bleak wooden bedstead, and on the wall hung a saber and a colored print of Garibaldi and also a withered wreath that had once figured in a club festival. I would have given much for pyjamas. At any rate there was water and a small towel and I could wash. Then I lay down on the bed in my clothes, and leaving the light on, gave myself up to my reflections. So I had settled accounts with Goethe. It was splendid that he had come to me in a dream. And this wonderful girl--if only I had known her name! All of a sudden there was a human being, a living human being, to shatter the death that had come down over me like a glass case, and to put out a hand to me, a good and beautiful and warm hand. All of a sudden there were things that concerned me again, which I could think of with joy and eagerness. All of a sudden a door was thrown open through which life came in. Perhaps I could live once more and once more be a human being. My soul that had fallen asleep in the cold and nearly frozen breathed once more, and sleepily spread its weak and tiny wings. Goethe had been with me. A girl had bidden me eat and drink and sleep, and had shown me friendship and had laughed at me and had called me a silly little boy. And this wonderful friend had talked to me of the saints and shown me that even when I had outdone myself in absurdity I was not alone. I was not an incomprehensible and ailing exception. There were people akin to me. I was understood. Should I see her again? Yes, for certain. She could be relied upon. "A promise is a promise."

And before I knew, I was asleep once more and slept four or five hours. It had gone ten when I woke. My clothes were all creases. I felt utterly exhausted. And in my head was the memory of yesterday's half-forgotten horror; but I had life, hope and happy thoughts. As I returned to my room I experienced nothing of that terror that this return had had for me the day before. On the stairs above the araucaria I met the "aunt," my landlady. I saw her seldom but her kindly nature always delighted me. The meeting was not very propitious, for I was still unkempt and uncombed after my night out, and I had not shaved. I greeted her and would have passed on. As a rule, she always respected my desire to live alone and unobserved. Today, however, as it turned out, a veil between me and the outer world seemed to be torn aside, a barrier fallen. She laughed and stopped.

"You have been on a spree, Mr. Haller. You were not in bed last night. You must be pretty tired!"

"Yes," I said, and was forced to laugh too. "There was something lively going on last night, and as I did not like to shock you, I slept at an hotel. My respect for the repose and dignity of your house is great. I sometimes feel like a 'foreign body' in it."

"You are poking fun, Mr. Haller."

"Only at myself."

"You ought not to do that even. You ought not to feel like a 'foreign body' in my house. You should live as best pleases you and do as best you can. I have had before now many exceedingly respectable tenants, jewels of respectability, but not one has been quieter or disturbed us less than you. And now--would you like some tea?"

I did not refuse. Tea was brought me in her drawing room with the old-fashioned pictures and furniture, and we had a little talk. In her friendly way she elicited this and that about my life and thoughts without actually asking questions and listened attentively to my confessions, while at the same time she did not give them more importance than an intelligent and motherly woman would to the peccadilloes of men. We talked, too, of her nephew and she showed me in a neighboring room his latest hobby, a wireless set. There the industrious young man spent his evenings, fitting together the apparatus, a victim to the charms of wireless, and kneeling on pious knees before the god of applied science whose might had made it possible to discover after thousands of years a fact which every thinker has always known and put to better use than in this recent and very imperfect development. We spoke about this, for the aunt had a slight leaning to piety and religious topics were not unwelcome to her. I told her that the omnipresence of all forces and facts was well known to ancient India, and that science had merely brought a small fraction of this fact into general use by devising for it, that is, for sound waves, a receiver and transmitter which were still in their first stages and miserably defective. The principal fact known to that ancient knowledge was, I said, the unreality of time. This science had not yet observed. Finally, it would, of course, make this "discovery," also, and then the inventors would get busy over it. The discovery would be made--and perhaps very soon--that there were floating round us not only the pictures and events of the transient present in the same way that music from Paris or Berlin was now heard in Frankfurt or Zurich, but that all that had ever happened in the past could be registered and brought back likewise. We might well look for the day when, with wires or without, with or without the disturbance of other sounds, we should hear King Solomon speaking, or Walter von der Vogelweide. And all this, I said, just as today was the case with the beginnings of wireless, would be of no more service to man than as an escape from himself and his true aims, and a means of surrounding himself with an ever closer mesh of distractions and useless activities. But instead of embarking on these familiar topics with my customary bitterness and scorn for the times and for science, I made a joke of them; and the aunt smiled, and we sat together for an hour or so and drank our tea with much content.

It was for Tuesday evening that I had invited the charming and remarkable girl of the Black Eagle, and I was a good deal put to it to know how to pass the time till then; and when at last Tuesday came, the importance of my relation to this unknown girl had become alarmingly clear to me. I thought of nothing but her. I expected everything from her. I was ready to lay everything at her feet. I was not in the least in love with her. Yet I had only to imagine that she might fail to keep the appointment, or forget it, to see where I stood. Then the world would be a desert once more, one day as dreary and worthless as the last, and the deathly stillness and wretchedness would surround me once more on all sides with no way out from this hell of silence except the razor. And these few days had not made me think any the more fondly of the razor. It had lost none of its terror. This was indeed the hateful truth: I dreaded to cut my throat with a dread that crushed my heart. My fear was as wild and obstinate as though I were the healthiest of men and my life a paradise. I realised my situation recklessly and without a single illusion. I realised that it was the unendurable tension between inability to live and inability to die that made the unknown girl, the pretty dancer of the Black Eagle, so important to me. She was the one window, the one tiny crack of light in my black hole of dread. She was my release and my way to freedom. She had to teach me to live or teach me to die. She had to touch my deadened heart with her firm and pretty hand, and at the touch of life it would either leap again to flame or subside in ashes. I could not imagine whence she derived these powers, what the source of her magic was, in what secret soil this deep meaning she had for me had grown up; nor did it matter. I did not care to know. There was no longer the least importance for me in any knowledge or perception I might have. Indeed it was just in that line that I was overstocked, for the ignominy under which I suffered lay just in this--that I saw my own situation so clearly and was so very conscious, too, of hers. I saw this wretch, this brute beast of a Steppenwolf as a fly in a web, and saw too the approaching decision of his fate. Entangled and defenceless he hung in the web. The spider was ready to devour him, and further off was the rescuing hand. I might have made the most intelligent and penetrating remarks about the ramifications and the causes of my sufferings, my sickness of soul, my general bedevilment of neurosis. The mechanism was transparent to me. But what I needed was not knowledge and understanding. What I longed for in my despair was life and resolution, action and reaction, impulse and impetus.

Although during the few days of waiting I never despaired of my friend keeping her word, this did not prevent my being in a state of acute suspense when the day arrived. Never in my life have I waited more impatiently for a day to end. And while the suspense and impatience were almost intolerable, they were at the same time of wonderful benefit to me. It was unimaginably beautiful and new for me who for a long while had been too listless to await anything or to find joy in anything--yes, it was wonderful to be running here and there all day long in restless anxiety and intense expectation, to be anticipating the meeting and the talk and the outcome that the evening had in store, to be shaving and dressing with peculiar care (new linen, new tie, new laces in my shoes). Whoever this intelligent and mysterious girl might be and however she got into this relation to myself was all one. She was there. The miracle had happened. I had found a human being once more and a new interest in life. All that mattered was that the miracle should go on, that I should surrender myself to this magnetic power and follow this star.

Unforgettable moment when I saw her once more! I sat in the old-fashioned and comfortable restaurant at a small table that I had quite unnecessarily engaged by telephone, and studied the menu. In a tumbler were two orchids I had bought for my new acquaintance. I had a good while to wait, but I was sure she would come and was no longer agitated. And then she came. She stopped for a moment at the cloakroom and greeted me only by an observant and rather quizzical glance from her clear gray eyes. Distrustful, I took care to see how the waiter behaved towards her. No, there was nothing confidential, no lack of distance. He was scrupulously respectful. And yet they knew each other. She called him Emil.

She laughed with pleasure when I gave her the orchids.

"That's sweet of you, Harry. You wanted to make me a present, didn't you, and weren't sure what to choose. You weren't quite sure you would be right in making me a present. I might be insulted, and so you chose orchids, and though they're only flowers, they're dear enough. So I thank you ever so much. And by the way I'll tell you now that I won't take presents from you. I live on men, but I won't live on you. But how you have altered! No one would know you. The other day you looked as if you had been cut down from a gallows, and now you're very nearly a man again. And now-have you carried out my orders?"

"What orders?"

"You've never forgotten? I mean, have you learned the fox trot? You said you wished nothing better than to obey my commands, that nothing was dearer to you than obeying me. Do you remember?"

"Indeed I do, and so it shall be. I meant it."

"And yet you haven't learned to dance yet?"

"Can that be done so quickly--in a day or two?"

"Of course. The fox trot you can learn in an hour. The Boston in two. The tango takes longer, but that you don't need."

"But now I really must know your name."

She looked at me for a moment without speaking.

"Perhaps you can guess it. I should be so glad if you did. Pull yourself together and take a good look at me. Hasn't it ever occurred to you that sometimes my face is just like a boy's? Now, for example."

Yes, now that I looked at her face carefully, I had to admit she was right. It was a boy's face. And after a moment I saw something in her face that reminded me of my own boyhood and of my friend of those days. His name was Herman. For a moment it seemed that she had turned into this Herman.

"If you were a boy," said I in amazement, "I should say your name was Herman."

"Who knows, perhaps I am one and am simply in woman's clothing," she said, joking.

"Is your name Hermine?"

She nodded, beaming, delighted at my guess. At that moment the waiter brought the food and we began to eat. She was as happy as a child. Of all the things that pleased and charmed me about her, the prettiest and most characteristic was her rapid changes from the deepest seriousness to the drollest merriment, and this without doing herself the least violence, with the facility of a gifted child. Now for a while she was merry and chaffed me about the fox trot, trod on my feet under the table, enthusiastically praised the meal, remarked on the care I had taken dressing, though she also had many criticisms to make on my appearance.

Meanwhile I asked her: "How did you manage to look like a boy and make me guess your name?"

"Oh, you did all that yourself. Doesn't your learning reveal to you that the reason why I please you and mean so much to you is because I am a kind of looking glass for you, because there's something in me that answers you and understands you? Really, we ought all to be such looking glasses to each other and answer and correspond to each other, but such owls as you are a bit peculiar. On the slightest provocation they give themselves over to the strangest notions that they can see nothing and read nothing any longer in the eyes of other men and then nothing seems right to them. And then when an owl like that after all finds a face that looks back into his and gives him a glimpse of understanding--well, then he's pleased, naturally."

"There's nothing you don't know, Hermine," I cried in amazement. "It's exactly as you say. And yet you're so entirely different from me. Why, you're my opposite. You have all that I lack."

"So you think.," she said shortly, "and it's well you should."

And now a dark cloud of seriousness spread over her face. It was indeed like a magic mirror to me. Of a sudden her face bespoke seriousness and tragedy and it looked as fathomless as the hollow eyes of a mask. Slowly, as though it were dragged from her word for word, she said:

"Mind, don't forget what you said to me. You said that I was to command you and that it would be a joy to you to obey my commands. Don't forget that. You must know this, my little Harry--just as something in me corresponds to you and gives you confidence, so it is with me. The other day when I saw you come in to the Black Eagle, exhausted and beside yourself and scarcely in this world any longer, it came to me at once: This man will obey me. All he wants is that I should command him. And that's what I'm going to do. That's why I spoke to you and why we made friends."

She spoke so seriously from a deep impulse of her very soul that I scarcely liked to encourage her. I tried to calm her down. She shook her head with a frown and with a compelling look went on: "I tell you, you must keep your word, my boy. If you don't you'll regret it. You will have many commands from me and you will carry them out. Nice ones and agreeable ones that it will be a pleasure to you to obey. And at the last you will fulfill my last command as well, Harry."

"I will," I said, half giving in. "What will your last command be?"

I guessed it already--God knows why.

She shivered as though a passing chill went through her and seemed to be waking slowly from her trance. Her eyes did not release me. Suddenly she became still more sinister.

"If I were wise, I shouldn't tell you. But I won't be wise, Harry, not for this time. I'll be just the opposite. So now mind what I say! You will hear it and forget it again. You will laugh over it, and you will weep over it. So look out! I am going to play with you for life and death, little brother, and before we begin the game I'm going to lay my cards on the table."

How beautiful she looked, how unearthly, when she said that! Cool and clear, there swam in her eyes a conscious sadness. These eyes of hers seemed to have suffered all imaginable suffering and to have acquiesced in it. Her lips spoke with difficulty and as though something hindered them, as though a keen frost had numbed her face; but between her lips at the corners of her mouth where the tip of her tongue showed at rare intervals, there was but sweet sensuality and inward delight that contradicted the expression of her face and the tone of her voice. A short lock hung down over the smooth expanse of her forehead, and from this corner of her forehead whence fell the lock of hair, her boyishness welled up from time to time like a breath of life and cast the spell of a hermaphrodite. I listened with an eager anxiety and yet as though dazed and only half aware.

"You like me," she went on, "for the reason I said before, because I have broken through your isolation. I have caught you from the very gates of hell and wakened you to a new life. But I want more from you--much more. I want to make you fall in love with me. No, don't interrupt me. Let me speak. You like me very much. I can see that. And you're grateful to me. But you're not in love with me. I mean to make you fall in love with me, and it is part of my calling. It is my living to be able to make men fall in love with me. But mind this, I don't do it because I find you exactly captivating. I'm as little in love with you as you with me. But I need you as you do me. You need me now, for the moment, because you're desperate. You're dying just for the lack of a push to throw you into the water and bring you to life again. You need me to teach you to dance and to laugh and to live. But I need you, not today--later, for something very important and beautiful too. When you are in love with me I will give you my last command and you will obey it, and it will be the better for both of us."

She pulled one of the brown and purple green-veined orchids up a little in the glass and bending over stared a moment at the bloom.

"You won't find it easy, but you will do it. You will carry out my command and--kill me. There--ask no more."

When she came to the end her eyes were still on the orchid, and her face relaxed, losing its strain like a flower bud unfolding its petals. In an instant there was an enchanting smile on her lips while her eyes for a moment were still fixed and spellbound. Then she gave a shake of her head with its little boyish lock, took a sip of water, and realizing of a sudden that we were at a meal fell to eating again with appetite and enjoyment.

I had heard her uncanny communication clearly word for word. I had even guessed what her last command was before she said it and was horrified no longer. All that she said sounded as convincing to me as a decree of fate. I accepted it without protest. And yet in spite of the terrifying seriousness with which she had spoken I did not take it all as fully real and serious. While part of my soul drank in her words and believed in them, another part appeased me with a nod and took note that Hermine too, for all her wisdom and health and assurance, had her fantasies and twilight states. Scarcely was her last word spoken before a layer of unreality and ineffectuality settled over the whole scene.

All the same I could not get back to realities and probabilities with the same lightness as Hermine.

"And so I shall kill you one day?" I asked, still half in a dream while she laughed, and attacked her fowl with great relish.

"Of course," she nodded lightly. "Enough of that. It is time to eat. Harry, be an angel and order me a little more salad. Haven't you any appetite? It seems to me you've still to learn all the things that come naturally to other people, even the pleasure of eating. So look, my boy, I must tell you that this is the celebration of the duck, and when you pick the tender flesh from the bone it's a festal occasion and you must be just as eager and glad at heart and delighted as a lover when he unhooks his lady love for the first time. Don't you understand? Oh, you're a sheep! Are you ready? I'm going to give you a piece off the little bone. So open your mouth. Oh, what a fright you are! There he goes, squinting round the room in case any one sees him taking a bite from my fork. Don't be afraid, you prodigal son, I won't make a scandal. But it's a poor fellow who can't take his pleasure without asking other people's permission."

The scene that had gone before became more and more unreal. I was less and less able to believe that these were the same eyes that a moment before had been fixed in a dread obsession. But in this Hermine was like life itself, one moment succeeding to the next and not one to be foreseen. Now she was eating, and the duck and the salad, the sweet and the liqueur were the important thing, and each time the plates were changed a new chapter began. Yet though she played at being a child she had seen through me completely, and though she made me her pupil there and then in the game of living for each fleeting moment, she seemed to know more of life than is known to the wisest of the wise. It might be the highest wisdom or the merest artlessness. It is certain in any case that life is quite disarmed by the gift to live so entirely in the present, to treasure with such eager care every flower by the wayside and the light that plays on every passing moment. Was I to believe that this happy child with her hearty appetite and the air of a gourmet was at the same time a victim of hysterical visions who wished to die? or a careful calculating woman who, unmoved herself, had the conscious intention of making me her lover and her slave? I could not believe it. No, her surrender to the moment was so simple and complete that the fleeting shadows and agitation to the very depths of the soul came to her no less than every pleasurable impulse and were lived as fully.

Though I saw Hermine only for the second time that day, she knew everything about me and it seemed to me quite impossible that I could ever have a secret from her. Perhaps she might not understand everything of my spiritual life, might not perhaps follow me in my relation to music, to Goethe, to Novalis or Baudelaire. This too, however, was open to question. Probably it would give her as little trouble as the rest. And anyway, what was there left of my spiritual life? Hadn't all that gone to atoms and lost its meaning? As for the rest, my more personal problems and concerns, I had no doubt that she would understand them all. I should very soon be talking to her about the Steppenwolf and the treatise and all the rest of it, though till now it had existed for myself alone and never been mentioned to a single soul. Indeed, I could not resist the temptation of beginning forthwith.

"Hermine," I said, "an extraordinary thing happened to me the other day. An unknown man gave me a little book, the sort of thing you'd buy at a fair, and inside I found my whole story and everything about me. Rather remarkable, don't you think?"

"What was it called," she asked lightly.

"Treatise on the Steppenwolf!"

"Oh, *Steppenwolf* is magnificent! And are you the Steppenwolf? Is that meant for you?"

"Yes, it's me. I am one who is half-wolf and half-man, or thinks himself so at least."

She made no answer. She gave me a searching look in the eyes, then looked at my hands, and for a moment her face and expression had that deep seriousness and sinister passion of a few minutes before. Making a guess at her thoughts I felt she was wondering whether I were wolf enough to carry out her last command.

"That is, of course, your own fanciful idea," she said, becoming serene once more, "or a poetical one, if you like. But there's something in it. You're no wolf today, but the other day when you came in as if you had fallen from the moon there was really something of the beast about you. It is just what struck me at the time."

She broke off as though surprised by a sudden idea.

"How absurd those words are, such as beast and beast of prey. One should not speak of animals in that way. They may be terrible sometimes, but they're much more right than men."

"How do you mean--right?"

"Well, look at an animal, a cat, a dog, or a bird, or one of those beautiful great beasts in the zoo, a puma or a giraffe. You can't help seeing that all of them are right. They're never in any embarrassment. They always know what to do and how to behave themselves. They don't flatter and they don't intrude. They don't pretend. They are as they are, like stones or flowers or stars in the sky. Don't you agree?"

I did.

"Animals are sad as a rule," she went on. "And when a man is sad--I don't mean because he has a toothache or has lost some money, but because he sees, for once in a way, how it all is with life and everything, and is sad in earnest--he always looks a little like an animal. He looks not only sad, but more right and more beautiful than usual. That's how it is, and that's how you looked, Steppenwolf, when I saw you for the first time."

"Well, Hermine, and what do you think about this book with a description of me in it?"

"Oh, I can't always be thinking. Well talk about it another time. You can give it to me to read one day. Or, no, if I ever start reading again, give me one of the books you've written yourself."

She asked for coffee and for a while seemed absent minded and distraught. Then she suddenly beamed and seemed to have found the clue to her speculations.

"Hullo," she cried, delighted, "now I've got it!"

"What have you got?"

"The fox trot. I've been thinking about it all the evening. Now tell me, have you a room where we two could dance sometimes? It doesn't matter if it's small, but there mustn't be anybody underneath to come up and play hell if his ceiling rocks a bit. Well, that's fine, you can learn to dance at home.""Yes," I said in alarm, "so much the better. But I thought music was required."

"Of course it's required. You've got to buy that. At the most it won't cost as much as a course of lessons. You save that because I'll give them myself. This way we have the music whenever we like and at the end we have the gramophone in the bargain."

"The gramophone?"

"Of course. You can buy a small one and a few dance records--"

"Splendid," I cried, "and if you bring it off and teach me to dance, the gramophone is yours as an honorarium. Agreed?"

I brought it out very pat, but scarcely from the heart. I could not picture the detested instrument in my study among my books, and I was by no means reconciled to the dancing either. It had been in my mind that I might try how it went for a while, though I was convinced that I was too old and stiff and would never learn now. But to plunge into it all at once seemed a bit too much. As an old and fastidious connoisseur of music, I could feel my gorge rising against the gramophone and jazz and modern dance-music. It was more than any one could ask of me to have dance tunes that were the latest rage of America let loose upon the sanctum where I took refuge with Novalis and Jean Paul and to be made to dance to them. But it was not any one who asked it of me. It was Hermine, and it was for her to command, and for me to obey. Of course, I obeyed.

We met at a café on the following afternoon. Hermine was there before me, drinking tea, and she pointed with a smile to my name which she had found in a newspaper. It was one of the reactionary jingo papers of my own district in which from time to time violently abusive references to me were circulated. During the war I had been opposed to it and, after, I had from time to time counseled quiet and patience and humanity and a criticism that began at home; and I had resisted the nationalist jingoism that became every day more pronounced, more insane and unrestrained. Here, then, was another attack of this kind, badly written, in part the work of the editor himself and in part stolen from articles of a similar kind in papers of similar tendencies to his own. It is common knowledge that no one writes worse than these defenders of decrepit ideas. No one plies his trade with less of decency and conscientious care. Hermine had read the article, and it had informed her that Harry Haller was a noxious insect and a man who disowned his native land, and that it stood to reason that no good could come to the country so long as such persons and such ideas were tolerated and the minds of the young turned to sentimental ideas of humanity instead of to revenge by arms upon the hereditary foe.

"Is that you?" asked Hermine, pointing to my name. "Well, you've made yourself some enemies and no mistake. Does it annoy you?"

I read a few lines. There was not a single line of stereotyped abuse that had not been drummed into me for years till I was sick and tired of it.

"No," I said, "it doesn't annoy me. I was used to it long ago. Now and again I have expressed the opinion that every nation, and even every person, would do better, instead of rocking himself to sleep with political catchwords about war guilt, to ask himself how far his own faults and negligences and evil tendencies are guilty of the war and all the other wrongs of the world, and that therein lies the only possible means of avoiding the next war. They don't forgive me that, for, of course, they are themselves all guiltless, the Kaiser, the generals, the trade magnates, the politicians, the papers. Not one of them has the least thing to blame himself for. Not one has any guilt. One might believe that everything was for the best, even though a few million men lie under the ground. And mind you, Hermine, even though such abusive articles cannot annoy me any longer, they often sadden me all the same. Two-thirds of my countrymen read this kind of newspaper, read things written in this tone every morning and every night, are every day worked up and admonished and incited, and robbed of their peace of mind and better feelings by them, and the end and aim of it all is to have the war over again, the next war that draws nearer and nearer, and it will be a good deal more horrible than the last. All that is perfectly clear and simple. Any one could comprehend it and reach the same conclusion after a moment's reflection. But nobody wants to. Nobody wants to avoid the next war, nobody wants to spare himself and his children the next holocaust if this be the cost. To reflect for one moment, to examine himself for a while and ask what share he has in the world's confusion and wickedness--look you, nobody wants to do that. And so there's no stopping it, and the next war is being pushed on with enthusiasm by thousands upon thousands day by day. It has paralysed me since I knew it, and brought me to despair. I have no country and no ideals left. All that comes to nothing but decorations for the gentlemen by whom the next slaughter is ushered in. There is no sense in thinking or saying or writing anything of human import, to bother one's head with thoughts of goodness--for two or three men who do that, there are thousands of papers, periodicals, speeches, meetings in public and in private, that make the opposite their daily endeavor and succeed in it too."

Hermine had listened attentively.

"Yes," she said now, "there you're right enough. Of course, there will be another war. One doesn't need to read the papers to know that. And of course one can be sad about it, but it isn't any use. It is just the same as when a man is sad to think that one day, in spite of his utmost efforts to prevent it, he will inevitably die. The war against death, dear Harry, is always a beautiful, noble and wonderful and glorious thing, and so, it follows, is the war against war. But it is always hopeless and quixotic too."

"That is perhaps true," I cried heatedly, "but truths like that--that we must all soon be dead and so it is all one and the same--make the whole of life flat and stupid. Are we then to throw everything up and renounce the spirit altogether and all effort and all that is human and let ambition and money rule forever while we await the next mobilization over a glass of beer?"

Remarkable the look that Hermine now gave me, a look full of amusement, full of irony and roguishness and fellow feeling, and at the same time so grave, so wise, so unfathomably serious.

"You shan't do that," she said in a voice that was quite maternal. "Your life will not be flat and dull even though you know that your war will never be victorious. It is far flatter, Harry, to fight for something good and ideal and to know all the time that you are bound to attain it. Are ideals attainable? Do we live to abolish death? No--we live to fear it and then again to love it, and just for death's sake it is that our spark of life glows for an hour now and then so brightly. You're a child, Harry. Now, do as I tell you and come along. We've a lot to get done today. I am not going to bother myself any more today about the war or the papers either. What about you?"

Oh, no, I had no wish to.

We went together--it was our first walk in the town--to a music shop and looked at gramophones. We turned them on and off and heard them play, and when we had found one that was very suitable and nice and cheap I wanted to buy it. Hermine, however, was not for such rapid transactions. She pulled me back and I had to go off with her in search of another shop and there, too, look at and listen to gramophones of every shape and size, from the dearest to the cheapest, before she finally agreed to return to the first shop and buy the machine we first thought of.

"You see," I said, "it would have been as simple to have taken it at once."

"Think so? And then perhaps tomorrow we should have seen the very same one in a shop window at twenty francs less. And besides, it's fun buying things and you have to pay for your fun. You've a lot to learn yet."

We got a porter to carry the purchase home.

Hermine made a careful inspection of my room. She commended the stove and the sofa, tried the chairs, picked up the books, stood a long while in front of the photograph of Erica. We had put the gramophone on a chest of drawers among piles of books. And now my instruction began. Hermine turned on a fox trot and, after showing me the first steps, began to take me in hand. I trotted obediently around with her, colliding with chairs, hearing her directions and failing to understand them, treading on her toes, and being as clumsy as I was conscientious. After the second dance she threw herself on the sofa and laughed like a child.

"Oh! how stiff you are! Just go straight ahead as if you were walking. There's not the least need to exert yourself. Why, I should think you have made yourself positively hot, haven't you? No, let's rest five minutes! Dancing, don't you see, is every bit as easy as thinking, when you can do it, and much easier to learn. Now you can understand why people won't get the habit of thinking and prefer calling Herr Haller a traitor to his country and waiting quietly for the next war to come along."

In an hour she was gone, assuring me that it would go better next time. I had my own thoughts about that, and I was sorely disappointed over my stupidity and clumsiness. It did not seem to me that I had learned anything whatever and I did not believe that it would go better next time. No, one had to bring certain qualities to dancing that I was entirely without, gaiety, innocence, frivolity, elasticity. Well, I had always thought so.

But there, the next time it did in fact go better. I even got some fun out of it, and at the end of the lesson Hermine announced that I was now proficient in the fox trot. But when she followed it up by saying that I had to dance with her the next day at a restaurant, I was thrown into a panic and resisted the idea with vehemence. She reminded me coolly of my oath of obedience and arranged a meeting for tea on the following day at the Balance Hotel.

That evening I sat in my room and tried to read; but I could not. I was in dread of the morrow. It was a most horrible thought that I, an elderly, shy, touchy crank, was to frequent one of those modern deserts of jazz music, a *thé dansant,* and a far more horrible thought that I was to figure there as a dancer, though I did not in the least know how to dance. And I own I laughed at myself and felt shame in my own eyes when alone in the quiet of my study I turned on the machine and softly in stockinged feet went through the steps of my dance.

A small orchestra played every other day at the Balance Hotel and tea and whisky were served. I made an attempt at bribing Hermine, I put cakes before her and proposed a bottle of good wine, but she was inflexible.

"You're not here for your amusement today. It is a dancing lesson."

I had to dance with her two or three times, and during an interval she introduced me to the saxophone player, a dark and good-looking youth of Spanish or South American origin, who, she told me, could play on all instruments and talk every language in the world. This señor appeared to know Hermine well and to be on excellent terms with her. He had two saxophones of different sizes in front of him which he played on by turns, while his darkly gleaming eyes scrutinized the dancers and beamed with pleasure. I was surprised to feel something like jealousy of this agreeable and charming musician, not a lover's jealousy, for there was no question of love between Hermine and me, but a subtler jealousy of their friendship; for he did not seem to me so eminently worthy of the interest, and even reverence, with which she so conspicuously distinguished him. I apparently was to meet some queer people, I thought to myself in ill humor. Then Hermine was asked to dance again, and I was left alone to drink tea and listen to the music, a kind of music that I had never till that day known how to endure. Good God, I thought, so now I am to be initiated, and made to feel at home in this world of idlers and pleasure seekers, a world that is utterly strange and repugnant to me and that to this day I have always carefully avoided and utterly despised, a smooth and stereotyped world of marble-topped tables, jazz music, cocottes and commercial travelers! Sadly, I swallowed my tea and stared at the crowd of second-rate elegance. Two beautiful girls caught my eye. They were both good dancers. I followed their movements with admiration and envy. How elastic, how beautiful and gay and certain their steps!

Soon Hermine appeared once more. She was not pleased with me. She scolded me and said that I was not there to wear such a face and sit idling at tea tables. I was to pull myself together, please, and dance. What, I knew no one? That was not necessary. Were there, then, no girls there who met with my approval?

I pointed out one of the two, and the more attractive, who happened at the moment to be standing near us. She looked enchanting in her pretty velvet dress with her short luxuriant blonde hair and her rounded womanly arms. Hermine insisted that I should go up to her forthwith and ask her to dance. I shrank back in despair.

"Indeed, I cannot do it," I said in my misery. "Of course, if I were young and good-looking--but for a stiff old hack like me who can't dance for the life of him--she would laugh at me!"

Hermine looked at me contemptuously.

"And that I should laugh at you, of course, doesn't matter. What a coward you are! Every one risks being laughed at when he addresses a girl. That's always at stake. So take the risk, Harry, and if the worst come to the worst let yourself be laughed at. Otherwise it's all up with my belief in your obedience...."

She was obdurate. I got up automatically and approached the young beauty just as the music began again.

"As a matter of fact, I'm engaged for this one," she said and looked me up and down with her large clear eyes, "but my partner seems to have got stranded at the bar over there, so come along."

I grasped her and performed the first steps, still in amazement that she had not sent me about my business. She was not long in taking my measure and in taking charge of me. She danced wonderfully and I caught the infection. I forgot for the moment all the rules I had conscientiously learned and simply floated along. I felt my partner's taut hips, her quick and pliant knees, and looking in her young and radiant face I owned to her that this was the first time in my life that I had ever really danced. She smiled encouragement and replied to my enchanted gaze and flattering words with a wonderful compliance, not of words, but of movements whose soft enchantment brought us more closely and delightfully in touch. My right hand held her waist firmly and I followed every movement of her feet and arms and shoulders with eager happiness. Not once, to my astonishment, did I step on her feet, and when the music stopped, we both stood where we were and clapped till the dance was played again; and then with a lover's zeal I devoutly performed the rite once more.

When, too soon, the dance came to an end, my beautiful partner in velvet disappeared and I suddenly saw Hermine standing near me. She had been watching us.

"Now do you see?" she laughed approvingly. "Have you made the discovery that women's legs are not table legs? Well, bravo! You know the fox trot now, thank the Lord. Tomorrow we'll get on to the Boston, and in three weeks there's the Masked Ball at the Globe Rooms."

We had taken seats for the interval when the charming young Herr Pablo, with a friendly nod, sat down beside Hermine. He seemed to be very intimate with her. As for myself, I must own that I was not by any means delighted with the gentleman at this first encounter. He was good-looking, I could not deny, both of face and figure, but I could not discover what further advantages he had. Even his linguistic accomplishments sat very lightly on him--to such an extent, indeed, that he did not speak at all beyond uttering such words as please, thanks, you bet, rather and hallo. These, certainly, he knew in several languages. No, he said nothing, this Señor Pablo, nor did he even appear to think much, this charming caballero. His business was with the saxophone in the jazz-band and to this calling he appeared to devote himself with love and passion. Often during the course of the music he would suddenly clap with his hands, or permit himself other expressions of enthusiasm, such as, singing out "O O O, Ha Ha, Hallo." Apart from this, however, he confined himself to being beautiful, to pleasing women, to wearing collars and ties of the latest fashion and a great number of rings on his fingers. His manner of entertaining us consisted in sitting beside us, in smiling upon us, in looking at his wrist watch and in rolling cigarettes--at which he was an expert. His dark and beautiful Creole eyes and his black locks hid no romance, no problems, no thoughts. Closely looked at, this beautiful demigod of love was no more than a complacent and rather spoiled young man with pleasant manners. I talked to him about his instrument and about tone colors in jazz music, and he must have seen that he was confronted by one who had the enjoyment of a connoisseur for all that touched on music. But he made no response, and while I, in compliment to him, or rather, to Hermine, embarked upon a musicianly justification of jazz, he smiled amiably upon me and my efforts. Presumably, he had not the least idea that there was any music but jazz or that any music had ever existed before it. He was pleasant, certainly, pleasant and polite, and his large, vacant eyes smiled most charmingly. Between him and me, however, there appeared to be nothing whatever in common. Nothing of all that was, perhaps, important and sacred to him could be so for me as well. We came of contrasted races and spoke languages in which no two words were akin. (Later, nevertheless, Hermine told me a remarkable thing. She told me that Pablo, after a conversation about me, had said that she must treat me very nicely, for I was so very unhappy. And when she asked what brought him to that conclusion, he said: "Poor, poor fellow. Look at his eyes. Doesn't know how to laugh.")

When the dark-eyed young man had taken his leave of us and the music began again, Hermine stood up. "Now you might have another dance with me. Or don't you care to dance any more?"

With her, too, I danced more easily now, in a freer and more sprightly fashion, even though not so buoyantly and more self-consciously than with the other. Hermine had me lead, adapting herself as softly and lightly as the leaf of a flower, and with her, too, I now experienced all these delights that now advanced and now took wing. She, too, now exhaled the perfume of woman and love, and her dancing, too, sang with intimate tenderness the lovely and enchanting song of sex. And yet I could not respond to all this with warmth and freedom. I could not entirely forget myself in abandon. Hermine stood in too close a relation to me. She was my comrade and sister--my double, almost, in her resemblance not to me only, but to Herman, my boyhood friend, the enthusiast, the poet, who had shared with ardor all my intellectual pursuits and extravagances.

"I know," she said when I spoke of it. "I know that well enough. All the same, I shall make you fall in love with me, but there's no use hurrying. First of all we're comrades, two people who hope to be friends, because we have recognised each other. For the present we'll each learn from the other and amuse ourselves together. I show you my little stage, and teach you to dance and to have a little pleasure and be silly; and you show me your thoughts and something of all you know."

"There's little there to show you, Hermine, I'm afraid. You know far more than I do. You're a most remarkable person--and a woman. But do I mean anything to you? Don't I bore you?"

She looked down darkly to the floor.

"That's how I don't like to hear you talk. Think of that evening when you came broken from your despair and loneliness, to cross my path and be my comrade. Why was it, do you think, I was able to recognise you and understand you?"

"Why, Hermine? Tell me!"

"Because it's the same for me as for you, because I am alone exactly as you are, because I'm as little fond of life and men and myself as you are and can put up with them as little. There are always a few such people who demand the utmost of life and yet cannot come to terms with its stupidity and crudeness."

"You, you!" I cried in deep amazement. "I understand you, my comrade. No one understands you better than I. And yet you're a riddle. You are such a past master at life. You have your wonderful reverence for its little details and enjoyments. You are such an artist in life. How can you suffer at life's hands? How can you despair?"

"I don't despair. As to suffering--oh, yes, I know all about that! You are surprised that I should be unhappy when I can dance and am so sure of myself in the superficial things of life. And I, my friend, am surprised that you are so disillusioned with life when you are at home with the very things in it that are the deepest and most beautiful, spirit, art, and thought! That is why we were drawn to one another and why we are brother and sister. I am going to teach you to dance and play and smile, and still not be happy. And you are going to teach me to think and to know and yet not be happy. Do you know that we are both children of the devil?"

"Yes, that is what we are. The devil is the spirit, and we are his unhappy children. We have fallen out of nature and hang suspended in space. And that reminds me of something. In the Steppenwolf treatise that I told you about, there is something to the effect that it is only a fancy of his to believe that he has one soul, or two, that he is made up of one or two personalities. Every human being, it says, consists of ten, or a hundred, or a thousand souls."

"I like that very much," cried Hermine. "In your case, for example, the spiritual part is very highly developed, and so you are very backward in all the little arts of living. Harry, the thinker, is a hundred years old, but Harry, the dancer, is scarcely half a day old. It's he we want to bring on, and all his little brothers who are just as little and stupid and stunted as he is."

She looked at me, smiling; and then asked softly in an altered voice:

"And how did you like Maria, then?"

"Maria? Who is she?"

"The girl you danced with. She is a lovely girl, a very lovely girl. You were a little smitten with her, as far as I could see."

"You know her then?"

"Oh, yes, we know each other well. Were you very much taken with her?"

"I liked her very much, and I was delighted that she was so indulgent about my dancing."

"As if that were the whole story! You ought to make love to her a little, Harry. She is very pretty and such a good dancer, and you are in love with her already, I know very well. You'll succeed with her, I'm sure."

"Believe me, I have no such aspiration."

"Now you're lying a little. Of course, I know that you have an attachment. There is a girl somewhere or other whom you see once or twice a year in order to have a quarrel with her. Of course, it's very charming of you to wish to be true to this estimable friend of yours, but you must permit me not to take it so very seriously. I suspect you of taking love frightfully seriously. That is your own affair. You can love as much as you like in your ideal fashion, for all I care. All I have to worry about is that you should learn to know a little more of the little arts and lighter sides of life. In this sphere, I am your teacher, and I shall be a better one than your ideal love ever was, you may be sure of that! It's high time you slept with a pretty girl again, Steppenwolf."

"Hermine," I cried in torment, "you have only to look at me, I am an old man!"

"You're a child. You were too lazy to learn to dance till it was nearly too late, and in the same way you were too lazy to learn to love. As for ideal and tragic love, that, I don't doubt, you can do marvellously--and all honor to you. Now you will learn to love a little in an ordinary human way. We have made a start. You will soon be fit to go to a ball, but you must know the Boston first, and we'll begin on that tomorrow. I'll come at three. How did you like the music, by the way?"

"Very much indeed."

"Well, there's another step forward, you see. Up to now you couldn't stand all this dance and jazz music. It was too superficial and frivolous for you. Now you have seen that there's no need to take it seriously and that it can all the same be very agreeable and delightful. And, by the way, the whole orchestra would be nothing without Pablo. He conducts it and puts fire into it."

. . . . . . .

Just as the gramophone contaminated the esthetic and intellectual atmosphere of my study and just as the American dances broke in as strangers and disturbers, yes, and as destroyers, into my carefully tended garden of music, so, too, from all sides there broke in new and dreaded and disintegrating influences upon my life that, till now, bad been so sharply marked off and so deeply secluded. The Steppenwolf treatise, and Hermine too, were right in their doctrine of the thousand souls. Every day new souls kept springing up beside the host of old ones; making clamorous demands and creating confusion; and now I saw as clearly as in a picture what an illusion my former personality had been. The few capacities and pursuits in which I had happened to be strong had occupied all my attention, and I had painted a picture of myself as a person who was in fact nothing more than a most refined and educated specialist in poetry, music and philosophy; and as such I had lived, leaving all the rest of me to be a chaos of potentialities, instincts and impulses which I found an encumbrance and gave the label of Steppenwolf.

Meanwhile, though cured of an illusion, I found this disintegration of the personality by no means a pleasant and amusing adventure. On the contrary, it was often exceedingly painful, often almost intolerable. Often the sound of the gramophone was truly fiendish to my ears in the midst of surroundings where everything was tuned to so very different a key. And many a time, when I danced my one step in a stylish restaurant among pleasure seekers and elegant rakes, I felt that I was a traitor to all that I was bound to hold most sacred. Had Hermine left me for one week alone I should have fled at once from this wearisome and laughable trafficking with the world of pleasure. Hermine, however, was always there. Though I might not see her every day, I was all the same continually under her eye, guided, guarded and counseled--besides, she read all my mad thoughts of rebellion and escape in my face, and smiled at them.

As the destruction of all that I had called my personality went on, I began to understand, too, why it was that I had feared death so horribly in spite of all my despair. I began to perceive that this ignoble horror in the face of death was a part of my old conventional and lying existence. The late Herr Haller, gifted writer, student of Mozart and Goethe, author of essays upon the metaphysics of art, upon genius and tragedy and humanity, the melancholy hermit in a cell encumbered with books, was given over bit by bit to self-criticism and at every point was found wanting. This gifted and interesting Herr Haller had, to be sure, preached reason and humanity and had protested against the barbarity of the war; but he had not let himself be stood against a wall and shot, as would have been the proper consequence of his way of thinking. He had found some way of accommodating himself; one, of course, that was outwardly reputable and noble, but still a compromise and no more. He was, further, opposed to the power of capital and yet he had industrial securities lying at his bank and spent the interest from them without a pang of conscience. And so it was all through. Harry Haller had, to be sure, rigged himself out finely as an idealist and contemner of the world, as a melancholy hermit and growling prophet. At bottom, however, he was a bourgeois who took exception to a life like Hermine's and was much annoyed over the nights thrown away in a restaurant and the money squandered there, and had them on his conscience. Instead of longing to be freed and completed, he longed, on the contrary, most earnestly to get back to those happy times when his intellectual trifling had been his diversion and brought him fame. Just so those newspaper readers--whom he despised and scorned--longed to get back to the ideal time before the war, because it was so much more comfortable than taking a lesson from those who had gone through it. Oh, the devil, he made one sick, this Herr Haller! And yet I clung to him all the same, or to the mask of him that was already falling away, clung to his coquetting with the spiritual, to his bourgeois horror of the disorderly and accidental (to which death, too, belonged) and compared the new Harry--the somewhat timid and ludicrous dilettante of the dance rooms--scornfully and enviously with the old one in whose ideal and lying portrait he had since discovered all those fatal characteristics which had upset him that night so grievously in the professor's print of Goethe. He himself, the old Harry, had been just such a bourgeois idealization of Goethe, a spiritual champion whose all-too-noble gaze shone with the unction of elevated thought and humanity, until he was almost overcome by his own nobleness of mind! The devil! Now, at last, this fine picture stood badly in need of repairs! The ideal Herr Haller had been lamentably dismantled! He looked like a dignitary who had fallen among thieves--with his tattered breeches--and he would have shown sense if he had studied now the rôle that his rags appointed him, instead of wearing them with an air of respectability and carrying on a whining pretence to lost repute.

I was constantly finding myself in the company of Pablo, the musician, and my estimate of him had to be revised if only because Hermine liked him so much and was so eager for his company. Pablo had left on me the impression of a pretty nonentity, a little beau, and somewhat empty at that, as happy as a child for whom there are no problems, whose joy is to dribble into his toy trumpet and who is kept quiet with praises and chocolate. Pablo, however, was not interested in my opinions. They were as indifferent to him as my musical theories. He listened with friendly courtesy, smiling as he always did; but he refrained all the same from any actual reply. On the other hand, in spite of this, it seemed that I had aroused his interest. It was clear that he put himself out to please me and to show me good-will. Once when I showed a certain irritation, and even ill humor, over one of these fruitless attempts at conversation he looked in my face with a troubled and sorrowful air and, taking my left hand and stroking it, he offered me a pinch from his little gold snuffbox. It would do me good. I looked inquiringly at Hermine. She nodded and I took a pinch. The almost immediate effect was that I became clearer in the head and more cheerful. No doubt there was cocaine in the powder. Hermine told me that Pablo had many such drugs, and that he procured them through secret channels. He offered them to his friends now and then and was a master in the mixing and prescribing of them. He had drugs for stilling pain, for inducing sleep, for begetting beautiful dreams, lively spirits and the passion of love.

One day I met him in the street near the quay and he turned at once to accompany me. This time I succeeded at last in making him talk.

"Herr Pablo," I said to him as he played with his slender ebony and silver walking stick, "you are a friend of Hermine's and that is why I take an interest in you. But I can't say you make it easy to get on with you. Several times I have attempted to talk about music with you. It would have interested me to know your thoughts and opinions, whether they contradicted mine or not, but you have disdained to make me even the barest reply."

He gave me a most amiable smile and this time a reply was accorded me.

"Well," he said with equanimity, "you see, in my opinion there is no point at all in talking about music. I never talk about music. What reply, then, was I to make to your very able and just remarks? You were perfectly right in all you said. But, you see, I am a musician, not a professor, and I don't believe that, as regards music, there is the least point in being right. Music does not depend on being right, on having good taste and education and all that."

"Indeed. Then what does it depend on?"

"On making music, Herr Haller, on making music as well and as much as possible and with all the intensity of which one is capable. That is the point, Monsieur. Though I carried the complete works of Bach and Haydn in my head and could say the cleverest things about them, not a soul would be the better for it. But when I take hold of my mouthpiece and play a lively shimmy, whether the shimmy be good or bad, it will give people pleasure. It gets into their legs and into their blood. That's the point and that alone. Look at the faces in a dance hall at the moment when the music strikes up after a longish pause, how eyes sparkle, legs twitch and faces begin to laugh. *That* is why one makes music."

"Very good, Herr Pablo. But there is not only sensual music. There is spiritual also. Besides the music that is actually played at the moment, there is the immortal music that lives on even when it is not actually being played. It can happen to a man to lie alone in bed and to call to mind a melody from the *Magic Flute* or the *Matthew Passion,* and then there is music without anybody blowing into a flute or passing a bow across a fiddle."

"Certainly, Herr Haller. *Yearning* and *Valencia* are recalled every night by many a lonely dreamer. Even the poorest typist in her office has the latest one step in her head and taps her keys in time to it. You are right. I don't grudge all those lonely persons their mute music, whether it's *Yearning* or the *Magic Flute* or *Valencia.* But where do they get their lonely and mute music from? They get it from us, the musicians. It must first have been played and heard, it must have got into the blood, before any one at home in his room can think of it and dream of it."

"Granted," I said coolly, "all the same it won't do to put Mozart and the latest fox trot on the same level. And it is not one and the same thing whether you play people divine and eternal music or cheap stuff of the day that is forgotten tomorrow."

When Pablo observed from my tone that I was getting excited, he at once put on his most amiable expression and touching my arm caressingly he gave an unbelievable softness to his voice.

"Ah, my dear sir, you may be perfectly right with your levels. I have nothing to say to your putting Mozart and Haydn and *Valencia* on what levels you please. It is all one to me. It is not for me to decide about levels. I shall never be asked about them. Mozart, perhaps, will still be played in a hundred years and *Valencia* in two will be played no more--we can well leave that, I think, in God's hands. God is good and has the span of all our days in his hands and that of every waltz and fox trot too. He is sure to do what is right. We musicians, however, we must play our parts according to our duties and our gifts. We have to play what is actually in demand, and we have to play it as well and as beautifully and as expressively as ever we can."

With a sigh I gave it up. There was no getting past the fellow.

At many moments the old and the new, pain and pleasure, fear and joy were quite oddly mixed with one another. Now I was in heaven, now in hell, generally in both at once. The old Harry and the new lived at one moment in bitter strife, at the next in peace. Many a time the old Harry appeared to be dead and done with, to have died and been buried, and then of a sudden there he was again, giving orders and tyrannizing and contradictory till the little new young Harry was silent for very shame and let himself be pushed to the wall. At other times the young Harry took the old by the throat and squeezed with all his might. There was many a groan, many a death struggle, many a thought of the razor blade.

Often, however, suffering and happiness broke over me in one wave. One such moment was when a few days after my first public exhibition of dancing, I went into my bedroom at night and to my indescribable astonishment, dismay, horror and enchantment found the lovely Maria lying in my bed.

Of all the surprises that Hermine had prepared for me this was the most violent. For I had not a moment's doubt that it was she who had sent me this bird of paradise. I had not, as usually, been with Hermine that evening. I had been to a recital of old church music in the Cathedral, a beautiful, though melancholy, excursion into my past life, to the fields of my youth, the territory of my ideal self. Beneath the lofty Gothic of the church whose netted vaulting swayed with a ghostly life in the play of the sparse lights, I heard pieces by Buxtehude, Pachelbel, Bach and Haydn. I had gone the old beloved way once more. I had heard the magnificent voice of a Bach singer with whom, in the old days when we were friends, I had enjoyed many a memorable musical occasion. The notes of the old music with its external dignity and sanctity had called to life all the exalted enchantment and enthusiasm of youth. I had sat in the lofty choir, sad and abstracted, a guest for an hour of this noble and blessed world which once had been my home. During a Haydn duet the tears had come suddenly to my eyes. I had not waited for the end of the concert. Dropping the thought I had had of seeing the singer again (what evenings I had once spent with the artists after such concerts) and stealing away out of the Cathedral, I had wearily paced the dark and narrow streets, where here and there behind the windows of the restaurants jazz orchestras were playing the tunes of the life I had now come to live. Oh, what a dull maze of error I had made of my life!

For long during this night's walk I had reflected upon the significance of my relation to music, and not for the first time recognized this appealing and fatal relation as the destiny of the entire German spirit. In the German spirit the matriarchal link with nature rules in the form of the hegemony of music to an extent unknown in any other people. We intellectuals, instead of fighting against this tendency like men, and rendering obedience to the spirit, the Logos, the Word, and gaining a hearing for it, are all dreaming of a speech without words that utters the inexpressible and gives form to the formless. Instead of playing his part as truly and honestly as he could, the German intellectual has constantly rebelled against the word and against reason and courted music. And so the German spirit, carousing in music, in wonderful creations of sound, and wonderful beauties of feeling and mood that were never pressed home to reality, has left the greater part of its practical gifts to decay. None of us intellectuals is at home in reality. We are strange to it and hostile. That is why the part played by intellect even in our own German reality, in our history and politics and public opinion, has been so lamentable a one. Well, I had often pondered all this, not without an intense longing sometimes to turn to and do something real for once, to be seriously and responsibly active instead of occupying myself forever with nothing but esthetics and intellectual and artistic pursuits. It always ended, however, in resignation, in surrender to destiny. The generals and the captains of industry were quite right. There was nothing to be made of us intellectuals. We were a superfluous, irresponsible lot of talented chatterboxes for whom reality had no meaning. With a curse, I came back to the razor.

So, full of thoughts and the echoes of the music, my heart weighed down with sadness and the longing of despair for life and reality and sense and all that was irretrievably lost, I had got home at last; climbed my stairs; put on the light in my sitting room; tried in vain to read; thought of the appointment which compelled me to drink whisky and dance at the Cecil Bar on the following evening; thought with malice and bitterness not only of myself, but of Hermine too. She might have the best and kindest intentions and she might be a wonderful person, but she would have done better all the same to let me perish instead of drawing me down into this strange, dazzling, dizzying world of hers where I would always remain a stranger and where my real self pined and wasted away.

And so I had sadly put out the light and taken myself to my bedroom and sadly begun to undress; and then I was surprised by an unaccustomed smell. There was a faint aroma of scent, and looking round I saw the lovely Maria lying in my bed, smiling and a little startled, with large blue eyes.

"Maria!" I said. And my first thoughts were that my landlady would give me notice when she knew of it.

"I've come," she said softly. "Are you angry with me?"

"No, no. I see Hermine gave you the key. Isn't that it?"

"Oh, it does make you angry. I'll go again."

"No, lovely Maria, stay! Only, just tonight, I'm very sad. I can't be jolly tonight. Perhaps tomorrow I'll be better again."

I was bending over her and she took my head in her large firm hands and drawing it down gave me a long kiss. Then I sat down on the bed beside her and took her hands and asked her to speak low in case we were heard, and looked at her beautiful full rounded face that lay so strangely and wonderfully on my pillow like a large flower. She drew my hand slowly to her lips and laid it beneath the clothes on her warm and evenly breathing breast.

"You don't need to be jolly," she said. "Hermine told me that you had troubles. Any one can understand that. Tell me, then, do I please you still? The other day, when we were dancing, you were very much in love with me."

I kissed her eyes, her mouth and neck and breasts. A moment ago I had thought of Hermine with bitterness and reproach. Now I held her gift in my hands and was thankful. Maria's caresses did not harm the wonderful music I had heard that evening. They were its worthy fulfillment. Slowly I drew the clothes from her lovely body till my kisses reached her feet. When I lay down beside her, her flower face smiled back at me omniscient and bountiful.

During this night by Maria's side I did not sleep much, but my sleep was as deep and peaceful as a child's. And between sleeping I drank of her beautiful warm youth and heard, as we talked softly, a number of curious tales about her life and Hermine's. I had never known much of this side of life. Only in the theatrical world, occasionally, in earlier years had I come across similar existences--women as well as men who lived half for art and half for pleasure. Now, for the first time, I had a glimpse into this kind of life, remarkable alike for its singular innocence and singular corruption. These girls, mostly from poor homes, but too intelligent and too pretty to give their whole lives to some ill-paid and joyless way of gaining their living, all lived sometimes on casual work, sometimes on their charm and easy virtue. Now and then, for a month or two, they sat at a typewriter; at times were the mistresses of well-to-do men of the world, receiving pocket money and presents; lived at times in furs and motorcars, at other times in attics, and though a good offer might under some circumstances induce them to marry, they were not at all eager for it. Many of them had little inclination for love and gave themselves very unwillingly, and then only for money and at the highest price. Others, and Maria was one of them, were unusually gifted in love and unable to do without it. They lived solely for love and besides their official and lucrative friends had other love affairs as well. Assiduous and busy, care-ridden and light-hearted, intelligent and yet thoughtless, these butterflies lived a life at once childlike and *raffiné;* independent, not to be bought by every one, finding their account in good luck and fine weather, in love with life and yet clinging to it far less than the bourgeois, always ready to follow a fairy prince to his castle, always certain, though scarcely conscious of it, that a difficult and sad end was in store for them.

During that wonderful first night and the days that followed Maria taught me much. She taught me the charming play and delights of the senses, but she gave me, also, new understanding, new insight, new love. The world of the dance and pleasure resorts, the cinemas, bars and hotel lounges that for me, the hermit and esthete, had always about it something trivial, forbidden, and degrading, was for Maria and Hermine and their companions the world pure and simple. It was neither good nor bad, neither loved nor hated. In this world their brief and eager lives flowered and faded. They were at home in it and knew all its ways- They loved a champagne or a special dish at a restaurant as one of us might a composer or poet, and they lavished the same enthusiasm and rapture and emotion on the latest craze in dances or the sentimental cloying song of a jazz singer as one of us on Nietzsche or Hamsun. Maria talked to me about the handsome saxophone player, Pablo, and spoke of an American song that he had sung them sometimes, and she was so carried away with admiration and love as she spoke of it that I was far more moved and impressed than by the ecstasies of any highly cultured person over artistic pleasures of the rarest and most distinguished quality. I was ready to enthuse in sympathy, be the song what it might. Maria's loving words, her fond and tender looks tore large gaps in the bulwark of my esthetics. There was to be sure a beauty, one and indivisible, small and select, that seemed to me, with Mozart at the top, to be above all dispute and doubt, but where was the limit? Hadn't we all as connoisseurs and critics in our youth been consumed with love for works of art and for artists that today we regarded with doubt and dismay? Hadn't that happened to us with Liszt and Wagner, and, to many of us, even with Beethoven? Wasn't the blossoming of Maria's childish emotion over the song from America just as pure and beautiful an artistic experience and exalted as far beyond doubt as the rapture of any academic big-wig over Tristan, or the ecstasy of a conductor over the *Ninth Symphony?* And didn't this agree remarkably well with the views of Herr Pablo and prove him right?

Maria too appeared to love the beautiful Pablo extremely.

"He certainly is a beauty," said I. "I like him very much too. But tell me, Maria, how can you have a fondness for me as well, a tiresome old fellow with no looks, who even has grey hairs and doesn't play a saxophone and doesn't sing any English love songs?"

"Don't talk so horribly," she scolded. "It is quite natural. I like you too. You, too, have something nice about you that endears you and marks you out. I wouldn't have you different. One oughtn't to talk of these things and want them accounted for. Listen, when you kiss my neck or my ear, I feel that I please you, that you like me. You have a way of kissing as though you were shy, and that tells me: 'You please him. He is grateful to you for being pretty.' That gives me great, great pleasure. And then again with another man it's just the opposite that pleases me, that he kisses me as though he thought little of me and conferred a favor."

Again we fell asleep and again I woke to find my arm still about her, my beautiful, beautiful flower.

And this beautiful flower, strange to say, continued to be nonetheless the gift that Hermine had made me. Hermine continued to stand in front of her and to hide her with a mask. Then suddenly the thought of Erica intervened--my distant, angry love, my poor friend. She was hardly less pretty than Maria, even though not so blooming; and she was more constrained, and not so richly endowed in the little arts of making love. She stood a moment before my eyes, clearly and painfully, loved and deeply woven into my destiny; then fell away again in a deep oblivion, at a half regretted distance.

And so in the tender beauty of the night many pictures of my life rose before me who for so long had lived in a poor pictureless vacancy. Now, at the magic touch of Eros, the source of them was opened up and flowed in plenty. For moments together my heart stood still between delight and sorrow to find how rich was the gallery of my life, and how thronged the soul of the wretched Steppenwolf with high eternal stars and constellations. My childhood and my mother showed in a tender transfiguration like a distant glimpse over mountains into the fathomless blue; the litany of my friendships, beginning with the legendary Herman, soul-brother of Hermine, rang out as clear as trumpets; the images of many women floated by me with an unearthly fragrance like moist sea flowers on the surface of the water, women whom I had loved, desired and sung, whose love I had seldom won and seldom striven to win. My wife, too, appeared. I had lived with her many years and she had taught me comradeship, strife and resignation. In spite of all the shortcomings of our life, my confidence in her remained untouched up to the very day when she broke out against me and deserted me without warning, sick as I was in mind and body. And now, as I looked back, I saw how deep my love and trust must have been for her betrayal to have inflicted so deep and lifelong a wound.

These pictures--there were hundreds of them, with names and without--all came back. They rose fresh and new out of this night of love, and I knew again, what in my wretchedness I had forgotten, that they were my life's possession and all its worth. Indestructible and abiding as the stars, these experiences, though forgotten, could never be erased. Their series was the story of my life, their starry light the undying value of my being. My life had become weariness. It had wandered in a maze of unhappiness that led to renunciation and nothingness; it was bitter with the salt of all human things; yet it had laid up riches, riches to be proud of. It had been for all its wretchedness a princely life. Let the little way to death be as it might, the kernel of this life of mine was noble. It had purpose and character and turned not on trifles, but on the stars.

Time has passed and much has happened, much has changed; and I can only remember a little of all that passed that night, a little of all we said and did in the deep tenderness of love, a few moments of clear awakening from the deep sleep of love's weariness. That night, however, for the first time since my downfall gave me back the unrelenting radiance of my own life and made me recognize chance as destiny once more and see the ruins of my being as fragments of the divine. My soul breathed once more. My eyes were opened. There were moments when I felt with a glow that I had only to snatch up my scattered images and raise my life as Harry Haller and as the Steppenwolf to the unity of one picture, in order to enter myself into the world of imagination and be immortal. Was not this, then, the goal set for the progress of every human life?

In the morning, after we had shared breakfast, I had to smuggle Maria from the house. Later in the same day I took a little room in a neighboring quarter which was designed solely for our meetings.

True to her duties, Hermine, my dancing mistress, appeared and I had to learn the Boston. She was firm and inexorable and would not release me from a single lesson, for it was decided that I was to attend the Fancy Dress Ball in her company. She had asked me for money for her costume, but she refused to tell me anything about it. To visit her, or even to know where she lived, was still forbidden me.

This time, about three weeks before the Fancy Dress Ball, was remarkable for its wonderful happiness. Maria seemed to me to be the first woman I had ever really loved. I had always wanted mind and culture in the women I had loved, and I had never remarked that even the most intellectual and, comparatively speaking, educated woman never gave any response to the Logos in me, but rather constantly opposed it. I took my problems and my thoughts with me to the company of women, and it would have seemed to me utterly impossible to love a girl for more than an hour who had scarcely read a book, scarcely knew what reading was, and could not have distinguished Tschaikovsky from Beethoven. Maria had no education. She had no need of these circuitous substitutes. Her problems all sprang directly from the senses. All her art and the whole task she set herself lay in extracting the utmost delight from the senses she had been endowed with, and from her particular figure, her color, her hair, her voice, her skin, her temperament; and in employing every faculty, every curve and line and every softest modeling of her body to find responsive perceptions in her lovers and to conjure up in them an answering quickness of delight. The first shy dance I had had with her had already told me this much. I had caught the scent and the charm of a brilliant and carefully cultivated sensibility and had been enchanted by it. Certainly, too, it was no accident that Hermine, the all-knowing, introduced me to this Maria. She had the scent and the very significance of summer and of roses.

It was not my fortune to be Maria's only lover, nor even her favorite one. I was one of many. Often she had no time for me, often only an hour at midday, seldom a night. She took no money from me. Hermine saw to that. She was glad of presents, however, and when I gave her, perhaps, a new little purse of red lacquered leather there might be two or three gold pieces inside it. As a matter of fact, she laughed at me over the red purse. It was charming, but a bargain, and no longer in fashion. In these matters, about which up to that time I was as little learned as in any language of the Eskimos, I learned a great deal from Maria. Before all else I learned that these playthings were not mere idle trifles invented by manufacturers and dealers for the purposes of gain. They were, on the contrary, a little or, rather, a big world, authoritative and beautiful, many sided, containing a multiplicity of things all of which had the one and only aim of serving love, refining the senses, giving life to the dead world around us, endowing it in a magical way with new instruments of love, from powder and scent to the dancing show, from ring to cigarette case, from waist-buckle to handbag. This bag was no bag, this purse no purse, flowers no flowers, the fan no fan. All were the plastic material of love, of magic and delight. Each was a messenger, a smuggler, a weapon, a battle cry.

I often wondered who it was whom Maria really loved. I think she loved the young Pablo of the saxophone, with his melancholy black eyes and his long, white, distinguished, melancholy hands. I should have thought Pablo a somewhat sleepy lover, spoiled and passive, but Maria assured me that though it took a long time to wake him up he was then more strenuous and forward and virile than prize fighter or riding master.

In this way I got to know many secrets about this person and that, jazz musicians, actors and many of the women and girls and men of our circle. I saw beneath the surface of the various alliances and enmities and by degrees (though I had been such an entire stranger to this world) I was drawn in and treated with confidence. I learned a good deal about Hermine, too. It was of Herr Pablo, however, of whom Maria was fond, that I saw the most. At times she, too, availed herself of his secret drugs and was forever procuring these delights for me also; and Pablo was always most markedly on the alert to be of service to me. Once he said to me without more ado: "You are so very unhappy. That is bad. One shouldn't be like that. It makes me sorry. Try a mild pipe of opium." My opinion of this jolly, intelligent, childlike and, at the same time, unfathomable person gradually changed. We became friends, and I often took some of his specifics. He looked on at my affair with Maria with some amusement. Once he entertained us in his room on the top floor of an hotel in the suburbs. There was only one chair, so Maria and I had to sit on the bed. He gave us a drink from three little bottles, a mysterious and wonderful draught. And then when I had got into a very good humor, he proposed, with beaming eyes, to celebrate a love orgy for three. I declined abruptly. Such a thing was inconceivable to me. Nevertheless I stole a glance at Maria to see how she took it, and though she at once backed up my refusal I saw the gleam in her eyes and observed that the renunciation cost her some regret. Pablo was disappointed by my refusal but not hurt. "Pity," he said. "Harry is too morally minded. Nothing to be done. All the same it would have been so beautiful, so very beautiful! But I've got another idea." He gave us each a little opium to smoke, and sitting motionless with open eyes we all three lived through the scenes that he suggested to us while Maria trembled with delight. As I felt a little unwell after this, Pablo laid me on the bed and gave me some drops, and while I lay with closed eyes I felt the fleeting breath of a kiss on each eyelid. I took the kiss as though I believed it came from Maria, but I knew very well it came from him.

And one evening he surprised me still more. Coming to me in my room he told me that he needed twenty francs and would I oblige him? In return he offered that I instead of him should have Maria for the night.

"Pablo," I said, very much shocked, "you don't know what you say. Barter for a woman is counted among us as the last degradation. I have not heard your proposal, Pablo."

He looked at me with pity. "You don't want to, Herr Harry. Very good. You're always making difficulties for yourself. Don't sleep tonight with Maria if you would rather not. But give me the money all the same. You shall have it back. I have urgent need of it."

"What for?"

"For Agostino, the little second violin, you know. He has been ill for a week and there's no one to look after him. He hasn't a sou, nor have I at the moment."

From curiosity and also partly to punish myself, I went with him to Agostino. He took milk and medicine to him in his attic, and a wretched one it was. He made his bed and aired the room and made a most professional compress for the fevered head, all quickly and gently and efficiently like a good sick nurse. The same evening I saw him playing till dawn in the City Bar.

I often talked at length and in detail about Maria with Hermine, about her hands and shoulders and hips and her way of laughing and kissing and dancing.

"Has she shown you this?" asked Hermine on one occasion, describing to me a peculiar play of the tongue in kissing. I asked her to show it me herself, but she was most earnest in her refusal. "That is for later. I am not your love yet."

I asked her how she was acquainted with Maria's ways of kissing and with many secrets as well that could be known only to her lovers.

"Oh," she cried, "we're friends, after all. Do you think we'd have secrets from one another? I must say you've got hold of a beautiful girl. There's no one like her."

"All the same, Hermine, I'm sure you have some secrets from each other, or have you told her everything you know about me?"

"No, that's another matter. Those are things she would not understand. Maria is wonderful. You are fortunate. But between you and me there are things she has not a notion of. Naturally I told her a lot about you, much more than you would have liked at the time. I had to win her for you, you see. But neither Maria nor anyone else will ever understand you as I understand you. I've learned something about you from her besides, for she's told me all about you as far as she knows you at all. I know you nearly as well as if we had often slept together."

It was curious and mysterious to know, when I was with Maria again, that she had had Hermine in her arms just as she had me ... New, indirect and complicated relations rose before me, new possibilities in love and life; and I thought of the thousand souls of the Steppenwolf treatise.

. . . . . . .

In the short interval between the time that I got to know Maria and the Fancy Dress Ball I was really happy; and yet I never had the feeling that this was my release and the attainment of felicity. I had the distinct impression, rather, that all this was a prelude and a preparation, that everything was pushing eagerly forward, that the gist of the matter was to come.

I was now so proficient in dancing that I felt quite equal to playing my part at the Ball of which everybody was talking. Hermine had a secret. She took the greatest care not to let out what her costume was to be. I would recognize her soon enough, she said, and should I fail to do so, she would help me; but beforehand

I was to know nothing. She was not in the least inquisitive to know my plans for a fancy dress and I decided that I should not wear a costume at all. Maria, when I asked her to go with me as my partner, explained that she had a cavalier already and a ticket too, in fact; and I saw with some disappointment that I should have to attend the festivity alone. It was the principal Fancy Dress Ball of the town, organized yearly by the Society of Artists in the Globe Rooms.

During these days I saw little of Hermine, but the day before the Ball she paid me a brief visit. She came for her ticket, which I had got for her, and sat quietly with me for a while in my room. We fell into a conversation so remarkable that it made a deep impression on me.

"You're really doing splendidly," she said. "Dancing suits you. Anyone who hadn't seen you for the last four weeks would scarcely know you."

"Yes," I agreed. "Things haven't gone so well with me for years. That's all your doing, Hermine."

"Oh, not the beautiful Maria's?"

"No. She is a present from you like all the rest. She is wonderful."

"She is just the girl you need, Steppenwolf--pretty, young, light hearted, an expert in love and not to be had every day. If you hadn't to share her with others, if she weren't always merely a fleeting guest, it would be another matter."

Yes, I had to concede this too.

"And so have you really got everything you want now?"

"No, Hermine. It is not like that. What I have got is very beautiful and delightful, a great pleasure, a great consolation. I'm really happy--"

"Well then, what more do you want?"

"I do want more. I am not content with being happy. I was not made for it. It is not my destiny. My destiny is the opposite."

"To be unhappy in fact? Well, you've had that and to spare, that time when you couldn't go home because of the razor."

"No, Hermine, it is something else. That time, I grant you, I was very unhappy. But it was a stupid unhappiness that led to nothing."

"Why?"

"Because I should not have had that fear of death when I wished for it all the same. The unhappiness that I need and long for is different. It is of the kind that will let me suffer with eagerness and lust after death. That is the unhappiness, or happiness, that I am waiting for."

"I understand that. There we are brother and sister. But what have you got against the happiness that you have found now with Maria? Why aren't you content?"

"I have nothing against it. Oh, no, I love it. I'm grateful for it. It is as lovely as a sunny day in a wet summer. But I suspect that it can't last. This happiness leads to nothing either. It gives content, but content is no food for me. It lulls the Steppenwolf to sleep and satiates him. But it is not a happiness to die for."

"So it's necessary to be dead, Steppenwolf?"

"I think so, yes. My happiness fills me with content and I can bear it for a long while yet. But sometimes when happiness leaves a moment's leisure to look about me and long for things, the longing I have is not to keep this happiness forever, but to suffer once again, only more beautifully and less meanly than before. I long for the sufferings that make me ready and willing to die."

Hermine looked tenderly in my eyes with that dark look that could so suddenly come into her face. Lovely, fearful eyes! Picking her words one by one and piecing them together, and speaking slowly and so low that it was an effort to hear her, she said:

"I want to tell you something today, something that I have known for a long while, and you know it too; but perhaps you have never said it to yourself. I am going to tell you now what it is that I know about you and me and our fate. You, Harry, have been an artist and a thinker, a man full of joy and faith, always on the track of what is great and eternal, never content with the trivial and petty. But the more life has awakened you and brought you back to yourself, the greater has your need been and the deeper the sufferings and dread and despair that have overtaken you, till you were up to your neck in them. And all that you once knew and loved and revered as beautiful and sacred, all the belief you once had in mankind and our high destiny, has been of no avail and has lost its worth and gone to pieces. Your faith found no more air to breathe. And suffocation is a hard death. Is that true, Harry? Is that your fate?"

I nodded again and again.

"You have a picture of life within you, a faith, a challenge, and you were ready for deeds and sufferings and sacrifices, and then you became aware by degrees that the world asked no deeds and no sacrifices of you whatever, and that life is no poem of heroism with heroic parts to play and so on, but a comfortable room where people are quite content with eating and drinking, coffee and knitting, cards and wireless. And whoever wants more and has got it in him--the heroic and the beautiful, and the reverence for the great poets or for the saints--is a fool and a Don Quixote. Good. And it has been just the same for me, my friend. I was a gifted girl. I was meant to live up to a high standard, to expect much of myself and do great things. I could have played a great part. I could have been the wife of a king, the beloved of a revolutionary, the sister of a genius, the mother of a martyr. And life has allowed me just this, to be a courtesan of fairly good taste, and even that has been hard enough. That is how things have gone with me. For a while I was inconsolable and for a long time I put the blame on myself. Life, thought I, must in the end be in the right, and if life scorned my beautiful dreams, so I argued, it was my dreams that were stupid and wrong headed. But that did not help me at all. And as I had good eyes and ears and was a little inquisitive too, I took a good look at this so-called life and at my neighbors and acquaintances, fifty or so of them and their destinies, and then I saw you. And I knew that my dreams had been right a thousand times over, just as yours had been. It was life and reality that were wrong. It was as little right that a woman like me should have no other choice than to grow old in poverty and in a senseless way at a typewriter in the pay of a money-maker, or to marry such a man for his money's sake, or to become some kind of drudge, as for a man like you to be forced in his loneliness and despair to have recourse to a razor. Perhaps the trouble with me was more material and moral and with you more spiritual--but it was the same road. Do you think I can't understand your horror of the fox trot, your dislike of bars and dancing floors, your loathing of jazz and the rest of it? I understand it only too well, and your dislike of politics as well, your despondence over the chatter and irresponsible antics of the parties and the press, your despair over the war, the one that has been and the one that is to be, over all that people nowadays think, read and build, over the music they play, the celebrations they hold, the education they carry on. You are right, Steppenwolf, right a thousand times over, and yet you must go to the wall. You are much too exacting and hungry for this simple, easygoing and easily contented world of today. You have a dimension too many. Whoever wants to live and enjoy his life today must not be like you and me. Whoever wants music instead of noise, joy instead of pleasure, soul instead of gold, creative work instead of business, passion instead of foolery, finds no home in this trivial world of ours--"

She looked down and fell into meditation.

"Hermine," I cried tenderly, "sister, how clearly you see! And yet you taught me the fox trot! But how do you mean that people like us with a dimension too many cannot live here? What brings it about? Is it only so in our days, or was it so always?"

"I don't know. For the honor of the world, I will suppose it to be in our time only--a disease, a momentary misfortune. Our leaders strain every nerve, and with success, to get the next war going, while the rest of us, meanwhile, dance the fox trot, earn money and eat chocolates--in such a time the world must indeed cut a poor figure. Let us hope that other times were better, and will be better again, richer, broader and deeper. But that is no help to us now. And perhaps it has always been the same--"

"Always as it is today? Always a world only for politicians, profiteers, waiters and pleasure-seekers, and not a breath of air for men?"

"Well, I don't know. Nobody knows. Anyway, it is all the same. But I am thinking now of your favorite of whom you have talked to me sometimes, and read me, too, some of his letters, of Mozart. How was it with him in his day? Who controlled things in his times and ruled the roost and gave the tone and counted for something? Was it Mozart or the business people, Mozart or the average man? And in what fashion did he come to die and be buried? And perhaps, I mean, it has always been the same and always will be, and what is called history at school, and all we learn by heart there about heroes and geniuses and great deeds and fine emotions, is all nothing but a swindle invented by the schoolmasters for educational reasons to keep children occupied for a given number of years. It has always been so and always will be. Time and the world, money and power belong to the small people and the shallow people. To the rest, to the real men belongs nothing. Nothing but death."

"Nothing else?"

"Yes, eternity."

"You mean a name, and fame with posterity?"

"No, Steppenwolf, not fame. Has that any value? And do you think that all true and real men have been famous and known to posterity?"

"No, of course not."

"Then it isn't fame. Fame exists in that sense only for the schoolmasters. No, it isn't fame. It is what I call eternity. The pious call it the kingdom of God. I say to myself: all we who ask too much and have a dimension too many could not contrive to live at all if there were not another air to breathe outside the air of this world, if there were not eternity at the back of time; and this is the kingdom of truth. The music of Mozart belongs there and the poetry of your great poets. The saints, too, belong there, who have worked wonders and suffered martyrdom and given a great example to men. But the image of every true act, the strength of every true feeling, belongs to eternity just as much, even though no one knows of it or sees it or records it or hands it down to posterity. In eternity there is no posterity."

"You are right."

"The pious," she went on meditatively, "after all know most about this. That is why they set up the saints and what they call the communion of the saints. The saints, these are the true men, the younger brothers of the Savior. We are with them all our lives long in every good deed, in every brave thought, in every love. The communion of the saints, in earlier times it was set by painters in a golden heaven, shining, beautiful and full of peace, and it is nothing else but what I meant a moment ago when I called it eternity. It is the kingdom on the other side of time and appearances. It is there we belong. There is our home. It is that which our heart strives for. And for that reason, Steppenwolf, we long for death. There you will find your Goethe again and Novalis and Mozart, and I my saints, Christopher, Philip of Neri and all. There are many saints who at first were sinners. Even sin can be a way to saintliness, sin and vice. You will laugh at me, but I often think that even my friend Pablo might be a saint in hiding. Ah, Harry, we have to stumble, through so much dirt and humbug before we reach home. And we have no one to guide us. Our only guide is our homesickness."

With the last words her voice had sunk again and now there was a stillness of peace in the room. The sun was setting; it lit up the gilt lettering on the back of my books. I took Hermine's head in my hands and kissed her on the forehead and leaned my cheek to hers as though she were my sister, and so we stayed for a moment. And so I should have liked best to stay and to have gone out no more that day. But Maria had promised me this night, the last before the great Ball.

But on my way to join Maria I thought, not of her, but of what Hermine had said. It seemed to me that it was not, perhaps, her own thoughts but mine. She had read them like a clairvoyant, breathed them in and given them back, so that they had a form of their own and came to me as something new. I was particularly thankful to her for having expressed the thought of eternity just at this time. I needed it, for without it I could not live and neither could I die. The sacred sense of beyond, of timelessness, of a world which had an eternal value and the substance of which was divine had been given back to me today by this friend of mine who taught me dancing.

I was forced to recall my dream of Goethe and that vision of the old wiseacre when he laughed so inhumanly and played his joke on me in the fashion of the immortals. For the first time I understood Goethe's laughter, the laughter of the immortals. It was a laughter without an object. It was simply light and lucidity. It was that which is left over when a true man has passed through all the sufferings, vices, mistakes, passions and misunderstandings of men and got through to eternity and the world of space And eternity was nothing else than the redemption of time, its return to innocence, so to speak, and its transformation again into space.

I went to meet Maria at the place where we usually dined. However, she had not arrived, and while I sat waiting at the table in the quiet and secluded restaurant, my thoughts still ran on the conversation I had had with Hermine. All these thoughts that had arisen between her and me seemed so intimate and well known, fashioned from a mythology and an imagery so entirely my own. The immortals, living their life in timeless space, enraptured, re-fashioned and immersed in a crystalline eternity like ether, and the cool starry brightness and radiant serenity of this world outside the earth--whence was all this so intimately known? As I reflected, passages of Mozart's *Cassations,* of Bach's *Well-tempered Clavier* came to my mind and it seemed to me that all through this music there was the radiance of this cool starry brightness and the quivering of this clearness of ether. Yes, it was there. In this music there was a feeling as of time frozen into space, and above it there quivered a never-ending and superhuman serenity, an eternal, divine laughter. Yes, and how well the aged Goethe of my dreams fitted in too! And suddenly I heard this fathomless laughter around me. I heard the immortals laughing. I sat entranced. Entranced, I felt for a pencil in my waistcoat pocket, and looking for paper saw the wine card lying on the table. I turned it over and wrote on the back. I wrote verses and forgot about them till one day I discovered them in my pocket. They ran:

## THE IMMORTALS

Ever reeking from the vales of earth
Ascends to us life's fevered surge,
Wealth's excess, the rage of dearth,
Smoke of death meals on the gallow's verge;
Greed without end, imprisoned air;
Murderers' hands, usurers' hands, hands of prayer;
Exhales in foetid breath the human swarm
Whipped on by fear and lust, blood raw, blood warm,
Breathing blessedness and savage heats,
Eating itself and spewing what it eats,
Hatching war and lovely art,
Decking out with idiot craze
Bawdy houses while they blaze,
Through the childish fair-time mart
Weltering to its own decay
In the glare of pleasure's way,
Rising for each newborn and then
Sinking for each to dust again.
But we above you ever more residing
In the ether's star translumined ice
Know not day nor night nor time's dividing,
Wear nor age nor sex for our device.
All your sins and anguish self-affrighting,
Your murders and lascivious delighting

Are to us but as a show
Like the suns that circling go,
Changing not our day for night;
On your frenzied life we spy,
And refresh ourselves thereafter
With the stars in order fleeing;
Our breath is winter; in our sight
Fawns the dragon of the sky;
Cool and unchanging is our eternal being,
Cool and star bright is our eternal laughter.

Then Maria came and after a cheerful meal I accompanied her to our little room. She was lovelier that evening, warmer and more intimate than she had ever been. The love she gave me was so tender that I felt it as the most complete abandon. "Maria," said I, "you are as prodigal today as a goddess. Don't kill us both quite. Tomorrow after all is the Ball. Whom have you got for a cavalier tomorrow? I'm very much afraid it is a fairy prince who will carry you off and I shall never see you any more. Your love tonight is almost like that of good lovers who bid each other farewell for the last time."

She put her lips close to my ear and whispered:

"Don't say that, Harry. Any time might be the last time. If Hermine takes you, you will come no more to me. Perhaps she will take you tomorrow."

Never did I experience the feeling peculiar to those days, that strange, bitter-sweet alternation of mood, more powerfully than on that night before the Ball. It was happiness that I experienced. There was the loveliness of Maria and her surrender. There was the sweet and subtle sensuous joy of inhaling and tasting a hundred pleasures of the senses that I had only begun to know as an elderly man. I was bathed in sweet joy like a rippling pool. And yet that was only the shell. Within all was significant and tense with fate, and while, love-lost and tender, I was busied with the little sweet appealing things of love and sank apparently without a care in the caress of happiness, I was conscious all the while in my heart how my fate raced on at breakneck speed, racing and chasing like a frightened horse, straight for the precipitous abyss, spurred on by dread and longing to the consummation of death. Just as a short while before I had started aside in fear from the easy thoughtless pleasure of merely sensual love and felt a dread of Maria's beauty that laughingly offered itself, so now I felt a dread of death, a dread, however, that was already conscious of its approaching change into surrender and release.

Even while we were lost in the silent and deep preoccupation of our love and belonged more closely than ever we had to one another, my soul bid adieu to Maria, and took leave of all that she had meant to me. I had learned from her, once more before the end, to confide myself like a child to life's surface play, to pursue a fleeting joy, and to be both child and beast in the innocence of sex, a state that (in earlier life) I had only known rarely and as an exception. The life of the senses and of sex had nearly always had for me the bitter accompaniment of guilt, the sweet but dread taste of forbidden fruit that puts a spiritual man on his guard. Now, Hermine and Maria had shown me this garden in its innocence, and I had been a guest there and thankfully. But it would soon be time to go on farther. It was too agreeable and too warm in this garden. It was my destiny to make another bid for the crown of life in the expiation of its endless guilt. An easy life, an easy love, an easy death--these were not for me.

From what the girls told me I gathered that for the Ball next day, or in connection with it, quite unusual delights and extravagances were on foot. Perhaps it was the climax, and perhaps Maria's suspicion was correct. Perhaps this was our last night together and perhaps the morning would bring a new unwinding of fate. I was aflame with longing and breathless with dread; I clung wildly to Maria; and there flared within me a last burst of wild desire...

. . . . . . .

I made up by day for the sleep I had lost at night. After a bath I went home dead tired. I darkened my bedroom and as I undressed I came on the verses in my pocket; but I forgot them again and lay down forthwith. I forgot Maria and Hermine and the Masked Ball and slept the clock round. It was not till I had got up in the evening and was shaving that I remembered that the Ball began in an hour and that I had to find a dress shirt. I got myself ready in very good humor and went out thereafter to have dinner.

It was the first masked ball I was to participate in. In earlier days, it is true, I had now and again attended such festivities and even sometimes found them very entertaining, but I had never danced. I had been a spectator merely. As for the enthusiasm with which others had talked and rejoiced over them in my hearing, it had always struck me as comic. And now the day had come for me too to find the occasion one of almost painful suspense. As I had no partner to take, I decided not to go till late. This, too, Hermine had counseled me.

I had seldom of late been to the Steel Helmet, my former refuge, where the disappointed men sat out their evenings, soaking in their wine and playing at bachelor life. It did not suit the life I had come to lead since. This evening, however, I was drawn to it before I was aware. In the mood between joy and fear that fate and parting imposed on me just now, all the stations and shrines of meditation in my life's pilgrimage caught once more that gleam of pain and beauty that comes from things past; and so too had the little tavern, thick with smoke, among whose patrons I had lately been numbered and whose primitive opiate of a bottle of cheap wine had lately heartened me enough to spend one more night in my lonely bed and to endure life for one more day. I had tasted other specifics and stronger stimulus since then, and sipped a sweeter poison. With a smile I entered the ancient hostel. The landlady greeted me and so, with a nod, did the silent company of habitués. A roast chicken was commended and soon set before me. The limpid Elsasser sparkled in the thick peasant glass. The clean white wooden tables and the old yellow paneling had a friendly look. And while I ate and drank there came over me that feeling of change and decay and of farewell celebrations, that sweet and inwardly painful feeling of being a living part of all the scenes and all the things of an earlier life that has never yet been parted from, and from which the time to part has come. The modern man calls this sentimentality. He has lost the love of inanimate objects. He does not even love his most sacred object, his motorcar, but is ever hoping to exchange it as soon as he can for a later model. This modern man has energy and ability. He is healthy, cool and strenuous--a splendid type, and in the next war he will be a miracle of efficiency. But all that was no concern of mine. I was not a modern man, nor an old-fashioned one either. I had escaped time altogether, and went my way, with death at my elbow and death as my resolve. I bad no objection to sentimentalities. I was glad and thankful to find a trace of anything like a feeling still remaining in my burned-out heart. So I let my memories of the old tavern and my attachment to the solid wooden chairs and the smell of smoke and wine and the air of use and wont and warmth and homeliness that the place had carry me away. There is beauty in farewells and a gentleness in their very tone. The hard seat was dear to me, and so was the peasant glass and the cool racy taste of the Elsasser and my intimacy with all and everything in this room, and the faces of the bent and dreaming drinkers, those disillusioned ones, whose brother I had been for so long. All this was bourgeois sentimentality, lightly seasoned with a touch of the old-fashioned romance of inns, a romance coming from my boyhood when inns and wine and cigars were still forbidden things--strange and wonderful. But no Steppenwolf rose before me baring his teeth to tear my sentiment to pieces. I sat there in peace in the glow of the past whose setting still shed a faint afterglow.

A street seller came in and I bought a handful of roasted chestnuts. An old woman came in with flowers and I bought a bunch of violets and presented them to the landlady. It was not till I was about to pay my bill and felt in vain for the pocket of the coat I usually wore that I realized once more that I was in evening dress. The Masked Ball. And Hermine!

It was still early enough, however. I could not convince myself to go to the Globe Rooms straight away. I felt too--as I had in the case of all the pleasures that had lately come my way--a whole array of checks and resistances. I had no inclination to enter the large and crowded and noisy rooms. I had a schoolboy's shyness of the strange atmosphere and the world of pleasure and dancing.

As I sauntered along I passed by a cinema with its dazzling lights and huge colored posters. I went on a few steps, then turned again and went in. There till eleven I could sit quietly and comfortably in the dark. Led by the usher's flashlight I stumbled through the curtains into the darkened hall, found a seat and was suddenly in the middle of the Old Testament. The film was one of those that are nominally not shown for money. Much expense and many refinements are lavished upon them in a more sacred and nobler cause, and at midday even school-children are brought to see them by their religious teachers. This one was the story of Moses and the Israelites in Egypt, with a huge crowd of men, horses, camels, palaces, splendors of the pharaohs and tribulations of the Jews in the desert. I saw Moses, whose hair recalled portraits of Walt Whitman, a splendidly theatrical Moses, wandering through the desert at the head of the Jews, with a dark and fiery eye and a long staff and the stride of a Wotan. I saw him pray to God at the edge of the Red Sea, and I saw the Red Sea parted to give free passage, a deep road between piled-up mountains of water (the confirmation classes conducted by the clergy to see this religious film could argue without end as to how the film people managed this). I saw the prophet and his awestruck people pass through to the other side, and behind them I saw the war chariots of Pharaoh come into sight and the Egyptians stop and start on the brink of the sea, and then, when they ventured courageously on, I saw the mountainous waters close over the heads of Pharaoh in all the splendor of his gold trappings and over all his chariots and all his men, recalling, as I saw it, Handel's wonderful duet for two basses in which this event is magnificently sung. I saw Moses, further, climbing Sinai, a gloomy hero in a gloomy wilderness of rocks, and I looked on as Jehovah in the midst of storm and thunder and lightning imparted the Ten Commandments to him, while his worthless people set up the golden calf at the foot of the mountain and gave themselves over to somewhat roisterous celebrations. I found it so strange and incredible to be looking on at all this, to be seeing the sacred writ, with its heroes and its wonders, the source in our childhood of the first dawning suspicion of another world than this, presented for money before a grateful public that sat quietly eating the provisions brought with it from home. A nice little picture, indeed, picked up by chance in the huge wholesale clearance of culture in these days! My God, rather than come to such a pass it would have been better for the Jews and every one else, let alone the Egyptians, to have perished in those days and forthwith of a violent and becoming death instead of this dismal pretence of dying by inches that we go in for today. Yes indeed!

My secret repressions and unconfessed fright in face of the Masked Ball were by no means lessened by the feelings provoked in me by the cinema. On the contrary, they had grown to uncomfortable proportions and I had to shake myself and think of Hermine before I could go to the Globe Rooms and dared to enter. It was late, and the Ball had been for a long time in full swing. At once before I had even taken off my things I was caught up, shy and sober as I was, in the swirl of the masked throng. I was accosted familiarly. Girls summoned me to the champagne rooms. Clowns slapped me on the back, and I was addressed on all sides as an old friend. I responded to none of it, but fought my way through the crowded rooms to the cloakroom, and when I got my cloakroom ticket I put it in my pocket with great care, reflecting that I might need it before very long when I had had enough of the uproar.

Every part of the great building was given over to the festivities. There was dancing in every room and in the basement as well. Corridors and stairs were filled to overflowing with masks and dancing and music and laughter and tumult. Oppressed in heart I stole through the throng, from the Negro orchestra to the peasant band, from the large and brilliantly lighted principal room into the passages and on to the stairs, to bars, buffets and champagne parlors. The walls were mostly hung with wild and cheerful paintings by the latest artists. All the world was there, artists, journalists, professors, business men, and of course every adherent of pleasure in the town. In one of the orchestras sat Pablo, blowing with enthusiasm in his curved mouthpiece. As soon as he saw me he sang out a greeting. Pushed hither and thither in the crowd I found myself in one room after another, upstairs here and downstairs there. A corridor in the basement had been staged as hell by the artists and there a band of devils played furiously. After a while, I began to look for Hermine or Maria and strove time after time to reach the principal room; but either I missed my way or had to meet the current. By midnight I had found no one, and though I had not danced I was hot and giddy. I threw myself into the nearest chair among utter strangers and ordered some wine, and came to the conclusion that joining in such rowdy festivals was no part for an old man like me. I drank my glass of wine while I stared at the naked arms and backs of the women, watched the crowd of grotesquely masked figures drifting by and silently declined the advances of a few girls who wished to sit on my knee or get me to dance. "Old Growler," one called after me; and she was right. I decided to raise my spirits with the wine, but even the wine went against me and I could scarcely swallow a second glass. And then the feeling crept over me that the Steppenwolf was standing behind me with his tongue out. Nothing pleased me. I was in the wrong place. To be sure, I had come with the best intentions, but this was no place for me to be merry in; and all this loud effervescence of pleasure, the laughter and the whole foolery of it on every side, seemed to me forced and stupid.

Thus it was that, at about one o'clock, in anger and disillusionment I steered a course for the cloakroom, to put on my coat again and go. It was surrender and backsliding into my wolfishness, and Hermine would scarcely forgive me for it. But I could not do otherwise. All the way as I squeezed through the throng to the cloakroom, I still kept a careful lookout in case I might yet see one of my friends, but in vain. Now I stood at the counter. Already the attendant was politely extending his hand for my number. I felt in my waistcoat pocket--the number was no longer there! The devil was in it if even this failed me. Often enough during my forlorn wanderings through the rooms and while I sat over my tasteless wine I had felt in my pocket, fighting back the resolve to go away again, and I had always found the round flat check in its place. And now it was gone. Everything was against me.

"Lost your number?" came in a shrill voice from a small red and yellow devil at my elbow. "Here, comrade, you can take mine," and he held it out to me without more ado. While I mechanically took it and turned it over in my fingers the brisk little fellow rapidly disappeared.

When, however, I examined the pasteboard counter for a number, no number was to be seen. Instead there was a scribble in a tiny hand. I asked the attendant to wait and went to the nearest light to read it. There in little crazy letters that were scarcely legible was scrawled:

TONIGHT AT THE MAGIC THEATER<br>
FOR MADMEN ONLY<br>
PRICE OF ADMITTANCE YOUR MIND.<br>
NOT FOR EVERYBODY. HERMINE IS IN HELL.

As a marionette whose thread the operator has let go for a moment wakes to new life after a brief paralysis of death and coma and once more plays its lively part, so did I at this jerk of the magic thread throw myself with the elasticity and eagerness of youth into the tumult from which I had just retreated in the listlessness and weariness of elderly years. Never did sinner show more haste to get to hell. A moment before my patent-leather shoes had galled me, the heavily scented air disgusted me, and the heat undone me. Now on my winged feet I nimbly one-stepped through every room on the way to hell. The very air had a charm. The warmth embedded me and wafted me on, and so no less did the riotous music, the intoxication of colors, the perfume of women's shoulders, the clamor of the hundred tongues, the laughter, the rhythm of the dance, and the glances of all the kindled eyes. A Spanish dancing girl flung herself into my arms: "Dance with me!" "Can't," said I. "I'm bound for hell. But I'll gladly take a kiss with me." The red mouth beneath the mask met mine and with the kiss I recognized Maria. I caught her tight in my arms and like a June rose bloomed her full lips.

By this time we were dancing, our lips still joined. Past Pablo we danced, who hung like a lover over his softly wailing instrument. Those lovely animal eyes embraced us with their half-abstracted radiance. But before we had gone twenty steps the music broke off and regretfully I let go of Maria.

"I'd have loved to have danced with you again," I said, intoxicated with her warmth. "Come with me a step or two, Maria. I'm in love with your beautiful arm. Let me have it a moment longer! But, you see, Hermine has summoned me. She is in hell."

"I thought so. Farewell, Harry. I won't forget you." She left me--left me indeed. Yes, it was autumn, it was fate, that had given the summer rose so full and ripe a scent.

On I went through the long corridors, luxuriously thronged, and down the stairs to hell. There, on pitch-black walls shone wicked garish lights, and the orchestra of devils was playing feverishly. On a high stool at the bar there was seated a pretty young fellow without a mask and in evening dress who scrutinized me with a cursory and mocking glance. Pressed to the wall by the swirl of dancers--about twenty couples were dancing in this very confined space--I examined all the women with eager suspense. Most were still in masks and smiled at me, but none was Hermine. The handsome youth on the high stool glanced mockingly at me. At the next pause, thought I, she will come and summon me. The dance ended but no one came.

I went over to the bar which was squeezed into a corner of the small and low room, and taking a seat near the young man ordered a whisky. While I drank it I saw his profile. It had a familiar charm, like a picture from long ago, precious for the very dust that has settled on it from the past. Oh, then it flashed through me. It was Herman, the friend of my youth.

"Herman!" I stammered.

She smiled. "Harry? Have you found me?"

It was Hermine, barely disguised by the make-up of her hair and a little paint. The stylish collar gave an unfamiliar look to the pallor of her intelligent face, the wide black sleeves of her dress coat and the white cuffs made her hands look curiously small, and the long black trousers gave a curious elegance to her feet in their black and white silk socks.

"Is this the costume, Hermine, in which you mean to make me fall in love with you?"

"So far," she said, "I have contented myself with turning the heads of the ladies. But now your turn has come. First, let's have a glass of champagne."

So we did, perched on our stools, while the dance went on around us to the lively and fevered strain of the strings. And without Hermine appearing to give herself the least trouble I was very soon in love with her. As she was dressed as a boy, I could not dance with her nor allow myself any tender advances, and while she seemed distant and neutral in her male mask, her looks and words and gestures encircled me with all her feminine charm. Without so much as having touched her I surrendered to her spell, and this spell itself kept within the part she played. It was the spell of a hermaphrodite. For she talked to me about Herman and about childhood, mine and her own, and about those years of childhood when the capacity for love, in its first youth, embraces not only both sexes, but all and everything, sensuous and spiritual, and endows all things with a spell of love and a fairylike ease of transformation such as in later years comes again only to a chosen few and to poets, and to them rarely. Throughout she kept up the part of a young man, smoking cigarettes and talking with a spirited ease that often had a little mockery in it; and yet it was all iridescent with the rays of desire and transformed, as it reached my senses, into a charming seduction.

How well and thoroughly I thought I knew Hermine, and yet what a completely new revelation of herself she opened up to me that night! How gently and inconspicuously she cast the net I longed for around me, and how playfully and how like a pixie she gave the sweet poison to drink!

We sat and talked and drank champagne. We strolled through the rooms and looked about us. We went on voyages of exploration to discover couples whose love-making it amused us to spy upon. She pointed out women whom she recommended me to dance with, and gave me advice as to the methods of attack to be employed with each. We took the floor as rivals and paid court for a while to the same girl, danced with her by turns and both tried to win her heart. And yet it was all only a carnival, only a game between the two of us that caught us more closely together in our own passion. It was all a fairy tale. Everything had a new dimension, a deeper meaning. Everything was fanciful and symbolic. There was one girl of great beauty but looking tragic and unhappy. Herman danced with her and drew her out. They disappeared to drink champagne together, and she told me afterwards that she had made a conquest of her not as a man but as a woman, with the spell of Lesbos. For my part, the whole building reverberated everywhere with the sound of dancing, and the whole intoxicated crowd of masks, became by degrees a wild dream of paradise. Flower upon flower wooed me with its scent. I toyed with fruit after fruit. Serpents looked at me from green and leafy shadows with mesmeric eyes. Lotus blossoms luxuriated over black bogs. Enchanted birds sang allurement from the trees. Yet all was a progress to one longed-for goal, the summons of a new yearning for one and one only. Once I was dancing with a girl I did not know. I had swept her with the ardor of a lover into the giddy swirl of dancers and while we hung in this unreal world, she suddenly remarked with a laugh: "One wouldn't know you. You were so dull and flat before." Then I recognized the girl who had called me "Old Growler" a few hours before. She thought she had got me now, but with the next dance it was another for whom my ardor glowed. I danced without ceasing for two hours or more--every dance and some, even, that I had never danced before. Every now and then Herman was near me, and gave me a nod and a smile as he disappeared in the throng.

An experience fell to my lot this night of the Ball that I had never known in all my fifty years, though it is known to every flapper and student--the intoxication of a general festivity, the mysterious merging of the personality in the mass, the mystic union of joy. I had often heard it spoken of. It was known, I knew, to every servant girl. I had often observed the sparkle in the eye of those who told me of it and I had always treated it with a half-superior, half-envious smile. A hundred times in my life I had seen examples of those whom rapture had intoxicated and released from the self, of that smile, that half-crazed absorption, of those whose heads have been turned by a common enthusiasm. I had seen it in drunken recruits and sailors, and also in great artists in the enthusiasm, perhaps, of a musical festival; and not less in young soldiers going to war. Even in recent days I had marveled at and loved and mocked and envied this gleam and this smile in my friend, Pablo, when he hung over his saxophone in the blissful intoxication of playing in the orchestra, or when, enraptured and ecstatic, he looked over to the conductor, the drum, or the man with the banjo. It had sometimes occurred to me that such a smile, such a childlike radiance could be possible only to quite young persons or among those peoples whose customs permitted no marked differences between one individual and another. But today, on this blessed night, I myself, the Steppenwolf, was radiant with this smile. I myself swam in this deep and childlike happiness of a fairy tale. I myself breathed the sweet intoxication of a common dream and of music and rhythm and wine and women--I, who had in other days so often listened with amusement, or dismal superiority, to its panegyric in the ballroom chatter of some student. I was myself no longer. My personality was dissolved in the intoxication of the festivity like salt in water. I danced with this woman or that, but it was not only the one I had in my arms and whose hair brushed my face that belonged to me. All the other women who were dancing in the same room and the same dance and to the same music, and whose radiant faces floated past me like fantastic flowers, belonged to me, and I to them. All of us had a part in one another. And the men too. I was with them also. They, too, were no strangers to me. Their smile was mine, and mine their wooing and theirs mine.

A new dance, a fox trot, with the title "Yearning," had swept the world that winter. Once we had beard it we could not have enough of it. We were all soaked in it and intoxicated with it and everyone hummed the melody whenever it was played. I danced without stop and with anyone who came in my way, with quite young girls, with women in their earlier or their later prime, and with those who had sadly passed them both; and with them all I was enraptured--laughing, happy, radiant. And when Pablo saw me so radiant, me whom he had always looked on as a very lamentable poor devil, his eyes beamed blissfully upon me and he was so inspired that he got up from his chair and blowing lustily in his horn climbed up on it. From this elevation he blew with all his might, while at the same time his whole body, and his instrument with it, swayed to the tune of "Yearning." I and my partner kissed our hands to him and sang loudly in response. Ah, thought I, meanwhile, let come to me what may, for once at least, I, too, have been happy, radiant, released from myself, a brother of Pablo's, a child.

I had lost the sense of time, and I don't know how many hours or moments the intoxication of happiness lasted. I did not observe either that the brighter the festal fire burned the narrower were the limits within which it was confined. Most people had already left. The corridors were silent and many of the lights out. The stairs were deserted and in the rooms above one orchestra after another had stopped playing and gone away. It was only in the principal room and in Hell below that the orgy still raged in a crescendo. Since I could not dance with Hermine as a boy, we had only had fleeting encounters in the pauses between the dances, and at last I lost sight of her entirely--and not only sight but thought. There were no thoughts left. I was lost in the maze and whirl of the dance. Scents and tones and sighs and words stirred me. I was greeted and kindled by strange eyes, encircled by strange faces, borne hither and thither in time to the music as though by a wave.

And then of a sudden I saw, half coming to my senses for a moment, among the last who still kept it up in one of the smaller rooms, and filled it to overflowing--the only one in which the music still sounded--of a sudden I saw a black Pierrette with face painted white. She was fresh and charming, the only masked figure left and a bewitching apparition that I had never in the whole course of the night seen before. While in everyone else the late hour showed itself in flushed and heated faces, crushed dresses, limp collars and crumpled ruffs, the black Pierrette stood there fresh and neat with her white face beneath her mask. Her costume had not a crease and not a hair was out of place. Her ruff and pointed cuffs were untouched. I rushed towards her, put my arms around her, and drew her into the dance. Her perfumed ruff tickled my chin. Her hair brushed my cheek. The young vigor of her body answered my movements as no one else's had done that night, yielding to them with an inward tenderness and compelling them to new contacts by the play of her allurements. I bent down to kiss her mouth as we danced. Its smile was triumphant and long familiar. Of a sudden I recognized the firm chin, the shoulders, arms and hands. It was Hermine, Herman no longer. Hermine in a change of dress, fresh, perfumed, powdered.

Our lips met passionately. For a moment her whole body to her knees clung in longing and surrender to mine. Then she drew her mouth away and, holding back, fled from me as we danced. When the music broke off we were still clasped where we stood. All the excited couples round us clapped, stamped, cried out and urged the exhausted orchestra to play "Yearning" over again. And now a feeling that it was morning fell upon us all. We saw the ashen light behind the curtains. It warned us of pleasure's approaching end and gave us symptoms of the weariness to come. Blindly, with bursts of laughter, we flung ourselves desperately into the dance once more, into the music and the light that began to flood the room. Our feet moved in time to the music as though we were possessed, every couple touching, and once more we felt the great wave of bliss break over us. Hermine abandoned her triumphant air, her mockery and coolness. She knew that there was no more to do to make me in love with her. I was hers, and her way of dancing, her looks and smiles and kisses all showed that she gave herself to me. All the women of this fevered night, all that I had danced with, all whom I had kindled or who had kindled me, all whom I had courted, all who had clung to me with longing, all whom I had followed with enraptured eyes were melted together and had become one, the one whom I held in my arms.

On and on went this nuptial dance. Time after time the music flagged. The winds let their instruments fall. The pianist got up from the piano. The first fiddle shook his head. And every time they were won over by the imploring persistence of the last intoxicated dancers and played once more. They played faster and more wildly. Then at last, as we stood, still entwined and breathless after the last eager dance, the piano was closed with a bang, and our arms fell wearily to our sides like those of the winds and strings and the flutist, blinking sleepily, put his flute away in its case. Doors opened, the cold air poured in, attendants appeared with cloaks and the bar waiter turned off the light. The whole scene vanished eerily away and the dancers who a moment ago had been all on fire shivered as they put on coats and cloaks and turned up their collars. Hermine was pale but smiling. Slowly she raised her arm and pushed back her hair. As she did so one arm caught the light and a faint and indescribably tender shadow ran from her armpit to her hidden breast, and this little trembling line of shadow seemed to me to sum up all the charm and fascination of her body like a smile.

We stood looking at one another, the last in the hall, the last in the whole building. Somewhere below I heard a door bang, a glass break, a titter of laughter die away, mixed with the angry hurried noise of motorcars starting up. And somewhere, at an indeterminable distance and height, I heard a laugh ring out, an extraordinarily clear and merry peal of laughter. Yet it was eerie and strange. It was a laugh, made of crystal and ice, bright and radiant, but cold and inexorable. Where had I heard this laugh before? I could not tell.

We stood and looked at one another. For a moment I came to my sober self. I felt a fearful weariness descend upon me. I felt with repugnance how moist and limp my clothing hung around me. I saw my hands emerging red and with swollen veins from my crumpled and wilted cuffs. But all at once the mood passed, banished by a look from Hermine. At this look that seemed to come from my own soul all reality fell away, even the reality of my sensuous love of her. Bewitched we looked at one another, while my poor little soul looked at me.

"You're ready?" asked Hermine, and her smile fled away like the shadows on her breast. Far up in unknown space rang out that strange and eerie laughter.

I nodded. Oh, yes, I was ready.

At this moment Pablo appeared in the doorway and beamed on us out of his jolly eyes that really were animal's eyes except that animal's eyes are always serious, while his always laughed, and this laughter turned them into human eyes. He beckoned to us with his usual friendly cordiality. He had put on a gorgeous silk smoking jacket. His limp collar and tired white face had a withered and pallid look above its red facings; but the impression was erased by his radiant black eyes. So was reality erased, for they too had the witchery.

We joined him when he beckoned and in the doorway he said to me in a low voice: "Brother Harry, I invite you to a little entertainment. For madmen only, and one price only--your mind. Are you ready?"

Again I nodded.

The dear fellow gave us each an arm with kind solicitude, Hermine his right, me his left, and conducted us upstairs to a small round room that was lit from the ceiling with a bluish light and nearly empty. There was nothing in it but a small round table and three easy chairs in which we sat ourselves.

Where were we? Was I asleep? Was I at home? Was I driving in a car? No, I was sitting in a blue light in a round room and a rare atmosphere, in a stratum of reality that had become rarefied in the extreme.

Why then was Hermine so white? Why was Pablo talking so much? Was it not perhaps I who made him talk, spoke, indeed, with his voice? Was it not, too, my own soul that contemplated me out of his black eyes like a lost and frightened bird, just as it had out of Hermine's gray ones?

Pablo looked at us good-naturedly as ever and with something ceremonious in his friendliness; and he talked much and long. He whom I had never heard say two consecutive sentences, whom no discussion nor thesis could interest, whom I had scarcely credited with a single thought, discoursed now in his good-natured warm voice fluently and without a fault.

"My friends, I have invited you to an entertainment that Harry has long wished for and of which he has long dreamed. The hour is a little late and no doubt we are all slightly fatigued. So, first, we will rest and refresh ourselves a little."

From a recess in the wall he took three glasses and a quaint little bottle, also a small oriental box inlaid with differently colored woods. He filled the three glasses from the bottle and taking three long thin yellow cigarettes from the box and a box of matches from the pocket of his silk jacket he gave us a light. And now we all slowly smoked the cigarettes whose smoke was as thick as incense, leaning back in our chairs and slowly sipping the aromatic liquid whose strange taste was so utterly unfamiliar. Its effect was immeasurably enlivening and delightful--as though one were filled with gas and had no longer any gravity. Thus we sat peacefully exhaling small puffs and taking little sips at our glasses, while every moment we felt ourselves growing lighter and more serene.

From far away came Pablo's warm voice.

"It is a pleasure to me, my dear Harry, to have the privilege of being your host in a small way on this occasion. You have often been sorely weary of your life. You were striving, were you not, for escape? You have a longing to forsake this world and its reality and to penetrate to a reality more native to you, to a world beyond time. You know, of course, where this other world lies hidden. It is the world of your own soul that you seek. Only within yourself exists that other reality for which you long. I can give you nothing that has not already its being within yourself. I can throw open to you no picture gallery but your own soul. All I can give you is the opportunity, the impulse, the key. I can help you to make your own world visible. That is all."

Again he put his hand into the pocket of his gorgeous jacket and drew out a round looking glass.

"Look, it is thus that you have so far seen yourself."

He held the little glass before my eyes (a childish verse came to my mind: "Little glass, little glass in the hand") and I saw, though indistinctly and cloudily, the reflection of an uneasy self-tormented, inwardly laboring and seething being--myself, Harry Haller. And within him again I saw the Steppenwolf, a shy, beautiful, dazed wolf with frightened eyes that smoldered now with anger, now with sadness. This shape of a wolf coursed through the other in ceaseless movement, as a tributary pours its cloudy turmoil into a river. In bitter strife, each tried to devour the other so that his shape might prevail. How unutterably sad was the look this fluid inchoate figure of the wolf threw from his beautiful shy eyes.

"There you see yourself," Pablo remarked and put the mirror away in his pocket. I was thankful to close my eyes and take a sip of the elixir.

"And now," said Pablo, "we have had our rest. We have had our refreshment and a little talk. If your fatigue has passed off I will conduct you to my peep show and show you my little theater. Will you come?"

We got up. With a smile Pablo led. He opened a door and drew a curtain aside, and we found ourselves in the horseshoe-shaped corridor of a theater, and exactly in the middle. On either side, the curving passage led past a large number, indeed an incredible number, of narrow doors into the boxes.

"This," explained Pablo, "is our theater, and a jolly one it is. I hope you'll find lots to laugh at." He laughed aloud as he spoke, a short laugh, but it went through me like a shot. It was the same bright and peculiar laugh that I had heard before from below.

"This little theater of mine has as many doors into as many boxes as you please, ten or a hundred or a thousand, and behind each door exactly what you seek awaits you. It is a pretty cabinet of pictures, my dear friend; but it would be quite useless for you to go through it as you are. You would be checked and blinded at every turn by what you are pleased to call your personality. You have no doubt guessed long since that the conquest of time and the escape from reality, or however else it may be that you choose to describe your longing, means simply the wish to be relieved of your so-called personality. That is the prison where you lie. And if you were to enter the theater as you are, you would see everything through the eyes of Harry and the old spectacles of the Steppenwolf. You are therefore requested to lay these spectacles aside and to be so kind as to leave your highly esteemed personality here in the cloakroom where you will find it again when you wish. The pleasant dance from which you have just come, the treatise on the Steppenwolf, and the little stimulant that we have only this moment partaken of may have sufficiently prepared you. You, Harry, after having left behind your valuable personality, will have the left side of the theater at your disposal, Hermine the right. Once inside, you can meet each other as you please. Hermine will be so kind as to go for a moment behind the curtain. I should like to introduce Harry first."

Hermine disappeared to the right past a gigantic mirror that covered the rear wall from floor to vaulted ceiling.

"Now, Harry, come along, be as jolly as you can. To make it so and to teach you to laugh is the whole aim in getting up this entertainment--I hope you will make it easy for me. You feel quite well, I trust? Not afraid? That's good, excellent. You will now, without fear and with unfeigned pleasure, enter our visionary world. You will introduce yourself to it by means of a trifling suicide, since this is the custom."

He took out the pocket mirror again and held it in front of my face. Again I was confronted by the same indistinct and cloudy reflection, with the wolf's shape encircling it and coursing through it. I knew it too well and disliked it too sincerely for its destruction to cause me any sorrow.

"You will now erase this superfluous reflection, my dear friend. That is all that is necessary. To do so, it will suffice that you greet it, if your mood permits, with a hearty laugh. You are here in a school of humor. You are to learn to laugh. Now, true humor begins when a man ceases to take himself seriously."

I fixed my eyes on the little mirror, where the man Harry and the wolf were going through their convulsions. For a moment there was a convulsion deep within me too, a faint but painful one like remembrance, or like homesickness, or like remorse. Then the slight oppression gave way to a new feeling like that a man feels when a tooth has been extracted with cocaine, a sense of relief and of letting out a deep breath, and of wonder, at the same time, that it has not hurt in the least. And this feeling was accompanied by a buoyant exhilaration and a desire to laugh so irresistible that I was compelled to give way to it.

The mournful image in the glass gave a final convulsion and vanished. The glass itself turned gray and charred and opaque, as though it had been burned. With a laugh Pablo threw the thing away and it went rolling down the endless corridor and disappeared.

"Well laughed, Harry," cried Pablo. "You will learn to laugh like the immortals yet. You have done with the Steppenwolf at last. It's no good with a razor. Take care that he stays dead. You'll be able to leave the farce of reality behind you directly. At our next meeting we'll drink to brotherhood, dear fellow. I never liked you better than I do today. And if you still think it worth your while we can philosophize together and argue and talk about music and Mozart and Gluck and Plato and Goethe to your heart's content. You will understand now why it was so impossible before. I wish you good riddance of the Steppenwolf for today at any rate. For naturally, your suicide is not a final one. We are in a magic theater; a world of pictures, not realities. See that you pick out beautiful and cheerful ones and show that you really are not in love with your highly questionable personality any longer. Should you still, however, have a hankering after it, you need only have another look in the mirror that I will now show you. But you know the old proverb: 'A mirror in the hand is worth two on the wall.' Ha! ha!" (Again that laugh, beautiful and frightful!) "And now there only remains one little ceremony and quite a jolly one. You have now to cast aside the spectacles of your personality. So come here and look in a proper looking glass. It will give you some fun."

Laughingly with a few droll caresses he turned me about so that I faced the gigantic mirror on the wall. There I saw myself.

I saw myself for a brief instant as my usual self, except that I looked unusually good-humored, bright and laughing. But I had scarcely had time to recognize myself before the reflection fell to pieces. A second, a third, a tenth, a twentieth figure sprang from it till the whole gigantic mirror was full of nothing but Harrys or bits of him, each of which I saw only for the instant of recognition. Some of these multitudinous Harrys were as old as I, some older, some very old. Others were young. There were youths, boys, schoolboys, scamps, children. Fifty-year-olds and twenty-year-olds played leap frog. Thirty-year-olds and five-year-olds, solemn and merry, worthy and comic, well-dressed and unpresentable, and even quite naked, long haired, and hairless, all were I and all were seen for a flash, recognized and gone. They sprang from each other in all directions, left and right and into the recesses of the mirror and clean out of it. One, an elegant young fellow, leaped laughing into Pablo's arms and embraced him and they went off together. And one who particularly pleased me, a good looking and charming boy of sixteen or seventeen years, sprang like lightning into the corridor and began reading the notices on the doors. I went after him and found him in front of a door on which was inscribed:

ALL GIRLS ARE YOURS
ONE QUARTER IN THE SLOT

The dear boy hurled himself forward, made a leap and, falling head first into the slot himself, disappeared behind the door.

Pablo too had vanished. So apparently had the mirror and with it all the countless figures. I realized that I was now left to myself and to the theater, and I went with curiosity from door to door and read on each its alluring invitation.

The inscription

JOLLY HUNTING
GREAT HUNT IN AUTOMOBILES

attracted me. I opened the narrow door and stepped in.

I was swept at once into a world of noise and excitement. Cars, some of them armored, were run through the streets chasing the pedestrians. They ran them down and either left them mangled on the ground or crushed them to death against the walls of the houses. I saw at once that it was the long-prepared, long-awaited and long-feared war between men and machines, now at last broken out. On all sides lay dead and decomposing bodies, and on all sides, too, smashed and distorted and half-burned cars. Airplanes circled above the frightful confusion and were being fired upon from many roofs and windows with rifles and machine guns. On every wall were wild and magnificently stirring placards, whose giant letters flamed like torches, summoning the nation to side with the men against the machines, to make an end at last of the fat and well-dressed and perfumed plutocrats who used machines to squeeze the fat from other men's bodies, of them and their huge fiendishly purring automobiles. Set factories afire at last! Make a little room on the crippled earth! Depopulate it so that the grass may grow again, and woods, meadows, heather, stream and moor return to this world of dust and concrete. Other placards, on the other hand, in wonderful colors and magnificently phrased, warned all those who had a stake in the country and some share of prudence (in more moderate and less childish terms which testified to the remarkable cleverness and intellect of those who bad composed them) against the rising tide of anarchy. They depicted in a truly impressive way the blessings of order and work and property and education and justice, and praised machinery as the last and most sublime invention of the human mind. With its aid, men would be equal to the gods. I studied these placards, both the red and the green, and reflected on them and marveled at them. The flaming eloquence affected me as powerfully as the compelling logic. They were right, and I stood as deeply convinced in front of one as in front of the other, a good deal disturbed all the time by the rather juicy firing that went on all round me. Well, the principal thing was clear. There was a war on, a violent, genuine and highly sympathetic war where there was no concern for Kaiser or republic, for frontiers, flags or colors and other equally decorative and theatrical matters, all nonsense at bottom; but a war in which every one who lacked air to breathe and no longer found life exactly pleasing gave emphatic expression to his displeasure and strove to prepare the way for a general destruction of this iron-cast civilization of ours. In every eye I saw the unconcealed spark of destruction and murder, and in mine too these wild red roses bloomed as rank and high, and sparkled as brightly. I joined the battle joyfully.

The best of all, however, was that my schoolfriend, Gustav, turned up close beside me. I had lost sight of him for dozens of years, the wildest, strongest, most eager and venturesome of the friends of my childhood. I laughed in my heart as I saw him blink at me with his bright blue eyes. He beckoned and at once I followed him joyfully.

"Good Lord, Gustav," I cried happily, "I haven't seen you in ages. Whatever has become of you?"

He gave a derisive snort, just as he used to do as a boy. "There you are again, you idiot, jabbering and asking questions. I'm a professor of theology if you want to know. But, the Lord be praised, there's no occasion for theology now, my boy. It's war. Come on!"

He shot the driver of a small car that came snorting towards us and leaping into it as nimbly as a monkey, brought it to a standstill for me to get in. Then we drove like the devil between bullets and crashed cars out of town and suburbs.

"Are you on the side of the manufacturers?" I asked my friend.

"Oh, Lord, that's a matter of taste, so we can leave it out of account--though now you mention it, I rather think we might take the other side, since at bottom it's all the same, of course. I'm a theologian and my predecessor, Luther, took the side of the princes and plutocrats against the peasants. So now we'll establish the balance a little. This rotten car, I hope it'll hold out another mile or two."

Swift as the wind, that child of heaven, we rattled on, and reached a green and peaceful countryside many miles distant. We traversed a wide plain and then slowly climbed into the mountains. Here we made a halt on a smooth and glistening road that led in bold curves between the steep wall of rock and the low retaining wall. Far below shone the blue surface of a lake.

"Lovely view," said I.

"Very pretty. We'll call it the Axle Way. A good many axles of one sort or another are going to crash here, Harry, my boy. So watch out!"

A tall pine grew by the roadside, and among the tall branches we saw something like a little hut made of boards to serve as an outlook and point of vantage. Gustav smiled with a knowing twinkle in his blue eyes. We hurried out of the car, climbed up the trunk and, breathing hard, concealed ourselves in the outlook post, which pleased us much. We found rifles and revolvers there and boxes of ammunition. We had scarcely cooled down when we heard the hoarse imperious horn of a big luxury car from the next bend of the road. It came purring at top speed up the smooth road. Our rifles were ready in our hands. The excitement was intense.

"Aim at the chauffeur," commanded Gustav quickly just as the heavy car went by beneath us. I aimed, and fired at the chauffeur in his blue cap. The man fell in a heap. The car careened on, charged the cliff face, rebounded, attacked the lower wall furiously with all its unwieldy weight like a great bumble bee and, tumbling over, crashed with a brief and distant report into the depths below.

"Got him!" Gustav laughed. "My turn next."

Another came as he spoke. There were three of four occupants packed in the back seat. From the head of a woman a bright blue veil streamed out behind. It filled me with genuine remorse. Who could say how pretty a face it might adorn? Good God, though we did play the brigand we might at least emulate the illustrious and spare pretty women. Gustav, however, had already fired. The driver shuddered and collapsed. The car leaped against the perpendicular cliff, fell back and overturned, wheels uppermost. Its engine was still running and the wheels turned absurdly in the air; but suddenly with a frightful explosion it burst into flames.

"A Ford," said Gustav. "We must get down and clear the road."

We climbed down and watched the burning heap. It soon burned out. Meanwhile we made levers of green wood and hoisted it to the side of the road and over the wall into the abyss, where for a long time it went crashing through the undergrowth. Two of the dead bodies had fallen out as we turned the car over and lay on the road with their clothing partly burned. One wore a coat which was still in fairly good condition. I searched the pockets to see who he was and came across a leather portfolio with some cards in it. I took one and read: Tat Twam Asi.

"Very witty," said Gustav. "Though, as a matter of fact, it is all one what our victims are called. They're poor devils just as we are. Their names don't matter. This world is done for and so are we. The least painful solution would be to hold it under water for ten minutes. Now to work--"

We threw the bodies after the car. Already another one was tooting. We shot it down with a volley where we stood. It made a drunken swerve and reeled on for a stretch: then turned over and lay gasping. One passenger was still sitting inside, but a pretty young girl got out uninjured, though she was white and trembling violently. We greeted her politely and offered our assistance. She was too much shaken to speak and stared at us for a while quite dazed.

"Well, first let us look after the old boy," said Gustav and turned to the occupant of the car who still clung to his seat behind the chauffeur. He was a gentleman with short grey hair. His intelligent, clear gray eyes were open, but he seemed to be seriously hurt; at least, blood flowed from his mouth and he held his neck askew and rigid.

"Allow me to introduce myself. My name is Gustav. We have taken the liberty of shooting your chauffeur. May we inquire whom we have the honor to address?"

The old man looked at us coolly and sadly out of his small gray eyes.

"I am Attorney-General Loering," he said slowly. "You have not only killed my poor chauffeur, but me too, I fancy. Why did you shoot on us?"

"For exceeding the speed limit."

"We were not traveling at more than normal speed."

"What was normal yesterday is no longer normal today, Mr. Attorney-General. We are of the opinion that whatever speed a motorcar travels is too great. We are destroying all cars and all other machines also."

"Your rifles too?"

"Their turn will come, granted we have the time. Presumably by tomorrow or the day after we shall all be done for. You know, of course, that this part of the world was shockingly overpopulated. Well, now we are going to let in a little air."

"Are you shooting every one, without distinction?"

"Certainly. In many cases it may no doubt be a pity. I'm sorry, for example, about this charming young lady. Your daughter, I presume."

"No. She is my stenographer."

"So much the better. And now will you please get out, or let us carry you out, as the car is to be destroyed."

"I prefer to be destroyed with it."

"As you wish. But allow me to ask you one more question. You are a public prosecutor. I never could understand how a man could be a public prosecutor. You make your living by bringing other men, poor devils mostly, to trial and passing sentence on them. Isn't that so?"

"It is. I do my duty. It was my office. Exactly as it is the office of the hangman to hang those whom I condemn to death. You too have assumed a like office. You kill people also."

"Quite true. Only we do not kill from duty, but pleasure, or much more, rather, from displeasure and despair of the world. For this reason we find a certain amusement in killing people. Has it never amused you?"

"You bore me. Be so kind as to do your work. Since the conception of duty is unknown to you--"

He was silent and made a movement of his lips as though to spit. Only a little blood came, however, and clung to his chin.

"One moment!" said Gustav politely. "The conception of duty is certainly unknown to me--now. Formerly I had a great deal of official concern with it. I was a professor of theology. Besides that, I was a soldier and went through the war. What seemed to me to be duty and what the authorities and my superior officers from time to time enjoined upon me was not by any means good. I would rather have done the opposite. But granting that the conception of duty is no longer known to me, I still know the conception of guilt--perhaps they are the same thing. In so far as a mother bore me, I am guilty. I am condemned to live. I am obliged to belong to a state, to serve as a soldier, to kill and to pay taxes for armaments. And now at this moment the guilt of life has brought me once more to the necessity of killing the people as it did in the war. And this time I have no repugnance. I am resigned to the guilt. I have no objection to this stupid congested world going to bits. I am glad to help and glad to perish with it."

The public prosecutor made an effort to smile a little with his lips on which the blood had coagulated. He did not succeed very well, though the good intention was manifest.

"Good," said he. "So we are colleagues. Well, as such, please do your duty."

The pretty girl had meanwhile sat down by the side of the road and fainted.

At this moment there was again the tooting of a car coming down the road at full speed. We drew the girl a little to one side and, standing close against the cliff, let the approaching car run into the ruins of the other. The brakes were applied violently and the car reared up in the air. It came to a standstill undamaged. We seized our rifles and quickly had the newcomers covered.

"Get out!" commanded Gustav. "Hands up!"

Three men got out of the car and obediently held up their hands.

"Is any one of you a doctor?" Gustav asked.

They shook their heads.

"Then be so good as to remove this gentleman. He is seriously hurt. Take him in your car to the nearest town. Forward, and get on with it."

The old gentleman was soon lying in the other car. Gustav gave the word and off they went.

The stenographer meanwhile had come to herself and had been watching these proceedings. I was glad we had made so fair a prize.

"Madam," said Gustav, "you have lost your employer. I hope you were not bound to the old gentleman by other ties. You are now in my service. So be our good comrade. So much for that; and now time presses. It will be uncomfortable here before long. Can you climb, Madam? Yes? Then go ahead and we'll help you up between us."

We all climbed up to our hut in the tree as fast as we could. The lady did not feel very well up there, but we gave her some brandy, and she was soon so much recovered that she was able to admire the wonderful view over lake and mountains and to tell us also that her name was Dora.

Immediately after this, there was another car below us. It steered carefully past the overturned one without stopping and then gathered speed.

"Poltroon!" laughed Gustav and shot the driver. The car zigzagged and dashing into the wall stove it in and hung suspended over the abyss.

"Dora," I said, "can you use firearms?"

She could not, but we taught her how to load. She was clumsy at first and hurt her finger and cried and wanted court-plaster. But Gustav told her it was war and that she must show her courage. Then it went better.

"But what's going to become of us?" she asked.

"Don't know," said Gustav. "My friend Harry is fond of pretty girls. He'll look after you."

"But the police and the soldiers will come and kill us."

"There aren't any police and such like any more. We can choose, Dora. Either we stay quietly up here and shoot down every car that tries to pass, or else we can take a car and drive off in it and let others shoot at us. It's all the same which side we take. I'm for staying here."

And now there was the loud tooting of another car beneath us. It was soon accounted for and lay there wheels uppermost.

Gustav smiled. "Yes, there are indeed too many men in the world. In earlier days it wasn't so noticeable. But now that everyone wants air to breathe, and a car to drive as well, one does notice it. Of course, what we are doing isn't rational. It's childishness, just as war is childishness on a gigantic scale. In time, mankind will learn to keep its numbers in check by rational means. Meanwhile, we are meeting an intolerable situation in a rather irrational way. However, the principle's correct--we eliminate."

"Yes," said I, "what we are doing is probably mad, and probably it is good and necessary all the same. It is not a good thing when man overstrains his reason and tries to reduce to rational order matters that are not susceptible of rational treatment. Then there arise ideals such as those of the Americans or of the Bolsheviks. Both are extraordinarily rational, and both lead to a frightful oppression and impoverishment of life, because they simplify it so crudely. The likeness of man, once a high ideal, is in process of becoming a machine-made article. It is for madmen like us, perhaps, to ennoble it again."

With a laugh Gustav replied: "You talk like a book, my boy. It is a pleasure and a privilege to drink at such a fount of wisdom. And perhaps there is even something in what you say. But now kindly reload your piece. You are a little too dreamy for my taste. A couple of bucks can come dashing by here again any moment, and we can't kill them with philosophy. We must have ball in our barrels."

A car came and was dropped at once. The road was blocked. A survivor, a stout red-faced man, gesticulated wildly over the ruins. Then he stared up and down and, discovering our hiding place, came for us bellowing and shooting up at us with a revolver.

"Get off with you or I'll shoot," Gustav shouted down. The man took aim at him and fired again. Then we shot him.

After this two more came and were bagged. Then the road was silent and deserted. Apparently the news had got about that it was dangerous. We had time to enjoy the beauty of the view. On the far side of the lake a small town lay in the valley. Smoke rose from it and soon we saw fire leaping from roof to roof. Shooting could be heard. Dora cried a little and I stroked her wet cheeks.

"Have we all got to die then?" she asked. There was no reply. Meanwhile a man on foot went past below. He saw the smashed-up cars and began nosing round them. Leaning over into one of them he pulled out a gay parasol, a lady's handbag and a bottle of wine. Then he sat down contentedly on the wall, took a drink from the bottle and ate something wrapped in tinfoil out of the handbag. After emptying the bottle he went on, well pleased, with the parasol clasped under his arm; and I said to Gustav: "Could you find it in you to shoot at this good fellow and make a hole in his head? God knows, I couldn't."

"You're not asked to," my friend growled. But he did not feel very comfortable either. We had no sooner caught sight of a man whose behavior was harmless and peaceable and childlike and who was still in a state of innocence than all our praise-worthy and most necessary activities became stupid and repulsive. Pah--all that blood! We were ashamed of ourselves. But in the war there must have been generals even who felt the same.

"Don't let us stay here any longer," Dora implored. "Let's go down. We are sure to find something to eat in the cars. Aren't you hungry, you Bolsheviks?"

Down in the burning town the bells began to peal with a wild terror. We set ourselves to climb down. As I helped Dora to climb over the breast work, I kissed her knee. She laughed aloud, and then the planks gave way and we both fell into vacancy--

. . . . . . .

Once more I stood in the round corridor, still excited by the hunting adventure. And everywhere on all the countless doors were the alluring inscriptions:

MUTABOR
TRANSFORMATION INTO ANY ANIMAL OR PLANT
YOU PLEASE

KAMASUTRAM
INSTRUCTION IN THE INDIAN ARTS OF LOVE
COURSE FOR BEGINNERS; FORTY-TWO DIFFERENT
METHODS AND PRACTICES

DELIGHTFUL SUICIDE
YOU LAUGH YOURSELF TO BITS

DO YOU WANT TO BE ALL SPIRIT?

THE WISDOM OF THE EAST.

DOWNFALL OF THE WEST
MODERATE PRICES. NEVER SURPASSED

COMPENDIUM OF ART
TRANSFORMATION FROM TIME INTO SPACE
BY MEANS OF MUSIC

LAUGHING TEARS
CABINET OF HUMOR

SOLITUDE MADE EASY
COMPLETE SUBSTITUTE FOR ALL FORMS OF
SOCIABILITY.

The series of inscriptions was endless. One was

GUIDANCE IN THE BUILDING UP OF THE
PERSONALITY. SUCCESS GUARANTEED

This seemed to me to be worth looking into and I went in at this door.

I found myself in a quiet twilit room where a man with something like a large chessboard in front of him sat in Eastern fashion on the floor. At the first glance I thought it was friend Pablo. He wore at any rate a similar gorgeous silk jacket and had the same dark and shining eyes.

"Are you Pablo?" I asked.

"I am not anybody," he replied amiably. "We have no names here and we are not anybody. I am a chess player. Do you wish for instruction in the building up of the personality?"

"Yes, please."

"Then be so kind as to place a few dozen of your pieces at my disposal."

"My pieces--?"

"Of the pieces into which you saw your so-called personality broken up. I can't play without pieces."

He held a glass up to me and again I saw the unity of my personality broken up into many selves whose number seemed even to have increased. The pieces were now, however, very small, about the size of chessmen. The player took a dozen or so of them in his sure and quiet fingers and placed them on the ground near the board. As he did so he began to speak in the monotonous way of one who goes through a recitation or reading that he has often gone through before.

"The mistaken and unhappy notion that a man is an enduring unity is known to you. It is also known to you that man consists of a multitude of souls, of numerous selves. The separation of the unity of the personality into these numerous pieces passes for madness. Science has invented the name schizomania for it. Science is in this so far right as no multiplicity may be dealt with unless there be a series, a certain order and grouping. It is wrong insofar as it holds that one only and binding and lifelong order is possible for the multiplicity of subordinate selves. This error of science has many unpleasant consequences, and the single advantage of simplifying the work of the state-appointed pastors and masters and saving them the labors of original thought. In consequence of this error many persons pass for normal, and indeed for highly valuable members of society, who are incurably mad; and many, on the other hand, are looked upon as mad who are geniuses. Hence it is that we supplement the imperfect psychology of science by the conception that we call the art of building up the soul. We demonstrate to anyone whose soul has fallen to pieces that he can rearrange these pieces of a previous self in what order he pleases, and so attain to an endless multiplicity of moves in the game of life. As the playwright shapes a drama from a handful of characters, so do we from the pieces of the disintegrated self build up ever new groups, with ever new interplay and suspense, and new situations that are eternally inexhaustible. Look!"

With the sure and silent touch of his clever fingers he took hold of my pieces, all the old men and young men and children and women, cheerful and sad, strong and weak, nimble and clumsy, and swiftly arranged them on his board for a game. At once they formed themselves into groups and families, games and battles, friendships and enmities, making a small world. For a while he let this lively and yet orderly world go through its evolutions before my enraptured eyes in play and strife, making treaties and fighting battles, wooing, marrying and multiplying. It was indeed a crowded stage, a moving breathless drama.

Then he passed his hand swiftly over the board and gently swept all the pieces into a heap; and, meditatively with an artist's skill, made up a new game of the same pieces with quite other groupings, relationships and entanglements. The second game had an affinity with the first, it was the same world built of the same material, but the key was different, the time changed, the motif was differently given out and the situations differently presented.

And in this fashion the clever architect built up one game after another out of the figures, each of which was a bit of myself, and every game had a distant resemblance to every other. Each belonged recognizably to the same world and acknowledged a common origin. Yet each was entirely new.

"This is the art of life," he said dreamily. "You may yourself as an artist develop the game of your life and lend it animation. You may complicate and enrich it as you please. It lies in your hands. Just as madness, in a higher sense, is the beginning of all wisdom, so is schizomania the beginning of all art and all fantasy. Even learned men have come to a partial recognition of this, as may be gathered, for example, from *Prince Wunderhorn,* that enchanting book, in which the industry and pains of a man of learning, with the assistance of the genius of a number of madmen and artists shut up as such, are immortalized. Here, take your little pieces away with you. The game will often give you pleasure. The piece that today grew to the proportions of an intolerable bugbear, you will degrade tomorrow to a mere lay figure. The luckless Cinderella will in the next game be the princess. I wish you much pleasure, my dear sir."

I bowed low in gratitude to the gifted chess player, put the little pieces in my pocket and withdrew through the narrow door.

My real intention was to seat myself at once on the floor in the corridor and play the game for hours, for whole eternities; but I was no sooner in the bright light of the circular theater passage than a new and irresistible current carried me along. A dazzling poster flashed before my eyes:

MARVELOUS TAMING OF THE STEPPENWOLF

Many different emotions surged up in me at the sight of this announcement. My heart was painfully contracted by all kinds of fears and repressions from my former life and the reality I had left behind. With trembling hand I opened the door and found myself in the booth of a fair with an iron rail separating me from a wretched stage. On the stage I saw an animal tamer--a cheap-jack gentleman with a pompous air--who in spite of a large moustache, exuberantly muscular biceps and his absurd circus getup had a malicious and decidedly unpleasant resemblance to myself. The strong man led on a leash like a dog--lamentable sight--a large, beautiful but terribly emaciated wolf, whose eyes were cowed and furtive; and it was as disgusting as it was intriguing, as horrible as it was all the same secretly entertaining, to see this brutal tamer of animals put the noble and yet so ignominiously obedient beast of prey through a series of tricks and sensational turns.

At any rate, the man, my diabolically distorted double, had his wolf marvelously broken. The wolf was obediently attentive to every command and responded like a dog to every call and every crack of the whip. He went down on his knees, lay for dead, and, aping the lord of creation, carried a loaf, an egg, a piece of meat, a basket in his mouth with cheerful obedience; and he even had to pick up the whip that the tamer had let fall and carry it after him in his teeth while he wagged his tail with an unbearable submissiveness. A rabbit was put in front of him and then a white lamb. He bared his teeth, it is true, and the saliva dropped from his mouth while he trembled with desire, but he did not touch either of the animals; and at the word of command he jumped over them with a graceful leap, as they cowered trembling on the floor. More--he laid himself down between the rabbit and the lamb and embraced them with his foremost paws to form a touching family group, at the same time eating a stick of chocolate from the man's hand. It was an agony to witness the fantastic extent to which the wolf had learned to belie his nature; and I stood there with my hair on end.

There was some compensation, however, both for the horrified spectator and for the wolf himself, in the second part of the program. For after this refined exhibition of animal taming and when the man with a winning smile had made his triumphant bow over the group of the wolf and the lamb, the roles were reversed. My engaging double suddenly with a low reverence laid his whip at the wolf's feet and became as agitated, as shrunken and wretched, as the wolf had been before. The wolf, however, licked his chops with a grin, his constraint and dissimulation erased. His eyes kindled. His whole body was taut and showed the joy he felt at recovering his wild nature.

And now the wolf commanded and the man obeyed. At the word of command the man sank on his knees, let his tongue loll out and tore his clothes off with his filed teeth. He went on two feet or all-fours just as the wolf ordered him, played the human being, lay for dead, let the wolf ride on his back and carried the whip after him. With the aptness of a dog he submitted gladly to every humiliation and perversion of his nature. A lovely girl came on to the stage and went up to the tamed man. She stroked his chin and rubbed her cheek against his; but he remained on all-fours, remained a beast. He shook his head and began to show his teeth at the charming creature--so menacingly and wolfishly at last, that she ran away. Chocolate was put before him, but with a contemptuous sniff he thrust it from him with his snout. Finally the white lamb and the fat mottled rabbit were brought on again and the docile man gave his last turn and played the wolf most amusingly. He seized the shrieking creatures in his fingers and teeth, tore them limb from limb, grinningly chewed the living flesh and rapturously drank their warm blood while his eyes closed in a dreamy delight.

I made for the door in horror and dashed out. This Magic Theater was clearly no paradise. All hell lay beneath its charming surface. O God, was there even here no release?

In fear I hurried this way and that. I had the taste of blood and chocolate in my mouth, the one as hateful as the other. I desired nothing but to be beyond this wave of disgust. I wrestled with myself for more bearable, friendlier pictures. "O Friend, not these notes!" sang in my head, and with horror I remembered those terrible photographs from the Front that one saw occasionally during the war--those heaps of bodies entangled with each other, whose faces were changed to grinning ghouls by their gas masks. How silly and childish of me, a humanely minded opponent of war though I was, to have been horrified by those pictures. Today I knew that no tamer of beasts, no general, no insane person could hatch a thought or a picture in his brain that I could not match myself with one every bit as frightful, every bit as savage and wicked, as crude and stupid.

With an immense relief I remembered the notice I had seen on first entering the theater, the one that the nice boy had stormed so furiously--

ALL GIRLS ARE YOURS

and it seemed to me, all in all, that there was really nothing else so desirable as this. I was greatly cheered at finding that I could escape from that cursed wolf world, and went in.

The fragrance of spring-time met me. The very atmosphere of boyhood and youth, so deeply familiar and yet so legendary, was around me and in my veins flowed the blood of those days. All that I had done and thought and been since, fell away from me and I was young again. An hour, a few minutes before, I had prided myself on knowing what love was and desire and longing, but it had been the love and the longing of an old man. Now I was young again and this glowing current of fire that I felt in me, this mighty impulse, this unloosening passion like that wind in March that brings the thaw, was young and new and genuine. How the flame that I had forgotten leaped up again, how darkly stole on my ears the tones of long ago! My blood was on fire, and blossomed forth as my soul cried aloud and sang. I was a boy of fifteen or sixteen with my head full of Latin and Greek and poetry. I was all ardor and ambition and my fancy was laden with the artist's dreams. But far deeper and stronger and more awful than all there burned and leaped in me the flame of love, the hunger of sex, the fever and the foreboding of desire.

I was standing on a spur of the hills above the little town where I lived. The wind wafted the smell of spring and violets through my long hair. Below in the town I saw the gleam of the river and the windows of my home, and all that I saw and heard and smelled overwhelmed me, as fresh and reeling from creation, as radiant in depth of color, swayed by the wind of spring in as magical a transfiguration, as when once I looked on the world with the eyes of youth--first youth and poetry. With wandering hand I pulled a half-opened leaf bud from a bush that was newly green. I looked at it and smelled it (with the smell everything of those days came back in a glow) and then I put it between my lips, lips that no girl had ever kissed, and began playfully to bite it. At the sour and aromatically bitter taste I knew at once and exactly what it was that I was living over again. It all came back. I was living again an hour of the last years of my boyhood, a Sunday afternoon in early spring, the day that on a lonely walk I met Rosa Kreisler and greeted her so shyly and fell in love with her so madly.

She came, that day, alone and dreamingly up the hill towards me. She had not seen me and the sight of her approaching filled me with apprehension and suspense. I saw her hair, tied in two thick plaits, with loose strands on either side, her cheeks blown by the wind. I saw for the first time in my life how beautiful she was, and how beautiful and dreamlike the play of the wind in her delicate hair, how beautiful and provocative the fall of her thin blue dress over her young limbs; and just as the bitter spice of the chewed bud coursed through me with the whole dread pleasure and pain of spring, so the sight of the girl filled me with the whole deadly foreboding of love, the foreboding of woman. In that moment was contained the shock and the forewarning of enormous possibilities and promises, nameless delight, unthinkable bewilderments, anguish, suffering, release to the innermost and deepest guilt. Oh, how sharp was the bitter taste of spring on my tongue! And how the wind streamed playfully through the loose hair beside her rosy cheeks! She was close now. She looked up and recognized me. For a moment she blushed a little and looked aside; but when I took off my school cap, she was self-possessed at once and, raising her head, returned my greeting with a smile that was quite grown-up. Then, entirely mistress of the situation, she went slowly on, in a halo of the thousand wishes, hopes and adorations that I sent after her.

So it had once been on a Sunday thirty-five years before, and all that had been then came back to me in this moment. Hill and town, March wind and buddy taste, Rosa and her brown hair, the welling-up of desire and the sweet suffocation of anguish. All was as it was then, and it seemed to me that I had never in my life loved as I loved Rosa that day. But this time it was given me to greet her otherwise than on that occasion. I saw her blush when she recognized me, and the pains she took to conceal it, and I knew at once that she had a liking for me and that this encounter meant the same for her as for me. And this time instead of standing ceremoniously cap in hand till she had gone by, I did, in spite of anguish bordering on obsession, what my blood bade me do. I cried: "Rosa! Thank God, you've come, you beautiful, beautiful girl. I love you so dearly." It was not perhaps the most brilliant of all the things that might have been said at this moment, but there was no need for brilliance, and it was enough and more. Rosa did not put on her grown-up air, and she did not go on. She stopped and looked at me and, growing even redder than before, she said: "Heaven be praised, Harry--do you really like me?" Her brown eyes lit up her strong face, and they showed me that my past life and loves had all been false and perplexed and full of stupid unhappiness from that very moment on a Sunday afternoon when I had let Rosa pass me by. Now, however, the blunder was put right. Everything went differently and everything was good.

We clasped hands, and hand in hand walked slowly on as happy as we were embarrassed. We did not know what to do or to say, so we began to walk faster from embarrassment and then broke into a run, and ran till we lost our breath and had to stand still. But we did not let go our hands. We were both still children and did not know quite what to do with each other. That Sunday we did not even kiss, but we were immeasurably happy. We stood to get our breath. We sat on the grass and I stroked her hand while she passed the other one shyly over my hair. And then we got up again and tried to measure which of us was the taller. In reality, I was the taller by a finger's breath, but I would not have it so. I maintained that we were of exactly the same height and that God had designed us for each other and that later on we would marry. Then Rosa said that she smelled violets and we knelt in the short spring grass and looked for them and found a few with short stalks and I gave her mine and she gave me hers, and as it was getting chill and the sun slanted low over the cliffs, Rosa said she must go home. At this we both became very sad, for I dared not accompany her. But now we shared a secret and it was our dearest possession. I stayed behind on the cliffs and lying down with my face over the edge of the sheer descent, I looked down over the town and watched for her sweet little figure to appear far below and saw it pass the spring and over the bridge. And now I knew that she had reached her home and was going from room to room, and I lay up there far away from her; but there was a bond between her and me. The same current ran in both of us and a secret passed to and fro.

We saw each other again here and there all through this spring, sometimes on the cliffs, sometimes over the garden hedge; and when the elder began to bloom we gave each other the first shy kiss. It was little that children like us had to give each other and our kiss lacked warmth and fullness. I scarcely ventured to touch the strands of her hair about her ears. But all the love and all the joy that was in us were ours. It was a shy emotion and the troth we plighted was still unripe, but this timid waiting on each other taught us a new happiness. We climbed one little step up on the ladder of love. And thus, beginning from Rosa and the violets, I lived again through all the loves of my life--but under happier stars. Rosa I lost, and Irmgard appeared; and the sun was warmer and the stars less steady, but Irmgard no more than Rosa was mine. Step by step I had to climb. There was much to live through and much to learn; and I had to lose Irmgard and Anna too. Every girl that I had once loved in youth, I loved again, but now I was able to inspire each with love. There was something I could give to each, something each could give to me. Wishes, dreams and possibilities that had once had no other life than my own imagination were lived now in reality. They passed before me like beautiful flowers, Ida and Laura and all whom I had loved for a summer, a month, or a day.

I was now, as I perceived, that good-looking and ardent boy whom I had seen making so eagerly for love's door. I was living a bit of myself only--a bit that in my actual life and being had not been expressed to a tenth or a thousandth part, and

I was living it to the full. I was watching it grow unmolested by any other part of me. It was not perturbed by the thinker, nor tortured by the Steppenwolf, nor dwarfed by the poet, the visionary or the moralist. No--I was nothing now but the lover and I breathed no other happiness and no other suffering than love. Irmgard had already taught me to dance and Ida to kiss, and it was Emma first, the most beautiful of them all, who on an autumn evening beneath a swaying elm gave me her brown breasts to kiss and the cup of passion to drink.

I lived through much in Pablo's little theater and not a thousandth part can be told in words. All the girls I had ever loved were mine. Each gave me what she alone had to give and to each I gave what she alone knew how to take. Much love, much happiness, much indulgence, and much bewilderment, too, and suffering fell to my share. All the love that I had missed in my life bloomed magically in my garden during this hour of dreams. There were chaste and tender blooms, garish ones that blazed, dark ones swiftly fading. There were flaring lust, inward reverie, glowing melancholy, anguished dying, radiant birth. I found women who were only to be taken by storm and those whom it was a joy to woo and win by degrees. Every twilit corner of my life where, if but for a moment, the voice of sex had called me, a woman's glance kindled me or the gleam of a girl's white skin allured me, emerged again and all that had been missed was made good. All were mine, each in her own way. The woman with the remarkable dark brown eyes beneath flaxen hair was there. I had stood beside her for a quarter of an hour in the corridor of an express and afterwards she often appeared in my dreams. She did not speak a word, but what she taught me of the art of love was unimaginable, frightful, deathly. And the sleek, still Chinese, from the harbor of Marseilles, with her glassy smile, her smooth dead-black hair and swimming eyes--she too knew undreamed-of things. Each had her secret and the bouquet of her soil. Each kissed and laughed in a fashion of her own, and in her own peculiar way was shameful and in her own peculiar way shameless. They came and went. The stream carried them towards me and washed me up to them and away. I was a child in the stream of sex, at play in the midst of all its charm, its danger and surprise. And it astonished me to find how rich my life--the seemingly so poor and loveless life of the Steppenwolf--had been in the opportunities and allurements of love. I had missed them. I had fled before them. I had stumbled on over them. I had made haste to forget them. But here they all were stored up in their hundreds, and not one missing. And now that I saw them I gave myself up to them without defence and sank down into the rosy twilight of their underworld. Even that seduction to which Pablo had once invited me came again, and other, earlier ones which I had not fully grasped at the time, fantastic games for three or four, caught me up in their dance with a smile. Many things happened and many games, best unmentioned, were played.

When I rose once more to the surface of the unending stream of allurement and vice and entanglement, I was calm and silent. I was equipped, far gone in knowledge, wise, expert--ripe for Hermine. She rose as the last figure in my populous mythology, the last name of an endless series; and at once I came to myself and made an end of this fairy tale of love; for I did not wish to meet her in this twilight of a magic mirror. I belonged to her not just as this one piece in my game of chess--I belonged to her wholly. Oh, I would now so lay out the pieces in my game that all was centered in her and led to fulfillment.

The stream had washed me ashore. Once again I stood in the silent theater passage. What now? I felt for the little figures in my pocket--but already this impulse died away. Around me was the inexhaustible world of doors, notices and magic mirrors. Listlessly I read the first words that caught my eye, and shuddered.

HOW ONE KILLS FOR LOVE

was what it said.

Swiftly a picture was flashed upon my memory with a jerk and remained there one instant. Hermine at the table of a restaurant, turning all at once from the wine and food, lost in an abyss of speech, with a terrifying earnestness in her face as she said that she would have one aim only in making me her lover, and it was that she should die by my hand. A heavy wave of anguish and darkness flooded my heart. Suddenly everything confronted me once more. Suddenly once more the sense of the last call of fate gripped my heart. Desperately I felt in my pocket for the little figures so that I might practise a little magic and rearrange the layout of the board. The figures were no longer there. Instead of them I pulled out a knife. In mortal dread I ran along the corridor, past every door. I stood opposite the gigantic mirror. I looked into it. In the mirror there stood a beautiful wolf as tall as myself. He stood still, glancing shyly from unquiet eyes. As he leered at me, his eyes blazed and he grinned a little so that his chops parted and showed his red tongue.

Where was Pablo? Where was Hermine? Where was that clever fellow who had discoursed so pleasantly about the building up of the personality?

Again I looked into the mirror. I had been mad. I must have been mad. There was no wolf in the mirror, lolling his tongue in his maw. It was I, Harry. My face was gray, forsaken of all fancies, wearied by all vice, horribly pale. Still it was a human being, someone one could speak to.

"Harry," I said, "what are you doing there?"

"Nothing," said he in the mirror, "I am only waiting. I am waiting for death."

"Where is death then?"

"Coming," said the other. And I heard from the empty spaces within the theater the sound of music, a beautiful and awful music, that music from *Don Giovanni* that heralds the approach of the guest of stone. With an awful and an iron clang it rang through the ghostly house, coming from the other world, from the immortals.

"Mozart," I thought, and with the word conjured up the most beloved and the most exalted picture that my inner life contained.

At that, there rang out behind me a peal of laughter, a dear and ice-cold laughter out of a world unknown to men, a world beyond all suffering, and born of divine humor. I turned about, frozen through with the blessing of this laughter, and there came Mozart. He passed by me laughing as he went and, strolling quietly on, he opened the door of one of the boxes and went in. Eagerly I followed the god of my youth, the object, all my life long, of love and veneration. The music rang on. Mozart was leaning over the front of the box. Of the theater nothing was to be seen. Darkness filled the boundless space.

"You see," said Mozart, "it goes all right without the saxophone--though to be sure, I shouldn't wish to tread on the toes of that famous instrument."

"Where are we?" I asked.

"We are in the last act of *Don Giovanni.* Leporello is on his knees. A superb scene, and the music is fine too. There is a lot in it, certainly, that's very human, but you can hear the other world in it--the laughter, eh?"

"It is the last great music ever written," said I with the pomposity of a schoolmaster. "Certainly, there was Schubert to come. Hugo Wolf also, and I must not forget the poor, lovely Chopin either. You frown, Maestro? Oh, yes, Beethoven--he is wonderful too. But all that--beautiful as it may be--has something rhapsodical about it, something of disintegration. A work of such plentitude and power as *Don Giovanni* has never since arisen among men."

"Don't overstrain yourself," laughed Mozart, in frightful mockery. "You're a musician yourself, I perceive. Well, I have given up the trade and retired to take my ease. It is only for amusement that I look on at the business now and then."

He raised his hands as though he were conducting, and a moon, or some pale constellation, rose somewhere. I looked over the edge of the box into immeasurable depths of space. Mist and clouds floated there. Mountains and seashores glimmered, and beneath us extended world-wide a desert plain. On this plain we saw an old gentleman of a worthy aspect, with a long beard, who drearily led a large following of some ten thousand men in black. He had a melancholy and hopeless air; and Mozart said:

"Look, there's Brahms. He is striving for redemption, but it will take him all his time."

I realized that the thousands of men in black were the players of all those notes and parts in his scores which according to divine judgment were superfluous.

"Too thickly orchestrated, too much material wasted," Mozart said with a nod.

And thereupon we saw Richard Wagner marching at the head of a host just as vast, and felt the pressure of those thousands as they clung and closed upon him. Him, too, we watched as he dragged himself along with slow and sad step.

"In my young days," I remarked sadly, "these two musicians passed as the most extreme contrasts conceivable."

Mozart laughed.

"Yes, that is always the way. Such contrasts, seen from a little distance, always tend to show their increasing similarity. Thick orchestration was in any case neither Wagner's nor Brahms' personal failing. It was a fault of their time."

"What? And have they got to pay for it so dearly?" I cried in protest.

"Naturally. The law must take its course. Until they have paid the debt of their time it cannot be known whether anything personal to themselves is left over to stand to their credit."

"But they can't either of them help it!"

"Of course not. They cannot help it either that Adam ate the apple. But they have to pay for it all the same."

"But that is frightful."

"Certainly. Life is always frightful. We cannot help it and we are responsible all the same. One's born and at once one is guilty. You must have had a remarkable sort of religious education if you did not know that."

I was now thoroughly miserable. I saw myself as a dead-weary pilgrim, dragging myself across the desert of the other world, laden with the many superfluous books I had written, and all the articles and essays; followed by the army of compositors who had had the type to set up, by the army of readers who had had it all to swallow. My God--and over and above it all there was Adam and the apple, and the whole of original sin. All this, then, was to be paid for in endless purgatory. And only then could the question arise whether, behind all that, there was anything personal, anything of my own, left over; or whether all that I had done and all its consequences were merely the empty foam of the sea and a meaningless ripple in the flow of what was over and done.

Mozart laughed aloud when he saw my long face. He laughed so hard that he turned a somersault in the air and played trills with his heels. At the same time he shouted at me: "Hey, my young fellow, does your tongue smart, man, do your lungs really pinch, man? You think of your readers, those carrion feeders, and all your typesetters, those wretched abettors, and saber-whetters. You dragon, you make me laugh till I shake me and burst the stitches of my breeches. O heart of a gull, with printer's ink dull, and soul sorrow-full. A candle I'll leave you, if that'll relieve you. Belittled, betattled, spectacled and shackled, and pitifully snagged and by the tail wagged, with shilly and shally no more shall you dally. For the devil, I pray, who will bear you away and slice you and splice you till that shall suffice you for your writings and rotten plagiarisings ill-gotten."

This, however, was too much for me. Anger left me no time for melancholy. I caught hold of Mozart by the pigtail and off he flew. The pigtail grew longer and longer like the tail of a comet and I was whirled along at the end of it. The devil--but it was cold in this world we traversed! These immortals put up with a rarefied and glacial atmosphere. But it was delightful all the same--this icy air. I could tell that, even in the brief moment that elapsed before I lost my senses. A bitter-sharp and steel-bright icy gaiety coursed through me and a desire to laugh as shrilly and wildly and unearthly as Mozart had done. But then breath and consciousness failed me.

. . . . . . .

When I came to myself I was bewildered and exhausted. The white light of the corridor shone in the polished floor. I was not among the immortals, not yet. I was still, as ever, on this side of the riddle of suffering, of wolf-men and torturing complexities. I had found no happy spot, no endurable resting place. There must be an end of it.

In the great mirror, Harry stood opposite me. He did not appear to be very flourishing. His appearance was much the same as on that night when he visited the professor and sat through the dance at the Black Eagle. But that was far behind, years, centuries behind. He had grown older. He had learned to dance. He had visited the magic theater. He had heard Mozart laugh. Dancing and women and knives had no more terrors for him. Even those who have average gifts, given a few hundred years, come to maturity. I looked for a long time at Harry in the looking glass. I still knew him well enough, and he still bore a faint resemblance to the boy of fifteen who one Sunday in March had met Rosa on the cliffs and taken off his school cap to her. And yet he had grown a few centuries older since then. He had pursued philosophy and music and had his fill of war and his Elsasser at the Steel Helmet and discussed Krishna with men of honest learning. He had loved Erica and Maria, and had been Hermine's friend, and shot down motorcars, and slept with the sleek Chinese, and encountered Mozart and Goethe, and made sundry holes in the web of time and rents in reality's disguise, though it held him a prisoner still. And suppose he had lost his pretty chessman again, still he had a fine blade in his pocket. On then, old Harry, old weary loon.

Bah, the devil--how bitter the taste of life! I spat at Harry in the looking glass. I gave him a kick and kicked him to splinters. I walked slowly along the echoing corridor, carefully scanning the doors that had held out so many glowing promises. Not one now showed a single announcement. Slowly I passed by all the hundred doors of the Magic Theater. Was not this the day I had been to a masked ball? Hundreds of years had passed since then. Soon years would cease altogether. Something, though, was still to be done. Hermine awaited me. A strange marriage it was to be, and a sorrowful wave it was that bore me on, drearily bore me on, a slave, a wolf-man. Bah, the devil!

I stopped at the last door. So far had the sorrowful wave borne me. O Rosa! O departed youth! O Goethe! O Mozart!

I opened it. What I saw was a simple and beautiful picture. On a rug on the floor lay two naked figures, the beautiful Hermine and the beautiful Pablo, side by side in a sleep of deep exhaustion after love's play. Beautiful, beautiful figures, lovely pictures, wonderful bodies. Beneath Hermine's left breast was a fresh round mark, darkly bruised--a love bite of Pablo's beautiful, gleaming teeth. There, where the mark was, I plunged in my knife to the hilt. The blood welled out over her white and delicate skin. I would have kissed away the blood if everything had happened a little differently. As it was, I did not. I only watched how the blood flowed and watched her eyes open for a little moment in pain and deep wonder. What makes her wonder? I thought. Then it occurred to me. that I had to shut her eyes. But they shut again of themselves. So all was done. She only turned a little to one side, and from her armpit to her breast I saw the play of a delicate shadow. It seemed that it wished to recall something, but what I could not remember. Then she lay still.

For long I looked at her and at last I waked with a shudder and turned to go. Then I saw Pablo stretch himself. I saw him open his eyes and stretch his limbs and then bend over the dead girl and smile. Never, I thought, will this fellow take anything seriously. Everything makes him smile. Pablo, meanwhile, carefully turned over a corner of the rug and covered Hermine up as far as her breast so that the wound was hidden, and then he went silently out of the box. Where was he going? Was everybody leaving me alone? I stayed there, alone with the half-shrouded body of her whom I loved--and envied. The boyish hair hung low over the white forehead. Her lips shone red against the dead pallor of her blanched face and they were a little parted. Her hair diffused its delicate perfume and through it glimmered the little shell-like ear.

Her wish was fulfilled. Before she had ever been mine, I had killed my love. I had done the unthinkable, and now I kneeled and stared and did not know at all what this deed meant, whether it was good and right or the opposite. What would the clever chess player, what would Pablo have to say to it? I knew nothing and I could not think. The painted mouth glowed more red on the growing pallor of the face. So had my whole life been. My little happiness and love were like this staring mouth, a little red upon a mask of death.

And from the dead face, from the dead white shoulders and the dead white arms, there exhaled and slowly crept a shudder, a desert wintriness and desolation, a slowly, slowly increasing chill in which my hands and lips grew numb. Had I quenched the sun? Had I stopped the heart of all life? Was it the coldness of death and space breaking in?

With a shudder I stared at the stony brow and the stark hair and the cool pale shimmer of the ear. The cold that streamed from them was deathly and yet it was beautiful, it rang, it vibrated. It was music!

Hadn't I once felt this shudder before and found it at the same time a joy? Hadn't I once caught this music before? Yes, with Mozart and the immortals.

Verses came into my head that I had once come upon somewhere:

We above you ever more residing
In the ether's star translumined ice
Know nor day nor night nor time's dividing,
Wear nor age nor sex as our device.
Cool and unchanging is our eternal being,
Cool and star bright is our eternal laughter.

Then the door of the box opened and in came Mozart. I did not recognize him at the first glance, for he was without pigtail, knee breeches and buckled shoes, in modern dress. He took a seat close beside me, and I was on the point of holding him back because of the blood that had flowed over the floor from Hermine's breast. He sat there and began busying himself with an apparatus and some instruments that stood beside him. He took it very seriously, tightening this and screwing that, and I looked with wonder at his adroit and nimble fingers and wished that I might see them playing a piano for once. I watched him thoughtfully, or in a reverie rather, lost in admiration of his beautiful and skillful hands, warmed too, by the sense of his presence and a little apprehensive as well. Of what he was actually doing and of what it was that he screwed and manipulated, I took no heed whatever.

I soon found, however, that he had fixed up a radio and put it in going order, and now he inserted the loudspeaker and said: "Munich is on the air. *Concerto Grosso in F Major* by Handel."

And in fact, to my indescribable astonishment and horror, the devilish tin trumpet spat out, without more ado, a mixture of bronchial slime and chewed rubber; that noise that owners of gramophones and radios have agreed to call music. And behind the slime and the croaking there was, sure enough, like an old master beneath a layer of dirt, the noble outline of that divine music. I could distinguish the majestic structure and the deep wide breath and the full broad bowing of the strings.

"My God," I cried in horror, "what are you doing, Mozart? Do you really mean to inflict this mess on me and yourself, this triumph of our day, the last victorious weapon in the war of extermination against art? Must this be, Mozart?"

How the weird man laughed! And what a cold and eerie laugh! It was noiseless and yet everything was shattered by it. He marked my torment with deep satisfaction while he bent over the cursed screws and attended to the tin trumpet. Laughing still, he let the distorted, the murdered and murderous music ooze out and on; and laughing still, he replied:

"Please, no pathos, my friend! Anyway, did you observe the ritardando? An inspiration, eh? Yes, and now you tolerant man, let the sense of this ritardando touch you. Do you hear the basses? They stride like gods. And let this inspiration of old Handel penetrate your restless heart and give it peace. Just listen, you poor creature, listen without either pathos or mockery, while far away behind the veil of this hopelessly idiotic and ridiculous apparatus the form of this divine music passes by. Pay attention and you will learn something. Observe how this crazy funnel apparently does the most stupid, the most useless and the most damnable thing in the world. It takes hold of some music played where you please, without distinction, stupid and coarse, lamentably distorted, to boot, and chucks it into space to land where it has no business to be; and yet after all this it cannot destroy the original spirit of the music; it can only demonstrate its own senseless mechanism, its inane meddling and marring. Listen, then, you poor thing. Listen well. You have need of it. And now you hear not only a Handel who, disfigured by radio, is, all the same, in this most ghastly of disguises still divine; you hear as well and you observe, most worthy sir, a most admirable symbol of all life. When you listen to radio you are a witness of the everlasting war between idea and appearance, between time and eternity, between the human and the divine. Exactly, my dear sir, as the radio for ten minutes together projects the most lovely music without regard into the most impossible places, into respectable drawing rooms and attics and into the midst of chattering, guzzling, yawning and sleeping listeners, and exactly as it strips this music of its sensuous beauty, spoils and scratches and beslimes it and yet cannot altogether destroy its spirit, just so does life, the so-called reality, deal with the sublime picture-play of the world and make a hurley-burley of it. It makes its unappetizing tone--slime of the most magic orchestral music. Everywhere it obtrudes its mechanism, its activity, its dreary exigencies and vanity between the ideal and the real, between orchestra and ear. All life is so, my child, and we must let it be so; and, if we are not asses, laugh at it. It little becomes people like you to be critics of radio or of life either. Better learn to listen first! Learn what is to be taken seriously and laugh at the rest. Or is it that you have done better yourself, more nobly and fitly and with better taste? Oh, no, Mr. Harry, you have not. You have made a frightful history of disease out of your life, and a misfortune of your gifts. And you have, as I see, found no better use for so pretty, so enchanting a young lady than to stick a knife into her body and destroy her. Was that right, do you think?"

"Right?" I cried in despair. "No! My God, everything is so false, so hellishly stupid and wrong! I am a beast, Mozart, a stupid, angry beast, sick and rotten. There you're right a thousand times. But as for this girl--it was her own desire. I have only fulfilled her own wish."

Mozart laughed his noiseless laughter. But he had the great kindness to turn off the radio.

My self-extenuation sounded unexpectedly and thoroughly foolish even to me who had believed in it with all my heart. When Hermine had once, so it suddenly occurred to me, spoken about time and eternity, I had been ready forthwith to take her thoughts as a reflection of my own. That the thought, however, of dying by my hand had been her own inspiration and wish and not in the least influenced by me I had taken as a matter of course. But why on that occasion had I not only accepted that horrible and unnatural thought, but even guessed it in advance. Perhaps because it had been my own. And why had I murdered Hermine just at the very moment when I saw her lying naked in another's arms? All-knowing and all-mocking rang Mozart's soundless laughter.

"Harry," said he, "you're a great joker. Had this beautiful girl really nothing to desire of you but the stab of a knife? Keep that for someone else! Well, at least you have stabbed her properly. The poor child is stone dead. And now perhaps would be an opportune moment to realize the consequences of your gallantry towards this lady. Or do you think of evading the consequences?"

"No," I cried. "Don't you understand at all? I evade the consequences? I have no other desire than to pay and pay and pay for them, to lay my head beneath the axe and pay the penalty of annihilation."

Mozart looked at me with intolerable mockery.

"How pathetic you always are. But you will learn humor yet, Harry. Humor is always gallows-humor, and it is on the gallows you are now constrained to learn it. You are ready? Good. Then off with you to the public prosecutor and let the law take its course with you till your head is coolly hacked off at break of dawn in the prison yard. You are ready for it?"

Instantly a notice flashed before my eyes:

HARRY'S EXECUTION

and I consented with a nod. I stood in a bare yard enclosed by four walls with barred windows, and shivered in the air of a gray dawn. There were a dozen gentlemen there in morning coats and gowns, and a newly erected guillotine. My heart was contracted with misery and dread, but I was ready and acquiescent. At the word of command I stepped forward and at the word of command I knelt down. The public prosecutor removed his cap and cleared his throat and all the other gentlemen cleared their throats. He unfolded an official document and held it before him and read out:

"Gentlemen, there stands before you Harry Haller, accused and found guilty of the willful misuse of our Magic Theater. Haller has not alone insulted the majesty of art in that he confounded our beautiful picture gallery with so-called reality and stabbed to death the reflection of a girl with the reflection of a knife; he has in addition displayed the intention of using our theater as a mechanism of suicide and shown himself devoid of humor. Wherefore we condemn Haller to eternal life and we suspend for twelve hours his permit to enter our theater. The penalty also of being laughed out of court may not be remitted. Gentlemen, all together, one-two-three!"

On the word "three" all who were present broke into one simultaneous peal of laughter, a laughter in full chorus, a frightful laughter of the other world that is scarcely to be borne by the ears of men.

When I came to myself again, Mozart was sitting beside me as before. He clapped me on the shoulder and said: "You have heard your sentence. So, you see, you will have to learn to listen to more of the radio music of life. It'll do you good. You are uncommonly poor in gifts, a poor blockhead, but by degrees you will come to grasp what is required of you. You have got to learn to laugh. That will be required of you. You must apprehend the humor of life, its gallows-humor. But of course you are ready for everything in the world except what will be required of you. You are ready to stab girls to death. You are ready to be executed with all solemnity. You would be ready, no doubt, to mortify and scourge yourself for centuries together. Wouldn't you?"

"Oh, yes, ready with all my heart," I cried in my misery.

"Of course! When it's a question of anything stupid and pathetic and devoid of humor or wit, you're the man, you tragedian. Well, I am not. I don't care a fig for all your romantics of atonement. You wanted to be executed and to have your head chopped off, you lunatic! For this imbecile ideal you would suffer death ten times over. You are willing to die, you coward, but not to live. The devil, but you shall live! It would serve you right if you were condemned to the severest of penalties."

"Oh, and what would that be?"

"We might, for example, restore this girl to life again and marry you to her."

"No, I should not be ready for that. It would bring unhappiness."

"As if there were not enough unhappiness in all you have designed already! However, enough of pathos and death-dealing. It is time to come to your senses. You are to live and to learn to laugh. You are to learn to listen to the cursed radio music of life and to reverence the spirit behind it and to laugh at its distortions. So there you are. More will not be asked of you."

Gently from behind clenched teeth I asked: "And if I do not submit? And if I deny your right, Mozart, to interfere with the Steppenwolf, and to meddle in his destiny?"

"Then," said Mozart calmly, "I should invite you to smoke another of my charming cigarettes." And as he spoke and conjured up a cigarette from his waistcoat pocket and offered it me, he was suddenly Mozart no longer. It was my friend Pablo looking warmly at me out of his dark exotic eyes and as like the man who had taught me to play chess with the little figures as a twin.

"Pablo!" I cried with a convulsive start. "Pablo, where are we?"

"We are in my Magic Theater," he said with a smile, "and if you wish at any time to learn the Tango or to be a general or to have a talk with Alexander the Great, it is always at your service. But I'm bound to say, Harry, you have disappointed me a little. You forgot yourself badly. You broke through the humor of my little theater and tried to make a mess of it, stabbing with knives and spattering our pretty picture-world with the mud of reality. That was not pretty of you. I hope, at least, you did it from jealousy when you saw Hermine and me lying there. Unfortunately, you did not know what to do with this figure. I thought you had learned the game better. Well, you will do better next time."

He took Hermine who at once shrank in his fingers to the dimensions of a toy figure and put her in the very same waistcoat pocket from which he had taken the cigarette.

Its sweet and heavy smoke diffused a pleasant aroma. I felt hollow, exhausted, and ready to sleep for a whole year.

I understood it all. I understood Pablo. I understood Mozart, and somewhere behind me I heard his ghastly laughter. I knew that all the hundred thousand pieces of life's game were in my pocket. A glimpse of its meaning had stirred my reason and I was determined to begin the game afresh. I would sample its tortures once more and shudder again at its senselessness. I would traverse not once more, but often, the hell of my inner being.

One day I would be a better hand at the game. One day I would learn how to laugh. Pablo was waiting for me, and Mozart too.

9 789361 909177

Printed at Repro India Ltd.